Not So Much the Fall

Kerry Hart

Cover art, "The Edge of Past," copyright © 1993 by Chris Rose
Author photo by Denis Doyon
Cover design by Midge Stocker
Interior design and production by Midge Stocker

Printed on recycled, acid-free paper with vegetable-based inks in the United States of America.

Library of Congress Cataloging -in-Publication Data

Hart, Kerry, 1956-
    Not so much the fall / Kerry Hart. — 1st ed.
      p. cm.
    ISBN 1-879427-24-9 (alk. paper)
    I. Title.
    PS3558.A68344N68 1996
    813'.54—dc20   95-49298
                                  CIP

Third Side Press
2250 W. Farragut
Chicago, IL 60625-1802

First edition, May 1996

10 9 8 7 6 5 4 3 2 1

For my mother
who gave me my first breath.

For my father
who gave me my first typewriter.

And for Echo,
my first dream come true.

Acknowledgments

I can't possibly name everybody responsible for being there along my long road and contributing to my becoming a person capable of thinking this stuff up. But I would never forgive myself, nor, in some cases would I ever be forgiven, for not acknowledging the instrumental roles of the following:

I am indebted to my family of origin, the living and the dead, for never squelching their Southern quirks and Yankee oddities, or hiding them from us little ones. I owe the most to my witchy mother who could make it rain only on the golf course on which my father was playing as opposed to babysitting the kids. I wish you were alive to read this, but I suspect you have read it, wherever you are. Thanks to my father who encouraged me, at age six, to write my first story, gave it a serious read, then said the magic words, "Kerry. Publishable!"—Daddy, your sticking around to see this means the world to me.

Thanks to Aunt Rainey for being a role model way before her time to a little niece, who, without you, might not have learned for many years that a woman can be smart and successful and free to choose any alternative path she wishes in this world. I have to thank my older brother Randy for sharing with me his pioneering courage and perverse take on life—and Lynda for always showing me in so many ways that she loves me for exactly who I am, and for being my older sister who taught me that overcoming all the damn odds and obstacles was entirely possible.

Thanks to my publisher, Midge Stocker—you couldn't have known you were echoing my father. Thanks for saying those magical words to me again, for helping make my dream come true, and for being an inhabitant of the inexplicable geographical karma that relentlessly colors my life.

Thanks to all of you who were there in times of intense joy and deep despair—Lynn, Oberon, Zephyr, and Echo, the sweetest family I could have lucked into; Bess (and her baptism by fire), Melinda, and Mary Jayne who gave me memories to last a lifetime; Annie, Marcia, and Heather who befriended me when I most assuredly was not in Kansas anymore; and Patty, who introduced me to homosexual soup and helped me navigate a mine field I couldn't have imagined existed.

I'd like to extend my gratitude to Philadelphia for being a place that finally feels like home, and to all of you here who read this manuscript when it was brand new and needed you the most—Alix, David, Larry, Marj, and the wonderful women of the Windsor Avenue Writers' Group—Marie, Pam, Elliott, and Carolyn. Thanks to Ann in Memphis for letting me borrow her keen eyes and for boosting my ego with the greatest compliments, and to Denis for making my day and keeping my secrets.

Finally, special thanks and hugs to Pamela, my angel who always appears when I most need her; to Tammie, my loyal friend who puts up with a good handful of my idiosyncracies on a daily basis and who doesn't mind sitting on my couch in black pants despite the white dog hair; and to Bonnie, who has contributed generously to insuring that I make it down the last leg of this road safely.

MOJAVE

———

I was in the middle of nowhere. The sky had cleared and a crescent moon barely illuminated the terrain to the right and left of the highway. It looked vast in the pale light; and soon my eyes started playing tricks on me and I imagined it was an ocean's rhythmically-moving, whitecapped waves. Then I suffered a massive panic attack and realized the last thing I needed to think was that the ground beneath my wheels was anything less than earth solid.

I was exhausted and had no idea how far I was from Needles. I followed the taillights of an eighteen-wheeler for twenty miles and developed this fantasy about what the driver looked like and how he might help me if I got desperate—a fantasy that was harshly interrupted when I saw his right turn signal blinking. When he exited I burst into tears and laid on my horn until the flashing red square disappeared.

I drove alone and cried through Bruce Springsteen singing "Thunder Road," recognizing that I was neither sitting tight nor taking hold.

There were no lights around me but my own. I finally stopped crying and realized I had to make a decision. I figured I should pull off the road and sleep in my truck, serial killers be damned. Then I drove for a few minutes listening to Tom Petty's "Freefallin'."

My mind flashed to President Kennedy saying, "If not now, when?"—then I wondered if he made that up or if somebody else did. I remembered being seven and watching the film over and over of that piece of the president's head flying across the back of the limo—but mostly I remembered the wrenching crush I had on John-John, how manly I thought he was standing so still in his short pants, saluting his dead father's flag-draped coffin.

If not now, when?

I pulled off the highway, bumped across the soft shoulder, and came to rest in dry, crunchy soil. I rolled down my window and glanced back up at the road. Totally deserted. I peered ahead, still couldn't tell what was out there, opened my door, leaned out and touched the ground. Sand. Okay. I wished I had a flashlight. I had forgotten all about Kris' carefully packed provisions box.

I got out, extinguishing my headlights, and I saw little by the faint light of the sliver of moon. Some sagebrush, or tumbleweeds, or whatever you call them. It looked like a desert. My impaired short-term memory blinked a subliminal message—a sign I saw some time ago. *Mojave.*

The air was still and cold. I leaned against the toasty hood of my truck and I dragged the toes of my shoes through the sand. Suddenly, I thought of scorpions. *"There are no scorpions out here,"* a city voice said.

"There damn well could be," I snapped back. "I'm in the fucking Mojave Desert!" Then I thought, *rattlesnakes*, and I hoisted my butt up on my truck. There are, I reasoned, better and worse ways to die.

I smoked a cigarette. The last time I had heard anything so quiet was when I spent a day in the ruined bottoms of the Toutle River on Mt. St. Helens. That repetitive "Freefallin'" song popped into my head again—then, just as quickly, vanished.

Silence.

I wondered what would happen if you stayed this quiet for a long time. I remembered the story about Jesus wandering in the desert which is when, I thought, the burning bush thing happened and he saw God, or heard him, or whatever. But maybe that wasn't such a big deal because he was his father, after all. Then I thought, *what would I do if all of a sudden I heard Daddy talking out here?* Then I recalled that Charles Manson did the wandering in the desert thing too, once, before the murders happened. I think he had some peyote buttons. Come to think of it, this may have been the very desert.

I wished I had somebody to talk to.

You do, a gentle male voice said.

I looked around me.

Talk to me.

"Who are you?"

Say whatever you want.

If not now, when? That was Kennedy's voice.

"I don't know what to say," I whispered. "I don't know where to start." I pulled my legs up, crossing them beneath me on the truck's cooling hood, and I shrugged and laughed, gesturing with my hands, and spoke to someone I wasn't sure was there. "Well, yesterday I left behind a haunted house in Portland, Oregon. It is haunted because of me. The family that lived there is dead." I imagined the Mojave cocked his huge sandy head. "I killed them all." A tumbleweed took off and spun toward me, lodging itself behind my front tire. "I can't exactly start at the beginning, okay?" I said, and interpreted the desert's silence as permission to continue.

HOME STRETCH

I'm lost. Lost.

I watched the dogs romp on Mt. Tabor on a blustery March day, knowing this would be their last time there, knowing they didn't know that, wondering if they'd care. Knowing they would. And these words became a chant in my head.

I was sitting on the hill overlooking the reservoir. The sun was disappearing behind the palatial homes in Portland's West Hills. Mechanically, I cocked my arm to throw the ball. Griffin, the chocolate Labrador, waited with total concentration. Harley, the Great Dane, was five months his junior but twice his size. She concentrated, too—on him. When I threw the ball, our retriever instinctively rushed to capture it; but Harley, who had no interest in chasing balls, charged and body slammed Griffin until he couldn't remember where the ball landed. This had been their game ever since Harley achieved her size advantage.

Kris was coming the next day to take the dogs to Memphis. And in a month I'd be leaving Oregon to join them. Then, and there, we said, we'll "work on our relationship." But I'm afraid we were lying.

I had to get out of Portland, though.

My nine-year tenure in the Pacific Northwest had been a long fall that began not with a careless misstep but with an impulsive leap—and the whole way down I grabbed at rocks and limbs that were never as steady as they seemed. Maybe in Memphis, I thought, Kris would become the safety net I've long mistaken her for. I looked at the pink-tinged hills ahead of me and visualized the magnificent Pacific that lay behind them. I remembered the first time I saw that ocean, when I was twenty-four and standing close enough for the rising tide to lick my toes, knowing I had reached the end of my road. For good, I thought. That day I started collecting souvenirs to decorate my new Northwest home—driftwood and sandstone and volcanic rock—and my prize was a perfect, unbroken shell. In my innocence, I didn't realize until a week later that the sea creature inside had not vacated, and I awoke to an odor that wouldn't be fully banished from my apartment for two days.

That's sort of what I felt like as I watched the city lights below me slowly rise to meet the falling darkness—ignorantly transported somewhere I'm not supposed to be, trapped in my shell, and putrescent.

A nippy breeze caressed the back of my neck and I remembered the awe I experienced the first time I saw the mammoth peak of Mt. Hood. I wondered, not for the first time, how the beauty of this corner of the country could have been the setting for such despair for me—and I made the optimistic assumption that, perhaps, returning to a place of geographical homeliness could produce some measure of peace I'd not had in almost a decade.

So, I thought, tomorrow the dogs will be gone and I'll have a month to sell everything that won't fit into my truck. I'd already found renters. We didn't sell the house we bought together five years ago because that is an important part of the lie. Real property validates our shattering bond.

The next day Kris would bring the maps from Triple-A. She called them my "Trip-Tik," which I will see is the auto club's version of distributing bread crumbs along the road so a person like me can find her way home. There is Triple A in

Portland, but Kris took care of the travel arrangements because that is her job—keeping me safe, making things easy. Or so we had both come to believe.

She made up a list of items to have a mechanic check before I hit the road, although the Toyota pick-up I bought to appease my other lover's passion for shiny new things acquired with other people's money was only three months old. Kris also had a list of *provisions* for me to pack in case of an emergency. I used to know what *provisions* meant but I couldn't remember, which didn't matter because Kris assured me they were necessary. If I feel like I need them and I can't figure out what they are, she said, just call.

Griffin had disappeared down the hill into the ivy. I couldn't see him but I had complete confidence he was okay and would find his way back. Griffin takes after Kris. Harley, my favorite, was twenty feet from me, in full view, standing still as a statue and staring at a squirrel she had treed. If Harley disappeared in the ivy, I would immediately form a search party.

When Harley was a puppy, Griff would lie on his back and spread his legs so she could cuddle up on his belly. Her gargantuan paws would rest heavily on his penis and his look would reveal discomfort, but he graciously allowed it. Now she body blocks him when he tries to play his favorite retriever games. Kris always maintained that Harley takes after me, even before I definitively proved her right.

The sun was gone and twilight blued the sky. I could have sat there longer and dwelled on my decade of horror, but it was getting cold and I would have a month alone in the house and seven days on unfamiliar roads to obsess on the past. I stood as Griffin reappeared and I called Harley off the tree. I took one last sweeping look across the still water. I knelt and the dogs were standing next to me as I blew three kisses and whispered goodbye. I was sobbing so hard as we wound down the path to the truck that my chest quaked and my throat lurched and I prayed no stranger was around to see me so weak. Griffin took no notice and pranced along picking up sticks and promptly dropping them. Harley looked wary and stayed close beside me. I took a Percodan with my Halcion that night because, I rationalized, no one should have to bear this pain twenty-four hours a day.

I woke up the next morning and my head felt like it was stuffed with bloody gauze. Even the diffused light of the cloudy Portland morning burned my eyes and a heavy taste of metal persisted in my mouth. I told the dogs in an excited voice that their other mother was coming home, and they wagged their trusting tails and had no idea what I was saying.

At the airport, Kris gave me one of her generous bear hugs, then ran her hands across my back and shoulders—finally pulling away and gazing in my eyes with a look of sheer pity. I had lost twenty pounds since she left Portland in October and had forgotten to mention this in our many phone conversations.

The dogs remembered her.

She was only there for ten hours. We had lunch and she fussed over my lack of appetite, encouraged me to eat, wrapped my food to go when I refused. Back home she spread out my travel package and traced with her finger my upcoming 2800 mile route, offering essential advice and a few suggested scenic possibilities. I didn't pay attention after realizing the route was boldly outlined in bright blue. It was I-5 South to I-40 East—major interstates. What could go wrong? While she spoke I rocked back and forth on my knees to quell the nausea that boiled up when I was still for too long.

I stared at her large-boned body hunched over the maps on the living room floor and I thought, *she's too big to be in this little house with me.* I was immediately horrified that I could feel this way about Kris—my can't-live-without-her Kris, my forever-and-ever-'til-death—where will you be—when will you be back—I love you—peck on the cheek—sexless touch—you fry perfect bacon—power of attorney—is this a hemorrhoid—sing me to sleep—pink puppy bellies—sea salt in our shorts—closing costs Kris.

But I did.

We napped and I was flat on my back, my stomach concave, ribs raised and pelvic bones protruding, when my restless fingers discovered a lump in my groin. Kris felt it and raised up on her elbow and we collapsed crying until both of us fell asleep. Death becomes me, and we both knew it.

REAL PROPERTY

—

Kris kissed me goodbye at the airport and made me promise I would see the doctor about my lump—another promise to her I didn't keep. An assortment of airline freight attendants kindly allowed us to watch them load our sedated children, in their respective crates, into the cargo hold.

Back home I couldn't stand the silence, so I went down to the basement and stared at three rooms full of our five years together for ten minutes before returning to the living room. I padded aimlessly around the lifeless house singing that Janis Joplin song about something being another word for nothing left to lose, but I couldn't remember what that something was. I sat on the couch and picked up wads of Harley's white and black and gray hairs with my fingertips. I pressed my face into the cushions and inhaled the doggie smell, an unappealing odor only a mother could love. I sprinkled the hairs onto the carpet and knew I should be crying but was too exhausted to try.

There was so much to do. I had to start somewhere.

I went into the bedroom and retrieved my black backpack and took it, with a pad and pen, into the dining room. I sat at what had been Kris' desk, a large solid oak table now clear of bills and sharp pencils. I emptied my bag and lined my prescription bottles up on the table, grouping them by types, then counting their contents. Before I left town I would make a last visit to my favorite of three Portland doctors, and it was essential I know how many refills to request to tide me over in Memphis until I could find a physician there.

I decided that could take up to three months. In addition to my seventy-seven Percodans, fifty-one Valiums, and ninety Halcions, I decided I should ask for thirty, sixty, and ninety more, respectively. Plus refills. I took a moment to practice what I would say to the doctor because this is something I often do—imagine possible questions and rehearse sensible answers—although usually the people don't ask the questions I thought they would or, if they do, I don't remember the answers I had planned. Also, when I do this I move my lips, but very rarely speak out loud.

The doctor would say, *So you're low on everything?*
Yes.

So you need . . . —here I place my order. *Migraines worse again?*

Well, yes. It's a little of everything. Graduation—Kris and I broke up, you know. Yeah. Well, I was seeing somebody else. Briefly. Then we broke up, too. Yeah, well . . . Kris is in Memphis. I'm leaving next month to meet her there. Yeah, well, hopefully . . . we'll see.

Before I left the desk I looked out the picture window in front of me. Several weeks of unseasonably warm days and frost-free nights had tricked the rhododendron and hydrangea bushes that lined our home into sprouting scores of delicate green buds.

"We own this home," I whispered. "Those are our bushes. We could have lived here forever and ever." I felt a burning behind my nose and the clouding of impending tears and my visual perception shallowed and I saw my face, eerily lit by the table lamp, reflected in the glass. My eyes were dark-rimmed, my hair uncombed, my cheeks sunken. My skin was doughy and shiny, like unbaked pie crust glazed with egg white.

I flipped over the paper on which I recorded my drug count and wrote: *Am I bracing for the landing? Was Kris another weak branch, another unstable rock? I know Alex was. Or is this another follow-through problem? Am I giving up? Too early? And how many times have I done* that *before? I am so fucked up.*

I built a fire and while drifting off to sleep on the floor I watched the flames and thought back to Thanksgiving night, 1985. It was Griff's first night in our home and a fire roared in the fireplace as we watched *Airplane* on the VCR. We were determined our second puppy would live to adulthood and we hardly took our eyes off him. He loved the fire but kept getting too close and an ember would pop out and we'd grab him and drag him back. Finally he lay sleeping a foot from the grate, his fat, bald belly and oversized pink paws facing the flames. We were engrossed in the film when suddenly Kris exclaimed, "Oh my God!" and we looked at Griff who was sleeping deeply as his side rose and fell in a rapid pant. Kris scooped him up and we ran into the kitchen and placed him in front of his water bowl, but he was too parched and groggy to stand up. We knelt down and I held the bowl off the ground. Kris cradled Griffin in her hands and stuck his nose to the water. He began drinking, and continued as we laughed while our eleven-pound puppy drained the huge bowl he'd still use as an adult.

Kris and I knee to knee on our kitchen floor, our puppy rehydrated, the smell of holiday turkey and stuffing still lingering in the air.

I suddenly and clearly remembered what Joplin would trade all her tomorrows for.

I laid my hand over my nose and eyes and pulled my knees to my chest to protect myself from my anguish and guilt. Many times in the night I awoke to the dead calm of a house with no one else in it, to the fire in various stages of dying and I knew but didn't care that sleeping without my drugs was impossible.

Over the next month the Percodan killed whatever pain I might have felt in my scrawny arms and weak back as I packed twenty boxes that would go in my truck and twenty more that would go to Goodwill. In the wee hours of the morning I filled countless garbage bags and hauled them out to the curb and felt nothing. The Valium extinguished my anxiety as I plowed through our house's contents, often making brutal decisions to discard or sell items that owed their very existence to the marriage of Kris and Casey. The hardest things to throw away ended up being a half-eaten box of Wheaties and two Weight Watcher's frozen entrees. Kris food.

Before it was over, people would respond to my ads and one by one our washer and dryer and couch and tables and chairs and desks and bed disappeared. The Halcion made it possible for me to sleep without dreaming of the faces of strangers who casually carted away our possessions. I had this chemical *ménage à trois* frolicking through my bloodstream, protecting me from having to face, on any consistent basis, the fact that I had gone too far, and had gotten caught.

ALEX

"Five hundred dollars," I said, not turning my head toward the young couple in our dining room. I stared straight ahead at my friend Allie, my wilted eyelids partially concealing the limpid pool that threatened to overflow behind them. The curly-haired husband played a decent version of "Ode to Joy" that nevertheless hurt my ears.

Allie sat with me for most of the two days of my garage sale, during which some people handed over large sums of cash for major items without asking questions and others haggled over the price of a coffee can full of used pencils.

"Would you take three-fifty?" the wife asked.

That was what Kris paid for it, and I stuck out my hand. She came over and put three one-hundred dollar bills in my hand while her husband gently closed the lid over the keys. "We'll bring the other fifty in the morning when we come back with a truck to pick it up, okay?" This woman was physically so plain and vocally so chipper she made me cringe.

By the time Allie left, the two Percodans I took had made me giddy and courageous enough to pull out the bench and pound out both parts of "Heart and Soul", one after the other, again and again—and to remember the twisted path that brought this piano into our home, only allowing it to stay long enough for me to learn this one happy-sad silly song.

I had already met Alex, but Kris was not yet suspicious on that evening in June when she and I rented and watched *Big* on the VCR. After they played "Heart and Soul" on the piano keys with their feet I paused the tape. "I wish I could play the piano," I said.

"If you had one, do you really think you'd learn how to play?" Kris was acutely aware by now of my tendency to not finish things I start.

"Oh, God, yeah!"

I had first met Alex in the middle of May. I was finishing my final internship—practicing the art of long-term therapy for the hopelessly neurotic. In three months, I would have my master's degree and be doing this for a decent living. My supervisor, who later was ousted from the profession for sleeping with his clients, assigned Alex to me.

My last client had left some minutes before and, when I went into the waiting room to call Alex in, she wasn't there. I looked out the window, on the porch, and no one was there either. I peeked into my supervisor's office, knowing he wasn't there, and Alex was sitting at his desk, awkwardly using her elbows to flip through a book on aversion therapy.

"Alex?" I said.

She jumped up and followed me to the counseling room. I stopped to allow her to enter first and she stopped, too, wedging us in the doorway, penetrating my personal space by about three inches. She squinted her midnight blue eyes and said, "Have I seen you somewhere before?"

"I don't know." I doubted it. What common ground could I possibly have shared with this butch little child?

She shyly lowered her eyes. "You look familiar."

She sat in the chair where my legal pad and pen lay, and I sat on the couch opposite her. I recall almost nothing of what Alex said to me that first day because my initial response to her was so sensory as to preclude all rational thought. Mostly I remember how she smelled—a striking combination of Obsession for Men, a petroleum-based antibiotic ointment, fresh gauze, and the ethereal aroma of occult blood.

Alex had been released from the hospital just the day before on the condition she seek therapy. Now, she sat across from me, a rookie student whose mind was rendered incapable of recalling anything I had learned in the past two years. Instead, my nose and eyes feasted on this adorable young woman with her stiff, assaulted limbs swaddled in bandages from fingers to elbows. I could have killed my supervisor for giving me an "attempt."

Over the next week I boned up on suicide and tried to forget my visceral reaction to my new client—my simultaneous revulsion and attraction to this cute kid who had opened up her arms and tried to die. When Alex arrived for her second session I started with what the texts suggested.

"I'm glad you came back," I said as Alex sat, this time, on the couch.

"There's no way I wouldn't have come back!" she said. Alex was wearing a white cut-off T-shirt that showed her belly. The upper tip of a crescent moon tattoo peeked out of the waistband of her black nylon gym shorts. Her legs were long and tanned, her blond and black-rooted hair staticky from coming over in her '69 Cougar convertible. She could drive again, she explained, happily holding out her arms with their abbreviated bandaging that had freed her fingers.

"What made you want to come back?"

"Well . . ." She breathed deeply and made me wait. "I love the sound of your voice. . . . And you don't know me."

Pre-verbal trauma, I noted on my pad.

Alex, I would discover over the months, had an abuse history as long as Clyde Barrow's record. It took me less time to notice that her presence unfailingly made my heart pound and my hands sweat.

I had begun to abuse drugs as my fear of the follow-through, of successfully finishing something I had started, loomed larger as graduation approached. But these piddly prescriptions didn't seem capable of orchestrating the sabotage I needed, so my unconscious began spinning a more complex web—just in time, it seemed, for Alex to have danced right into it.

At the end of that second session Alex asked, "What would happen to me if something happened to you?"

"Such as?"

"I mean, if you left your job to have a baby or something."

I laughed. "I'm not going to have a baby."

"Are you married?"

"No."

As I walked her to the door she turned and lifted her shirt to show me her sunburned back. "Look," she said. "We went to Sauvie's Island the other day and I got roasted."

When she was gone I went back into the counseling room, quickly closed the door and leaned against it, took a deep breath, then shook my upper body like a wet dog who hates the water.

INTERMITTENT REINFORCEMENT

I broke down and took a Valium before Alex came back for her third session. I had spent considerable time that week trying to destroy thoughts of her that sometimes brought me to the verge of nausea, sometimes to the brink of orgasm. In my fantasy I saw Alex sprawled on the counseling couch, swallowing tiny gulps of air in response to the pain of my removing her sticky bandages and reapplying the healing oil. I told myself I was transferring my therapist duties to an understandable desire to care for her physical wounds—she had, after all, made her internal pain so *visible*—but even I couldn't find any rationalization for what came next in my daydreams.

Alex is free of pain and sleeping—her dark eyelashes accentuating her snow white skin. I watch as her deep breathing causes the lump in her jeans to rise and fall rhythmically, watch as her lashes flutter when I kiss her neck, as the pressure of my hand against her inner thigh interrupts her even breath and gentle motion.

I blushed when she came to the door for her next session, and, for some reason, so did she. When we sat, Alex scooted to the edge of the couch so our knees almost touched. Her bandages were gone, stitches removed, and she laid her arms across my legs, wiggling her fingers just inches from my crotch. She smiled up at me.

"Go on and look for a minute. I know you want to—people can't help looking, and I'm not ashamed of it."

I looked. "You shouldn't be ashamed." I unconsciously touched her upturned palms with my fingertips as I examined the bright red lines.

"You know why I'm not ashamed?" I gazed at her and said nothing. "Because, number one, I didn't do this without thinking about it for a long time; and, number two, the scars won't ever let me forget that I did something really, really stupid."

"So you think trying to kill yourself was stupid?"

"Oh, absolutely! Totally stupid." She furrowed her brow, squinted her eyes, and continued. "Stupid, for one thing, because if I had died I wouldn't have been here to drink this great cup of espresso I had this morning."

"Hmmm," I smiled.

"And last night I, uh, um . . ." she rapidly raised and lowered an eyebrow. "Last night was worth living for, too."

I laughed. "Intermittent reinforcement."

"What?"

"My theory is that the only reason we don't *all* commit suicide is because life is the ultimate intermittent reinforcer. Like, with rats in a laboratory—the best way to keep them pushing a lever for a food pellet is to give them one just every once in a while, not on any regular basis—because if they get the reward too predictably and/or too often, they get fat and lazy. And if you never give it to them, they give up trying. I think something in the cosmos knows that so, lots of times, just when we least expect it, just when we're about to give up—"

"Something good happens! Like my cup of espresso . . . like meeting you."

I blushed and shrugged. "I hope so." There was an uncomfortably long silence that I betrayed my training by breaking. "What made you give up so young?" Alex leaned back and wrapped her healing arms around her breasts. "What made you pick up the knife?"

"It was a straight razor."

Another prolonged silence forced me to ask the correct question. "What made you pick up the straight razor?"

"You want me to tell you the truth?"

"Please."

"I believe . . ." she started slowly ". . . I had stopped believing . . . that I was ever . . . going to . . . find you."

———

That night I mentioned Alex, not by name, to Kris for the first time; and because when I did I couldn't stop grinning, Kris asked me if she was cute.

"She's cute," I said, "but she's very, very fucked up."

"Well, that's good," Kris said as she tore the plastic windows out of the junk mail envelopes so the paper could be recycled. "She'll be great practice for you."

After Kris went to bed, I fought the effects of my Halcion for a full two hours. Whispering through my bliss was a voice halcyon as the west wind.

When was the last time somebody who couldn't see your scars wanted you? When was the last time she needed you more than you needed her?

Behind my drooping eyelids I saw myself at seven, standing outside a dime store with my tall grandfather, holding his huge hand. I was staring through thick glass, coveting the Ringo trinket that rested at the very top inside a gumball machine. Grandpa left me for a moment and returned from the store with rolls of pennies and a paper bag. He squatted beside me while I turned the knob again and again until Ringo was in my hand and the bag was full of gum and less valuable prizes.

I remembered, for a second, how much more exciting it was getting the charm than having it.

So what? the west wind said, discouraging any second thoughts.

WILL YOU STILL LOVE ME?

Finally, I had played "Heart and Soul" for the last time. Its cheeriness had momentarily filled the cavernous house—its seductive buoyancy allowed me, briefly, to think Alex may have been worth it. Then I realized I had to pee and, sitting on the toilet surrounded by Kris' never-to-be-completed renovations, I was reminded how unlike my mother my partner had turned out to be.

I am very little, no more than five, and I'm sitting on the toilet while Mama takes her bath. I am fascinated by her pendulous breasts and, as usual, she has lifted them several times, indulging my request to see what lays beneath them. I am also intrigued by her pubic hair because I don't exactly understand what it is or why it's there, and, thus far, I've been bashful about asking.

Finally I figure out a way to incorporate it into my favorite game. I never tire of asking Mama, "Will you still love me if..." and filling in the blank. I never fail to be delighted when her response, always, is yes.

I once asked Mama, "Will you still love me if I throw up in church?"—and another time, "Will you still love me if I spill grape juice on my library book?" Tonight, I take a deep breath and say, "Mama, will you still love me if I grow feathers?"

For the first time, she hesitates, and my blood freezes.

"Feathers?" she says.

"Feathers," I whisper. Then I cup one hand over my mouth to muffle my voice and I point my finger in the vicinity of my bald genitals beneath my small blue shorts. "Down here."

Mama bursts out laughing. She doesn't bother to correct my mistake, merely says, "Oh yes, yes baby—I'll still love you when you grow your feathers!"

As I grew my questions often reflected my irrational fears and neuroses. Mama, will you still love me if I . . . fail arithmetic, decide I like somebody's cooking better than yours, get rabies, give somebody rabies, accidentally run over Sophie with my bike? Not until I was twelve did I come up with something, after a great deal of research, that I was almost positive would force Mama to admit her love was conditional.

"Mama," I said, feeling very grown up having just smoked a Camel in Martin's pup tent in the backyard.

"Yes?" she said in that lilting voice she always used with me.

I squinted my eyes, penetrating hers with the most sinister stare I could muster. "Will you still love me if I grow up to be a serial killer?"

"Yes," she said without pausing. "I will still love you, even if you're a serial killer." Then she leaned down and kissed the top of my head.

That night, sitting on Kris' and my toilet, I stared into the empty tub. My drug euphoria had been usurped by queasiness and vague itching—but I still could imagine Kris was there, pulling her knees up and slumping down, allowing the warm water to cover her chest, piloting the wash cloth through the suds with her fingertips, carefully scrubbing her toes, her neck, and her ears, laughing at my Mama stories—not seeming to mind the comparisons I drew. Kris, too, let me peek beneath her large breasts. Kris, too, seemed inclined to love me no matter who I was or what I did.

As her image disappeared from the bathtub, I shivered sitting there naked from the waist down surrounded by porcelain and tile. As I stood I thought—*maybe Kris is not the woman I thought she was, or maybe Mama just didn't live long enough for me to come up with the right question.*

THE REFRIGERATOR ACCIDENT

With Kris gone and Alex gone and the dogs gone, I was really alone for the first time in eight years. Portland had taken on its original look for me. But this time it was much worse. I felt like I did those first months in '81—miles and miles from home and totally alone. But now I was sitting in my own house. Why after all these years didn't anything feel like home? Surely Memphis wasn't still home. Is it Kris? How did another human being come to be, for me, the only safe place to go? A normal person, I told myself, would get up out of this rocking chair and start packing some of those empty boxes that are cluttering up the dining room. Though I have never been, nor aspired to be, particularly normal, I decided that night it might behoove me to try.

In the basement I picked up a box marked "PHOTOS" and was carrying it upstairs when its mildewed bottom gave way and spilled its contents all over the steps. I quickly scooped them up and tossed them into a fresh box, not giving myself even a moment to be frustrated by the extra work this mishap made for me. In the dining room I closed the flaps and labeled the box with an indelible black Magic Marker.

Six boxes later I was feeling so proud of my industriousness that I allowed myself a break. Back in the rocking chair, my stomach growled, and it occurred to me that normal people eat on some kind of regular basis.

I went into the kitchen and stared into our well-stocked refrigerator. My belly was demanding—but there was something wrong with my mouth. Or my brain. I couldn't imagine what it would be like to chew anything up. I'd rather have a Halcion. Finally, I reached for some peach yogurt, then decided against it. I opened the dairy box and saw that someone forgot to wrap the cheese, rendering it dark orange, hard, and inedible. The tossed salad in a Rubbermaid container had frozen and I cursed Kris' penchant for lowering the temperature to reduce the risk of salmonella. The eggs sweated out my indecision, and I finally slammed the door in disgust. When I did, three magnets leaped to the floor—one, a button that said: "Caution: I'm armed and have PMS"; another, a bright red lobster we bought at a souvenir shop in Depoe Bay; and the third, a Holstein cow dressed like Santa Claus. Directly behind them, three postcards fluttered down—pictures of a chocolate Lab like Griff, a harlequin Great Dane like Harley, and a group of sea lions sunning on a rock at Otter Crest. On the back of the latter, I knew, were words of endearment I wrote Kris from a bungalow on the sea where I spent three days by myself late last summer trying to figure out how to stop the tidal wave that was coming closer to obliterating our relationship.

I yanked the refrigerator door open again and roughly grabbed a bunch of white grapes off the top shelf. The bottom of the laden stem brushed against a plastic glass half full of murky juice and toppled it. I grabbed to catch it and knocked over a bowl of half-eaten cereal and milk. The spoon tumbled to the next shelf and splashed into an open jar of oily artichoke hearts, and when I tried to avert a bigger mess, my elbow knocked two eggs to the floor. In the flurry of hands and arms and falling food, two other half-full glasses spilled and in seconds it was over—but there was milk on the pickles and grape-nuts on my shoes and egg on my leg and sticky juice dripping down the air vent.

My first impulse was to cry. My second, to tear all the remaining food and drink from the refrigerator and smash it to the floor. I envisioned myself bleeding to death in the broken glass and finding there, on the yellow linoleum, some peace.

But instead, I closed the door, went to the bathroom, took two Valiums, then went back to my rocking chair. For the first time I spoke out loud a thought I had on occasion during those initial months in 1981, but never since. "What the fuck am I doing in Portland, Oregon?"

My eyelids relaxed, my breathing slowed, as the Valium took effect. I lit a cigarette and gestured with my hand toward the couch opposite me, as though someone were sitting there. "Mama," I said, "Why didn't you stop me?" The drug gave me the courage to remember that night in the funeral home. To my back, my mother's corpse lay silent in her coffin. In front of me, my gregarious brother painted an imaginary map that contained fifty states, but he only showed me two. And I picked this one.

I glanced toward the kitchen I knew I must face. That night in the funeral home, I realized, I innocently picked up what looked like a fresh, crisp, tasty bunch of white grapes, and the ensuing nine years had been a long, slow refrigerator accident. And now there I was, alone, with nobody home to help me clean it up.

KRIS

—

I pretended I was going to the kitchen to deal with the mess the refrigerator had made on the floor—but instead I kept walking, down the basement steps to a place where a lone photograph fell, a picture I had planned to leave behind. I sat on the cold, gray stone floor and looked at Kris as she was when we met—tall, heavy with mostly muscle, and young, twenty-five, with her bright smile and sturdy hands. For a while, that night, I forgot the frost that covers her eyes now when she looks at me—her disinclination to wrap me up in her safe strength. And I remembered how it started and grew into something we believed was indestructible.

Things were going to hell in Portland when I met Kris.

I had finally stood my ground with Judith. I was going to Memphis to visit my family and nothing she did was stopping me again. The night before I left, Judith yanked all my clothes out of the closet and threw them out the front door. I dragged them back inside while she reiterated that when I came back I could expect to be unemployed and homeless.

Probably better than working for you and living here, I thought but didn't dare say. No sense getting into a shouting match in front of the baby.

The next morning I didn't turn on any lights, hoping Judith would sleep until I was gone. In the process of getting dressed in my dark bedroom I slammed my bare foot against the nightstand leg and broke my toe. As I was heading out the door, Judith stomped down the hallway with Penn on her hip, stood scowling six inches from my face, and said, "Good. Bye."

I picked up Penn and gave her a big kiss and rubbed my nose against hers. "I love you sweetie. I'll be back soon."

I took a cab to the airport.

It was February 2, 1984.

I was on speaking terms again with my last Memphis lover, Amy, who had exacted her revenge for my leaving town in 1981 by not saying a word to me for the next two years. She was now night manager of the restaurant where we had worked together. After I settled into my grandmother's house and visited with her and my father for a while, I called Amy and she told me to come up around eleven. I arrived at the restaurant and Amy was in the office starting the books. She grinned and jumped up and gave me a huge hug and a sloppy kiss.

"You're still skinny, girl," she said, ruffling my hair.

"Skinny again," I shrugged. "Relationships, you know. Who's closing tonight?"

"Kris. Kris Brantley. You know Kris?"

"I don't think so."

"Oh, she's great. Go up to the bar and get us a couple drinks and say hi. She should be up there."

As I approached the bar I saw several waitresses I didn't know sitting on the stools and I heard a resonant female voice say something that made them burst into laughter. I turned the corner to see a robust woman with short silky hair and piercing azure eyes gesture with a bottle of Dewar's in her right hand and say, "You laugh, but it's true!"

When they noticed I was there I looked at the woman behind the bar and extended my hand. "You must be Kris." She took my hand and crushed it. "I'm Casey."

"Oh my God!" Kris said. "The infamous Casey! We've heard all about you, and none of it good!"

I grinned. "Amy never could keep her mouth shut."

Kris' face softened. "It's great to finally get to meet you."

I asked her for the drinks and, as she put down the Dewar's bottle and made us two Chivas and waters, I watched her and a curious thought popped into my mind out of nowhere. *I've never made love to a woman that powerful before.*

Kris was a five-foot-ten, 190-pound steel ball of boundless energy. I sat like a tranquil lake as her stormy sea thrashed and whirled around the restaurant executing closing procedures. Her booming baritone engaged me in conversation whether she was two feet or two hundred away. Amy was still finishing up in the office when Kris was done, so we sat at the employee table and started a conversation that wouldn't end for six years.

"So, what's it like being back in Memphis?"

"Well, I just got here a couple hours ago but, good. It feels good. I needed a break."

"Are you going back?"

"Yeah, back to Portland. Not back to the woman I've been living with for two years."

"Uh-oh . . ."

I shrugged. "Well, you know how it is. Sometimes you just have to say 'it's time to go'."

"Is she seeing somebody else?"

I laughed. "Yeah, her two-year-old."

"She's got a kid?"

"Yeah."

"Are you seeing somebody else?"

"No. And I don't intend to—not for a while."

The next day, Amy told me Kris thought I was cute. I propped my feet up on the arm of her couch and tucked my hands behind my neck. "Well, I think she's cute, too." Amy grinned and raised her eyebrows. I threw back my head and laughed. "Hey, it's easy to think somebody's cute when you live 2500 miles away and you don't have to deal with their shit twenty-four hours a day!"

"You suck," Amy said.

"Hmmph, not recently."

"Judith really fried you, didn't she?"

"Yeah, I'm totally gun-shy again. And I have a feeling I'm gonna be ducking for a long time."

KRIS COMES

I wasn't exactly telling the truth to Amy when I said I thought Kris was cute. I did think she was attractive, but she wasn't the physical type I was normally interested in. Tall was okay. Defensive tackles I could do without. What usually turned my head was the rare "haunted, hunted" look that Pontius Pilate saw in the son of God in *Jesus Christ Superstar*. *What I couldn't say to Amy or anyone else because I couldn't explain it to myself was how I was drawn to Kris, more inexplicably than I had ever been to anyone else. It wasn't her body, but she had something I wanted; I just didn't know what.*

That first night we met she noticed my limp and demanded I show her my broken toe. She was an athlete since childhood who had suffered her share of injuries, and she wasn't at all reluctant to pull my bare foot into her lap and diagnose the damage. She noticed my jaw, too—laughed and didn't question my explanation that Penn had slammed me with a toy truck. Her advice was aspirin and ice for both bruises—and it worked like magic. We talked nonstop. I thought, *this is a woman who can take care of things—this is a woman I'd like to be with if I was drowning.* Kris knew how to repair cars, how to save money on a bartender's salary, how to give the best back rubs. We talked politics, religion, dreams, and desires and we seemed to be a perfect match.

I stayed with my brother, who had moved to Portland a year after me, for the two weeks it took me to find an apartment after I returned from Memphis. Judith and I barely spoke during my transition from her home to my own. I held Penn when we were together and fought back tears as she lay her curly-haired head against my shoulder and drooled down my shirt. She was only twenty months old. I didn't know how much she understood, but I was haunted by the feeling that sometime, maybe years from now, my leaving her would matter.

I thought about Kris and felt certain our lives would never cross again. I had always been frightened of wanting anything that was virtually unattainable. I would rather forget than try and fail. I needed to exorcise these feelings for Kris and abandon my fruitless cognitions, so I bought a card that had, on the front, a picture of a horrified gorilla sitting up in bed in a New York City high-rise as a huge blond woman peered in his window. Inside it said, *"They met under the most unlikely circumstances."*

I added, *"Thank you for being my friend, even if it can't last forever. A week is better than never having met you at all. Love, Casey."* Case closed.

Two weeks later, Kris called me as I was closing Judith's bar and asked if she could visit for a week in April. On the night of her twenty-sixth birthday, April 19, 1984, Kris and I made love for the first time in the tiny attic bedroom of my apartment in southeast Portland.

We had simultaneous orgasms, a first for me and for her—a sign, we believed, that our bodies were in agreement with our minds that had been coming together since the night we met in Memphis.

We said I love you. I said please don't leave. She said I don't want to leave. I said stay. She said I can't. I said come back. She said I will. And she did.

DIGGING IN

In the attic, as Kris and I touched for the first time, I lost all consciousness of physical details. In the dark, I forgot what we looked like. After our first orgasms, I briefly remembered the self who always said what she imagined a woman wanted to hear and I thought: *I love you, that was so good, you are so good . . .* Then I snapped back out of myself and said to this woman who just a few months ago had not existed, "This feels like coming home."

She said, "I didn't think I'd ever find you."

After we made love again, we lay with our lips just inches apart. I held the gaze of her pale eyes and I recognized the timbre of a voice husky from cigarettes and passion, but not the author of the words. "We're going to die together."

"I know," said Kris.

Beneath the sloping roof of my bedroom Kris and I got as close to the stars as we were ever going to come. The stellar transcendence of our new love quickly collapsed and, for the next five years we methodically, if unknowingly, plotted our return to the fundament. At some point we began digging our graves side by side with all of the adoration and commitment of true partnership. It was not until October of 1989 that we discovered with horror that our hard work had led us well past six feet, to a place where the earth itself gave way to a void so empty and gaping it would not allow our tender drifting, but would fling us violently apart, forever.

GOODBYE EVERYBODY

I took a deep breath and held it. Nothing in the Mojave stirred. Nothing blew or slithered or rumbled or sighed approval or disapproval.

"Okay," I said, "I'll take you back to the beginning."

It was already ninety degrees and horribly humid at seven a.m. when I awoke and prepared to leave Memphis in July of 1981. Like very other Memphian born and raised, I didn't expect anything better on a mid-summer day—so I did what I had always done, prepared to sweat. The night before I had kissed my grandmother, my father, my lover of six months, and my hamster goodbye.

My grandmother had said, "Here's a thousand dollars in traveler's checks, but I still think you're making a big mistake."

My father said, "Here's five one-hundred dollar bills. Go West young woman!"

My lover said, "I loved you, you bitch," and wouldn't look at me again.

My hamster said nothing, and she was the only one who made me cry.

I threw on my skimpiest clothes, didn't bother drying my freshly-shorn hair, and gathered up the remains of my apartment—a sleeping bag, one pillow, my toothbrush, toothpaste, and a towel—and climbed into my two-year-old unairconditioned Toyota Corolla whose rearview was completely obstructed by the small portion of possessions I couldn't bear to throw out.

I stopped at a Steak 'N' Eggs on Poplar Avenue for pancakes and at a Union 76 station for a fill up. I didn't notice the undifferentiated attendant until he grinned in my window and said, "You must be goin' on a long trip."

"I'm moving to Portland, Oregon," I boasted.

His eyebrows arched and his grin widened. "No shit! I just moved here from there!"

"From Portland, Oregon?"

"Yeah!"

"Why!?"

"I wanted to live in a city that was a little more excitin'," he said. "It's pretty out there though, you'll see."

As I headed toward the Memphis-Arkansas bridge, I pondered the statistical probability that what just happened would happen and I allowed myself to ponder too deeply and I got lost, ending up across the street from Graceland—way out on Elvis Presley Boulevard in South Memphis. In this, the only city I had ever known, I had to stop and ask directions to the bridge.

As my Toyota started across the steel expanse, I glanced at the wide, muddy Mississippi below me disappearing into the horizon in both directions, and I broke without warning into a torrent of tears. Losing sight of the river, I touched my fingers to my lips and whispered, "Goodbye, Mama. I love you."

My tears obscured my vision, so I held my breath, choking them off. *The next hundred miles will be boring,* I thought. Didn't somebody say our family had made this short trip once, after I was born? If so, I had seen it before, even if I didn't consciously remember it. No need to look again. I pulled myself up in the seat and said to the person swallowing her tears, "Go through it one more time if you need to, because after Little Rock, you're not going to ever think about it again."

UNLEASHED

On February 8, 1956, my parents became one of thousands of couples responsible for making that the most prolific year of the post-World War II baby boom. The morning was dreary and frigid and Mama awoke, as she put it, "feeling frisky"—so they bundled up four-year-old Martin and two-year-old Clara and sent them off to Grandma's house for the day.

"I made us a big breakfast," my mother told me fondly and often, with just a hint of shyness. "Then we made love right there in the kitchen. Then we made love on the couch. Then I don't know how many times in the bedroom. I didn't put my thing in, you know, for protection—and when I told your Daddy he said, 'Seize the day, Bear, seize the day.'"

Whenever my mother remembered this day of my conception to me, it was always with affection in her voice—but, as the years passed, she would usually add with dismay, "His attitude was good for making love and making babies, but not for making money . . . I pray to God someday your Daddy will stop living his whole life that way."

I never thought to ask my mother if they picked that day on purpose—it being exactly nine months before my father's birthday—but if they did, I didn't comply with their calculations. With haste, I disconnected myself from my mother's womb on Halloween, displaying an early determination to do things my way, on my time schedule, without warning. The doctor, my mother claimed, didn't believe she was in labor until I was discovered lying serenely between her legs, beneath the sheet in the delivery bed.

It would be twenty years before I would attempt another disengagement from my mother.

Mama was my first love, and my sister, my second. Although my brother and sister were somewhat perturbed that their trick-or-treating was disrupted that first Halloween night, Clara immediately perceived this baby was more interesting than a plastic pumpkin full of candy. She played with my fingers and toes and, alongside Mama, learned to understand and respond perfectly to my tiny cries and piercing screams, to my playful kicks and wild thrashing. When the attention did not stop as I grew older, I perfected my infant self and assumed my nurturers would always be there to fulfill their role. Implicit in their actions was the message: *You are loved just the way you are. Don't change and we will never leave you.*

No wonder it reached a point in my early adulthood where men and boys could not satisfy my core whose definition of love lay in the gaze of a woman.

My mother gave me plenty of freedom on a long leash, so long I came to believe I had no master at all. As a child, and even as a teenager, I never strayed so far that Mama had to pull me back. I always came back on my own. In those early days, whether it was a bloodied knee, a spat with my best friend, or anguish in the face of learning to tie my shoestrings, my mother was always there with her rocking chair and ample lap, her warm hands and soothing voice. Even when she was incapable of fully eliminating the source of my pain, she colluded in my schemes to manipulate the world in my favor. I wasn't quite six when I started first grade. I was absolutely not ready to be separated from my mother for such long periods of time. She knew, but I didn't, that going to school was an inevitability—so she did everything to enhance my pleasure prior to coercing me into the car each morning. She allowed me time before my bath to rock on my horse, which I did so violently his nose crashed into the floor, and to sing Elvis songs at the top of my lungs. She always cooked my favorite "dunkin' egg" breakfast with toast and grape jelly; and she let me choose my attire no matter how scruffy, mismatched, and/or unladylike it might be. Still, no matter how nice my morning had been up to that point, when we were sitting in the parking lot behind the school I would refuse to get out of the car. Often my mother would herself be in tears as I hung onto the steering wheel with both hands, shrieking as she pulled me out by my feet.

It didn't take me long to realize she was going to be a lot stronger than me for a long time, so I began faking illness to get out of going to school as many days as possible. My favorite ploy was mixing cornstarch and water with chunks of my breakfast eggs and tossing the concoction in the toilet. Mama seemed, on these mornings, as relieved as I that illness was, unfortunately, going to make me absent from school.

My mother and I made an unspoken pact very early—and it would be years before either of us would break the other's trust. I would be the perennial baby—always cute, happy-go-lucky, witty, and charming, always willing to let her pull me into her lap and pet my head—always the peacemaker, or at least the mischievous distraction, in a family filled with disruption and discontent.

My family's roles were quite clear. Daddy was the prodigal son—never capable of bringing in a steady income, always quick to spend the little money that was there, an act he preferred to call "investing"—never abusive, but never willing to compromise himself for the family's good. Daddy would say, "I go my own way, you're welcome along, seize the day."

Mama was the eternally-suffering martyr—willing to forsake all that was pleasurable in life to keep the family from dissolving, always working jobs tirelessly inside and outside our home to keep us out of that most dreadful place of all, "The Poor Farm"—always careful, always planning for the day when things would be easier. Seize the century.

Martin was the little boy-king, rudely dethroned when Clara was born. He hated her and was not afraid to show it in every way imaginable from the day she arrived in the Harper house. Martin compensated for his early losses by eating everything in sight, often before anybody else could even get a shot at it, frequently forking others' hands to secure the last pork chop for himself.

Clara was the unenviable middle child and the preeminent girl, whose anger at not being protected from her vicious brother hid beneath huge, frilly skirts and shiny patent-leather shoes. Clara's ability to withdraw from the fray into a safer world of her own making was second only to her ability to fly from behind her closed door now and then like a demon bad seed to boldly blurt the well-kept family secrets to anyone who would listen.

With all this exquisite choreography already in place by the time I was born, the obvious role left to fill seemed to be the chameleon. I was Clara's ally against Martin, sometimes physically able to step between them and thwart their fighting—other times skillful at distracting him or removing her from the line of fire with some real or imaginary pressing need that only she could satisfy. I was no threat to Martin, his worst nightmare of being joined in the center of the universe already having been embodied by Clara, so I became his confidante. He talked to me and I paid attention in this family where no one really listened to anybody else—where usually no one could even be heard above the fracas.

I was the androgynous child my father needed to satisfy his desire for rough and tumble play which was unfulfilled by his enormous and bookish son. And I was Mama's baby, promising I would never grow up, never leave her, never take from her the delight of caring for someone who truly loved and needed her. In exchange, she would never leave me either, would always be there to pick up my pieces, catch my fall, love me no matter who I became or what I did.

Our family aged, and Martin was the first to defect, leaving home at eighteen to attend college up state. Two years later, Clara sought asylum in her own apartment across town—leaving our house under a black cloud after a particularly contemptuous barrage of unwelcomed secret-sharing.

For three years I was home alone with my parents, living free, in relative peace. My mother would awake some mornings to find my boyfriend still in my room, and she would smile cheerily and fix extra breakfast for him. Mark and I made the rounds of rock concerts, often three or four a week, and on one occasion my mother informed me the next day that she had put the "little thing" I had left on the television on top of my dresser—the "little thing," to my horror, being a partially smoked joint. She never acted like she knew anything. I was upholding my part of the bargain—coming home every night, sooner or later, and still never feeling the slightest tug.

There was a little jerk of the leash when I was eighteen and decided to move out. I got an apartment just two miles from home, and I religiously called Mama daily and joined her and my father every week for Sunday dinner. Mama wasn't happy at first, but she learned quickly that my physical absence from her home had no effect on the emotional bond we shared that was unseverable.

I was a junior in college when I decided I would leave the theater arts degree I was soon to receive behind me and embark on a graduate career in psychology. My parents were delighted, reminding me how valuable my psychiatric services had been to the family over the years, noting that getting paid for these services might not be a bad idea.

I took my graduate exams early and did well. Martin, by this time, was working on a fine arts degree in Arkansas and Clara was beginning a doctoral program in New Orleans. Trusting that they knew the scoop on academia, I took their advice and began writing to and receiving applications from schools all across the United States. I homed in on Duke in North Carolina, Amherst in Massachusetts, and Stanford in California. Then I told my mother what I had done and something horrible began to happen.

She burst into tears, asked me what was wrong with Memphis State. She couldn't possibly have heard my informed explanations through her sobbing. "What if you leave and something happens to me?" she wailed. I went to my apartment that night stunned, trying to figure out why she said that, what she meant by that. I got into bed and tried to shut out these impossible questions by relaxing with my latest serial killer book. I read the words of a homicide detective, explaining how he knew the cause of the victim's death prior to the autopsy. "The ligature method was still in place. . . ." I awoke the next morning with a stiff, sore neck, having fallen asleep with the light on, with my arm crooked under my head and the book resting on my fingertips.

My mother had a bad case of the flu the winter of my senior year in college—and her cough wouldn't go away. She had ceased trying to talk me out of my plans, and I had stopped telling her what they might be. Our time together was strained. For the first time in my life, our conversations didn't flow as we carefully chose the words we spoke to each other and delivered them through clenched teeth and tight lips. Mama looked tired all the time. Her blue eyes lost their luster. I missed their twinkle, the endless chatter we had shared, but I didn't know what to do. I was twenty-two, about to receive my college degree. What was I supposed to do after that if not move on?

During my last semester, I was worried about my mother all the time and not even sure why. I was deeply involved with my second girlfriend. My joys and worries resulted in my failure to complete my final project, delaying my graduation until August. I didn't talk much to Melissa about my mother because I didn't know what to say. She wasn't *sick* or anything, so why was I feeling so scared? And so guilty. I really couldn't explain this sudden bout of guilt. My lesbian affairs to date had been in the same category as my rock 'n' roll, pot-smoking, boyfriend-humping teenage escapades—yet another thing I was doing that Mama would turn a blind eye to, another thing that would not affect her love for me. But, suddenly, I felt like I was keeping something from her, doing something bad that would upset her.

Even though my lover didn't know why, she knew when I was feeling sad or scared or agitated—and her comfort was endless. Many times, to transport myself out of my strange new skin, I engaged in some of the most passionate, energetic lovemaking I had known—justifying that if I had to keep emotional secrets from Melissa, at least I could give her my sexual best.

For strength I turned to my first, now ex, girlfriend with whom I had managed to salvage a friendship after she tempestuously introduced me to the joys of lesbian love, then dumped me on my ass for another "straight" girl.

"Don't worry," Reed would say. "They always freak when the baby leaves home."

"But she looks so sad all the time."

"So, she's sad. It's not gonna kill her. She'll cry for a while, then she'll get over it. What's the option?"

On June 15, 1979, the day most of my classmates were attending spring graduation ceremonies, I spent the afternoon with my mother. Between episodes of unproductive coughing, she said to me, "I'm sorry, honey. I guess it's funny seeing your Mama acting like this." With tears in her eyes she held my hands and said, "You'll never know how hard it is to say goodbye to your baby until you have one of your own. I want you to be happy, no matter how bad it hurts me. . . ."

That night, in a dream, I saw my mother lying alone on a narrow bed in a room with barren walls and ghastly fluorescent lighting. I saw myself standing on a jagged cliff high above a stormy sea and she was in that room, somewhere behind me, whispering, "I love you." I woke up drenched with sweat in my twin bed in my tiny garage apartment, strangling on a cry lodged deep in my throat. *Mama's dying*, I thought, and bolted for the telephone, called a florist without thinking, and had delivered to her that day a bouquet of red roses with a note that said: *I love you. No matter where I go, no matter what I do, you will always be my mother, and I will always be your baby. C.*

One month later, on a sticky July afternoon, my phone rang, waking me from a nap. "Yeah," I said in my sleepy voice. I heard a click that sounded like it came from a human throat followed by the unmistakable sniffs of someone crying. "Hello?" I said, waking quickly.

"Baby?" It was a feather-light whisper. It was my mother. "I've got cancer."

As she and my father packed a small bag and drove to the hospital, I sat on the side of my bed, my face in my hands, sobbing. In my mind I saw a little girl, sitting in her mother's big lap, rocking in the wooden chair—her curly, sweaty hair pressed close against a warm, full bosom—and I wanted to be that lucky baby again more than anything else in the whole world.

I didn't even bother to be fitted for my cap and gown that August. I stopped applying to graduate schools, threw away responses that were coming in without even opening them. I held Mama's dry, icy hand as they wheeled her into surgery—sat listless in the waiting room with my father while the doctors took fourteen hours to remove all the diseased organs they could. For the next eighteen months, I watched her breeze through chemotherapy, then collapse from a series of radiation treatments. I became a nurturer, this most challenging role usurping the easier ones of lover and friend, and I lost Melissa in the process.

I changed Mama's colostomy bag, trying not to show my horror at the hole in her abdomen constructed by the surgeon to replace her cancerous anus, trying not to gag in front of this woman who changed my dirty diapers without complaint. I cooked. I cleaned. I lost weight right along with her. I talked about the past which evoked weak smiles from my sick mother—and when I got home, I shook and rocked and begged a God I hoped existed not to take my mother because I didn't know how to live without her. In the winter of 1980 my mother seemed to be getting stronger, and, with faith in her improving health, I took a new lover. Amy and I had great sex, and, with my stay in Memphis now indefinite, we dared muse about a long future together. But by March, my mother had taken a turn for the worse as her cancer came roaring back with a vengeance, attacking what little was left of her colon, exploding blood vessels along its relentless path and spewing their contents into the plastic bag she wore at her side.

Thus began a seemingly endless series of emergency trips to the hospital for transfusions of blood—my stoic mother finally succumbing to the pain of needle sticks in collapsing veins, crying softly while I held her hands and this nurse or that poked again and again trying to find another point of access. I would lie in my bed at night with my new lover kneeling between my legs, begging me for just one more time— while behind my closed eyes I saw glaring hospital lights and heard screaming scarlet sirens, saw the nurses clamping tubes under my mother's nose as she gasped for breath. *I can't come when my mother is dying.* I didn't have to say anything. My distraught lover cried at the foot of the bed.

My mother went to the hospital one more time at the end of May. As fast as they could fill her up, her ragged intestine poured the fresh blood back out, refusing to allow her enough strength to come home. My grandmother, father, and I began splitting each day into thirds so my mother would never be alone. On June 14th, I prepared to leave her hospital room at ten p.m. when my father arrived for his overnight shift. As always, I had spent the last eight hours curled next to her talking when she was awake, making sure the nurses gave her pain shots when she needed them, and, when she slept, staring out the window and weeping silently, careful not to let her see the depth of my terror.

Her diseased liver had yellowed her skin and eyes, the blood loss had weakened her to the point at which she couldn't get out of the bed at all anymore—but every night she managed to rally and return my goodnight kiss and give me a slight smile. On this night, I rose to leave and took her hand, kissed her lips and hers didn't move. I said my usual, "See you tomorrow. I love you." My mother closed her eyes, and I never saw them open again.

PICKING PORTLAND

The night before we buried my mother, a hoard of family and friends gathered at the funeral home. My sister was in from New Orleans, my brother from Arkansas, and my aunt from Atlanta. An hour before closing, only my family remained.

"We're all tired, we should go on and go," my grandmother said. She was standing by the coffin stroking her dead daughter's waxy hand.

"Who's got cars here?" my mother's sister said, allowing her practical business sensibility to control her grief.

My sister stood behind me massaging my shoulders. "We can stop on the way home and have a drink," she said, concerned about getting me through the night.

"I'm staying 'til they close," I said.

My father, understanding more than I realized, said, "Let Case have some time with her mother."

They all went toward the door, my aunt negotiating the car pool, and I grabbed my brother's arm and whispered, "Stay."

When everyone was gone, we went back inside and sat in the room where my mother's corpse lay clad in a pale green nightgown. I turned to Martin and said, "I've got to get the fuck out of here."

"I know," he said. "This is creepy."

"Not out of *here*. I mean out of *Memphis*, for good. Right away."

"Oh." My brother was the consummate risk-taker. To my father's dismay, he never took to team sports, but his love of solitary physical challenges knew no bounds. Weighing in at two hundred pounds by age twelve never stopped him from climbing trees, at least one of which ripped apart beneath his poundage. He spent his youth macheteing his way through the primeval forests of the Nonconnah Creek bottoms and his young adulthood exploring first the hills of the antediluvian Ozarks and later the rugged peaks of the Colorado Rockies.

Never in my whole life had my brother tried to dissuade me from embarking on an adventure, regardless of how unsafe it might appear—never had he said to me, as had so many others, "Be careful."

"Where can I go?" I said.

"Where do you want to go?"

"As far away as possible."

"Like where?"

"Somewhere pretty."

"You want mountains?"

"Yeah! And the ocean, too!"

He thought for a moment. "How about Seattle?"

"Where's Seattle?"

"It's in Washington State."

"Where's Washington State?"

He pointed into the air, up and to the left. "Way up in the northwest corner." He was talking to me like I was a baby. I wasn't stupid—I was a theater major. There is a difference.

"Do they have mountains and the ocean?"

"Oh, God. The Cascades are there, and the Pacific."

"Is it big?"

"Pretty big."

"I don't want anything too big."

"Then how about Portland?"

"Where's Portland?"

"In Oregon."

"Where's Oregon?"

"Right below Washington."

"Do they have mountains and the ocean, too?"

"Yeah."

The funeral director came in and told us they were closing for the night. My brother strolled out to the car, and I went to my mother's coffin. I slipped my hand beneath hers, curling my fingers around her cold, dead flesh. "Mama," I whispered. "I'm going to Portland." I imagined I saw her lips rise in a small smile. She was free now, and maybe I could be, too.

I leaned into the chilly air surrounding her body and kissed her goodbye.

———

A week after my mother's funeral, on the instructions provided by my brother, I spent the afternoon at Triple A. An older man laid out a U.S. map and individual state maps on a drafting table and slowly outlined my journey with a pale green marker. He described the roads that would take me through Arkansas, Missouri, Kansas, Colorado, Utah, Idaho, and Oregon to Portland. I listened as he explained this central route would be best—how the southern trek through Arizona and New Mexico would add a good three hundred miles to my trip and how, even in July, the northern route's Tetons could still be buried under the winter snow.

I had never seen a mountain.

I had never driven alone more than a hundred miles from Memphis.

As he led me to the door with my arms full of maps and guide books, he touched my shoulder and said, "I can't believe a little girl like you is going to take a trip like this. Take care of yourself."

I was twenty-four, and neither surprised nor annoyed at encountering surrogate mothers of both sexes along my life's path.

GOODBYE EVERYBODY
REVISITED

The night before I left Portland, I invited my three best
friends over and I took two Percodans before they arrived. All
the furniture was gone, so we sat on the floor and I opened
their farewell gifts. Marlena gave me a box of pastries from a
quaint and expensive bakeshop on Hawthorne. Elaine gave
me a book called *Sisters on the Road*, an anthology of travel
stories written by women. And Allie's present was a cut crystal
on a leather strap which, she said as she hung it around my
neck, would deflect any negative energy that might come my
way on my journey.

I had already said goodbye to my brother, and to Kris'
little brother, Paul, who had come to Portland in 1986 to
attend college. The guys spent the afternoon packing my truck
for me. Upon their departure, my brother said, "It's a little
out of the way, but definitely run up to the Grand Canyon if
you have time."

Paul folded me in his long arms and said, "I love you,
Casey. I'm gonna miss you. Be careful, okay?" I loved him like
the baby brother I always wanted and never had until he became mine by marriage.

It got late and the steady drone of reminiscing began to
die and the four of us knew it was time and the tears came.
We stood at the door and the first drops spilled down my

cheeks when I turned to Marlena. "Thank you for everything," I said.

"Please be careful. And eat those pastries. Gain some weight, okay?" We released each other and Marlena stepped out onto the porch.

I turned to Elaine. "I'm gonna make it. I always do."

"I know," she said, avoiding my eyes. "I know." She joined Marlena on the porch.

I looked at Allie, whom I had never seen cry, and her face was flushed, her eyes sad, and both of us lost our ability and desire to keep up our tough facades. I took her face in my hands and she gripped my wrists, and between huge, gulping sobs I giggled and said, "Now I know how Dorothy felt!" She laughed and we choked on our tears. I buried my face in her neck and she in mine and added, "I always lost it when she said goodbye to the scarecrow."

"I love you," we said to each other. We let go, and my three best friends disappeared into the night. Nothing was left in the house except my rocking chair, so I rocked and looked around at the emptiness. *I should take a Halcion and go to bed and get this over with.* The pain-free high of the Percodan had faded into the familiar, queasy itching. I stared at the empty rectangle above the fireplace mantle—whiter in its interior than the dingy wall surrounding it—where my framed poster of Jack the Ripper used to hang. It had been a special gift from Paul who visited Whitechapel, the actual scene of the unsolved century-old murders, on a senior class trip to England. The boy knew me well. Kris had graciously allowed me to feature it prominently in our living room.

The picture was gone, but I could still clearly see the alleged Jack, dashing in his fashionable black cape and tall hat. Like all his brothers, he looks normal, even appealing—the last person you would suspect until it was far too late.

Of all people, I thought, *I should have known that the killer isn't necessarily a man, and the murder isn't always as obvious as a skillful slash from ear to ear.* A sudden chill shot through my body from my scalp to my feet. "A 'coon just ran across your grave," my mother used to say, and, for the first time in my life, I got it. Over the next week I would be covering a lot of empty, available earth.

I bolted for the bathroom, tossed a Halcion into my mouth, and washed it down with a palmful of water from the sink. I rested my hands on the porcelain and looked at myself in the mirror. My hair was damp and curling from old sweat and no real sleep. Water droplets hung from my bottom lip and my cheekbones and brow were accentuated by black shadows and blue highlights from the moon's glow through the tiny window. A vision of Kris, so far from home in Memphis, helped finish the thought.

And I'm not always the victim.

COUNTERTRANSFERENCE

"I think Alex is in love with me."

A snap of gunfire erupted down the street as I sat dressed in my therapist clothes in the North Portland house that had been converted into a counseling center. It was stuffy inside and sweltering out, and the Bloods and Crips were doing their summer thing. My supervisor got up and closed the two windows that were open, checked the front door lock, then sat back down opposite me.

He glanced at his notes. "Alex is the suicide?"

"Yeah."

He laughed. "They all fall in love with their therapist."

"Suicides?"

"No, I mean *all* of them."

"Mine don't!"

"Yeah they do. Your others just hide it better."

"Dannn." I was whining.

"All right, all right, what makes you think she's in love with you?"

"Well," I said, crossing my legs to squeeze off the sticky tingling in my crotch. "She threatened to terminate today." Dan raised his eyebrows. "She bluntly told me first thing that she didn't plan on coming back because she felt like she was starting to 'have feelings for me'."

"Did you ask her what the feelings were?"

"Yeah. She said 'lust' and 'love'. She said she's been writing me letters and dreaming about me. She kept the tape from her answering machine where I left a message a few weeks ago when she didn't show for a session. She says she listens to it over and over, late at night when she's alone, and I have to believe her. She quoted it back to me verbatim. She says she thinks about me constantly and it's driving her crazy."

"And how does all this make you feel?"

I shrugged my padded shoulders and lit a cigarette. "Well, it kind of defeats the purpose of therapy, doesn't it, if the therapist is driving the client crazy?"

Dan laughed. "Hey, maybe we owe 'em one every now and then!"

I smiled, then remembered I needed this man's serious consideration. "I'm scared, a little. I'm not sure how to proceed." It sounded pretty cool, fairly professional. But inside, my heart throbbed, my groin tightened, and some more authentic part of me continued silently. *It makes me feel horny and insane and reckless and obsessed and addicted to the idea of throwing away the macaroni and cheese and letting in the wolves.*

Dan rattled on about ethical responsibility and using misguided client affections to facilitate therapy and polite ways of terminating a professional relationship and the whole time I sat with my ankle propped across my knee, calmly smoking, and thinking: *You stupid man. Can't you see I'm about to commit a crime here?* When he left, fully confident I would handle this situation competently, I was completely alone with my madness and desire—a long-forgotten state with which I would become, against a will I no longer possessed, reacquainted.

TERMINATION

I pulled my therapist clothes from the closet and started to slip on the black dress pants with their sharp crease and stylish belt. Then I carefully returned them to their hanger. I opened my drawer and removed a pair of mottled 501's my slimmer body could fit into again. They slid easily over my thighs and buttoned with room to spare across my stomach. I tucked in a starched buttondown blue-striped shirt and left the house. It was nine-thirty p.m., and I was meeting Alex at ten.

I stood on the dark porch of the counseling house, smoking and fighting a weakening desire to think. It was August and the sun had just set on the West Coast—its memory still pinking the indigo horizon. I was breathing hard. I heard the rumbling of a big, old car approaching and my lips were dry with anxiety. I ran my fingers through my hair which was curling from the humidity as Alex pulled up to the curb and hopped out without opening the door. She didn't see me as she strolled up the walkway.

"Hey," I said in a soft voice, a nervous croak that may have sounded like a sexy whisper. She gasped and turned to me, squinting through the night for a moment with her hand across her heart.

"God, I didn't see you," she said. I shrugged, a cool gesture that masked my inability to speak in her presence—this adorable young woman with a pocked past I no longer cared to explore, my client who I believed wanted to make love to me as much as I to her. "I didn't know you smoked," she said, licking her lips that, opposite of mine, moistened with sexual tension.

"Yep," I said, flicking the butt in the bushes. I opened the door and Alex turned to face me. "After you," I said, and she turned her back to me and didn't move. I was inches behind her. "Alex?" She raised her chin and I saw her hair tickle her collar.

"Oh." It was a gasp, like a tiny breath catching in her throat, and her right hand reached out to grasp the door frame.

I touched her back lightly. "Are you okay?" She shivered like a wet puppy and walked into the house. In the light, she turned to face me and her eyes looked glassy. I thought she might be drunk. "Are you okay?"

Her eyes flicked down my body quickly then met mine. "Uh, I'm okay. You look, uh, nice."

In the counseling room, this client who had told me stories for months about abuse, neglect, and abandonment sat down and began playing with the shoestring of one of her battered off-brand sneakers. "Do you think we'll live through this?" she asked. I looked puzzled. "There was a drive-by this afternoon right over here off Killingsworth."

"Oh, shit," I said. "Well, either we do or we don't."

She grinned and teased me. "Oh, that's right—and worrying about it won't change anything."

"Right!"

We had long since ceased therapy. Alex knew more about me than any client should. She asked direct questions about my personal life. I kidded her about not playing the game by the rules; then I gave her direct answers.

She looked at me and her face fell. "I want to tell you something . . . right away . . . uh, tonight. . . . This is the last night I'm coming here." My brow furrowed. "Casey, this isn't a snap decision or anything. Just the opposite. I've thought about this and thought about this until I've practically driven myself crazy. Crazier." She laughed, then shook her head and dropped her eyes back to her mutilated shoestring. "I'd love to, uh . . . I'd like to see you sometimes, like, some other way, like be your friend or something, but you can't be my therapist anymore. I can't stand it. It hurts too much."

"Hurts? Alex . . ."

She stood, lit a cigarette, and opened the window. Staring out into the cool night, she continued. "I'm serious. Please hear me out. The other night I listened to your message on my tape again. I wrote you a letter and tore it up. Then I got in my Cougar and went up to Rocky Butte and spun cookies in the parking lot 'til my tires were nearly ripped to shit. Then I felt like an idiot, so I stopped and sat looking at the city lights and cried for about an hour. Then I left and drove by your house. I swore to myself that if I ever drove by your house I would stop seeing you. So I did, and I am. Please don't try to talk me out of it."

"Alex," I said, rising. I approached her from behind and touched her hip.

She lowered her head. "Please don't," she said, bending just slightly to place her palms on the windowsill, moving her ass just an inch closer to me. "There's nothing you can do. I'll never feel better. I'll never have what I want." She turned around and her eyelashes were wet with tears I hadn't heard in her voice at all. "I love you," she said.

I brushed her shaggy hair from her eyes, tucking it behind her ears and she whimpered. I glanced at her mouth and she barely cocked her head. I touched my fingertips to her jaw, and kissed her gently on the lips. "You're gonna destroy me," she said.

"I'm gonna destroy *me*," I said, and kissed her again.

ALEX COMES

—

A week after I first kissed Alex, Kris and I went to my class graduation party. It was August 14, 1989, Alex's 21st birthday. We got home around ten and, at eleven, Alex called our house. She was at a party thrown in her honor and Prince's "Let's Go Crazy" boomed in the background.

"I hate it here," she shouted. "I hate these people. I have a headache, and it hurts."

"Take some aspirin."

"I did."

"Tylenol."

"Did. Nothing's helping."

"What can I do?"

"What are my choices?"

Kris was roughhousing with the dogs and filling their food bowls in the kitchen. "Anything," I said.

"Just come take me home, okay?"

I hadn't told Kris we had terminated therapy. I told her that night that Alex was in trouble and I knew it was unorthodox, but I was going to go see her, to help her out. As I walked out the door, Kris glared at me with a look of suspicion so justified and pain so genuine I was ashamed to look back at her. I pretended she didn't exist on one level of consciousness. On a deeper one, a meter started running that would one day ring up an amount so high I would consider suicide to get out of paying it.

By the time we got to Alex's, her headache was gone. It was quiet at her apartment. We sat on the floor, Alex at my feet playing with my shoestrings.

"Oh, happy birthday, by the way. I don't think I said that."

"I hate my birthday," she said.

"Why?"

"Something bad always happens on my birthday."

"Always?"

"Pretty much."

"Such as?"

She sighed and stared at my shoe, then grinned and peeked up at me. "Hey, am I paying for this?"

"You never paid for it." I playfully kicked her thigh with my Nike.

She sighed again. "Well, on my sixth birthday my father left and never came back." There was a long pause and I said nothing.

"My best friend and her father were killed in an car accident on their way to my party when I was seven. I swear. I don't remember what happened when I was eight. On my ninth birthday my mother married my stepfather. You know what he did to me. But the worst was my tenth. My mother, she was such a fucker sometimes—I don't know, maybe she was just an idiot. When I was ten she threw me this huge party. It wasn't really a kid party, you know. It was mostly adults, drinking and everything. I don't know where all these people came from. There were a few kids, but by that time I'd pretty much stopped being friends with anybody. We moved around so damn much 'cause, you know, first my dad and then my stepfather—neither one of them could stay in one fucking job for any length of time. Anyway, I hid out in the shed that day because my stepfather was loaded and had his hands all over me. After everybody was gone my mom found me out there and she sat me down and said, 'Now that you're ten you're old enough to know the truth. Your real dad is dead.'

"I'm serious; it was that blunt. For what reason did she tell me this, and why on that day? Hell if I know. Anyway, of course, it turns out she was lying which makes it even worse, I know. But the bottom line is, it totally ruined my goddamn tenth birthday. And a lot of years after that. I just found out he's alive, you know, two years ago, when he called me up out of the blue. I guess that was when the fucker thought it was safe to get in touch, after I was too old to get any child support or something."

My family was nutty, but they weren't vipers. Like so many times before at the counseling house, I didn't know what to say. As Alex spoke, I had taken her hands in mine and she was now playing with my mother's wedding band, which I had put on my right ring finger the day she died. "Alex, I'm sorry this day's so bad for you."

"Oh, there's more but I don't have the energy to go into it. Let's just say enough bad stuff has happened that now I'm always paranoid on my birthday. I know that's *irrational*," she said, mocking my therapist-speak.

I shrugged. "I don't know. That's a lot of bad stuff."

"Hey," she said, shaking her head as she often did, as though to throw off some imaginary dampness. "Let's talk about something else."

"Well, this isn't totally off the subject, but you know what? I remember what I was doing on your ninth birthday."

"You do?"

"Yeah."

"How old were you?"

"Twenty."

"Damn!"

"Oh, shut up."

"So, what were you doing?"

"You're not going to believe this, but on August 14, 1977, I saw Elvis."

Alex burst out laughing. "Let me guess, in a Chico's?"

"We didn't have Chico's in Memphis."

"Did you have shopping malls way back then?"

"No, I'm serious. I saw him at Graceland."

"What, hovering over the gates?"

"No, baby girl," I said, ruffling her hair. "He wasn't dead yet."

"Oh, wow!"

"But two days later he would be."

"Hey, he died on Madonna's birthday! Maybe Madonna *is* Elvis!"

"I don't think reincarnation works that way—she would've been, like, eighteen or something."

"Oh yeah, right. Shit," she said, "my headache's coming back. I wish I had some good drug that'd just knock my ass out and get this birthday over with once and for all." My better judgment apparently still hung on by one frayed thread and I chose not to share with Alex the corner pharmacy I carried in my bag. I suggested she take a hot shower, and she promptly stood and disappeared into the bathroom. Which was good, because during the last moments of this conversation, I was overwhelmed by anxiety I had so far hidden well. Once alone I began to feel claustrophobic, so I dry-swallowed a Halcion and turned on some music—but nothing kept me from remembering that fortune-teller in Idaho back in '81 with her oddball ashtray and the messages from Elvis. I hadn't thought about this since that day Kris and I were at the Devil's Churn. What had Elvis said? I felt insane even letting myself imagine any of this meant anything. I racked my brain. I had kept the paper the woman had given me with the message scrawled in her own hand. It was in my copy of *Being and Nothingness* at home. He had said something about three people in Portland doing something to me—taking something from me. . . . shit, I couldn't remember. Like it really mattered.

A warm breeze fluttered the curtains at the open window in Alex's dining room and I smelled death. I had first smelled it the night I turned ten, when my brother took me on a Halloween tour of an overgrown, abandoned graveyard way past the Memphis city limits.

The night was nippy and someone in a house we couldn't see must have had a roaring fire fueled by some aromatic wood that, ever since, I have always associated with death. But that night at Alex's it was warm, August. No one had a fire in the hearth—and that night, the initial whiff of burning wood was quickly followed by the odor of formaldehyde I had first encountered as I stood over my mother's coffin and noticed the pink droplets oozing from the pores of her dead hands.

I was past the point of thinking. I smelled death, listened to the hiss of the shower, felt like I was going to evaporate. When the shower stopped, sensation disappeared and thought returned. One simple sentence: *I think my time in Portland is coming to an end.* It was a vaporous thought, made excruciatingly dissonant by the ponderous facts of my solid spouse, my large canine children, my sturdy house, my promising career.

Alex emerged from the shower wearing a white terrycloth robe. George Michael sang on the tape and we sat in hard-backed chairs by the open dining room window, smoking, talking. At two a.m., Alex's roommate came home and went straight to bed, seemingly oblivious to the fact that her friend's former therapist was in the house.

We had exhausted safe topics long ago. Our conversation had collapsed into whispered fragments, disjointed confessions, subtle suggestions. Alex rubbed her eye and asked me if there was something in it, and, when she leaned toward me, her robe opened and I saw the crescent curve of her right breast.

"Yeah," I said, when my face was inches from hers.

"What is it?" she said.

"Hmmm, well . . ." I ran my thumb across her eyebrow and down her cheek. "It looks like lust, and love."

"Oh God," she said, her lashes fluttering as I kissed the outside of her ear, then barely touched my tongue inside. "At the door," she whispered, cocking her head to grant me deeper access, "last week in North Portland . . . when I saw you in your 501s . . . when I stopped just inside the door . . . and you were behind me. . . . I, oh, I uh . . . came." She sucked in air between her teeth and trembled as I slipped my warm hands beneath the folds of her robe and held them against her ribs. We kissed, and her tongue moved between my teeth. I parted her robe and pulled her to my lap. She continued. "Just looking at you, just knowing you were behind me. I swear I felt your heat against my ass. I couldn't stop it. . . . Nothing like that has ever happened to me before."

"Do it again, where I can see you," I said, wrapping one arm around her naked hips and slipping my other hand between her legs. She rocked herself upon my hand, the back of which pressed strategically against the crotch of my jeans. She buried her face in my hair as I sucked and nibbled her nipples. "Come while I'm inside of you." She cried out as I thrust three fingers deep inside of her, almost breaking my wrist as she came in violent waves. She rested her moist lips against my sweaty neck and, when she was calm, I started to withdraw from her. Her muscles clenched and she pressed herself hard against my hand, against my lap, locking us together.

"Oh God, please don't go," she said.

As the first pastel colors of dawn peeked over the eastern horizon and George Michael reminded us for the hundredth time that sometimes love and crime can be mistaken for one another, I closed my eyes and realized my world was in big, big trouble.

RATTLESNAKES AND DUNKIN' EGGS

I didn't recognize Little Rock, so I figured the stories were true—we must have driven through there when I was an infant. Otherwise, I would remember it, because I certainly remembered the only other two trips my family took during my childhood.

My mother had a phobia about traveling.

Once we went to Ft. Lauderdale where my aunt and uncle lived before they moved to Atlanta. I was four, my sister seven, and my brother nine. We had an army green Plymouth station wagon and my father did all the driving. My mother sat in front—my sister, grandmother, and I sat in the backseat, and my brother sat on a huge pillow in the cargo area. On some stretch of road, Martin was tickling the back of Clara's neck and telling her it was spiders; and she was slapping his hand and complaining, but no one was making him stop. I was singing Elvis songs and eating graham crackers. My father, who was never one to tackle problems head on, often adopted creative ways to end the incessant bickering of three bored children.

On this occasion, he squinted at the highway ahead of us and said, "Hey, what's that in the road?" The chatter didn't stop. "Oh my God!" he exclaimed. "That's a rattlesnake!"

We all threw ourselves over the front seat shouting "Where? Where?"

"Oh, man," he said. "I think we ran over it."

We all threw ourselves over the backseat and stared at the road behind us. There was nothing there. "He's not there, Daddy, he's not there!" we chanted.

Daddy peered into the rearview mirror. "Oh my God," he said.

"What?!" we shrieked.

"He must have jumped up into the car."

Martin, all 175 pounds of him, scrambled over the back seat, over Grandma whose shouting joined ours as her neck bent under the massive weight of her grandson. Clara, who always had a secret desire to escape from this family, saw her legitimate chance and madly grabbed at the door handle. Grandma caught her before she could open the door. I leaped into my mother's lap, crying. Kids' hysterical screams drowned Grandma's orders to pull over and the sharp sounds of Mama slapping Daddy on the arm and commanding, "Damn it, Harland, tell them you're lying, you son of a bitch, tell them you're lying!"

Daddy never said another word about the rattlesnake and, eventually, the panic subsided.

I don't remember the ocean. I do remember changing into our bathing suits and Grandma angrily ripping hers to shreds because she'd gotten too fat to pull it on. Maybe it was Grandma who taught me that tearing things to pieces was an appropriate response to frustration. I recall sitting on a large towel on the hot sand and Aunt Lillian cutting her foot on a discarded soda can tab and crying very loudly, which got her oodles of attention. And, I remember Uncle Bailey, a tiny man who had made a million from sound business deals and prudent investing, patiently teaching me how to drop crab nets—then becoming infuriated when I caught more than he did.

The other trip, which we took the next summer when I was five, was to Illinois to visit my father's family. One thing I remember about that trip was refusing to eat eggs for breakfast at a roadside diner because the waitress said I could have them over-easy or sunnyside-up. At home, Mama called these styles "dunkin' eggs", and nobody could convince me they were all one and the same.

When we ate dinner at my paternal grandparents' house, I refused to eat the fresh corn because my father's mother, who always called me Cindy for some reason, cut it off the cob.

———

The first thing I saw that morning when I left Memphis that was different from anything I had seen before was the blinking lights on the tall silos of a nuclear power plant at Minifee. Relieved to be finally entering uncharted territory, I was paying close attention as I came upon the Ouachitas, the first mountains I had ever seen. On one high ridge, someone had painted the Arkansas Razorbacks emblem and "GO HOGS!", and I knew I wasn't in Memphis anymore.

I saw the Ozarks for the first time at seven o'clock and I pulled over as soon as I could and got out to gaze across the fuzzy, green mounds that dipped and rose as far as I could see. *This was all under the sea*, I thought, squatting and running my fingers through the soil. *Dinosaurs walked here.*

I arrived at my brother's home in Fayetteville at nine and his wife fed me meatloaf, mashed potatoes and gravy, fresh green beans, and blackberry pie—and I stayed up longer than I should have. Martin had always been a collector, and he loved to show off any new acquisitions, be they rocks or model trains and ships and airplanes or dusty rare books. That night, when he knew I was getting too sleepy to stay up much longer, he pulled out his latest pride and joy. Martin had recently received his fine arts degree, and with it, a special governor's award for having developed a program to teach poetry to children in the Arkansas school system. He beamed when he handed me a framed photo of himself receiving a plaque from the head of state and shaking his hand.

"This is great," I said, staring at the picture of my rotund brother and the handsome politician with a head full of big, poofy hair. "Who is this guy?"

"He's the governor, Bill Clinton," Martin said.

"How old is he?"

"God, I don't know. Maybe thirty-five."

I stared at Governor Clinton and thought he was kind of cute with his chipmunk cheeks and brilliant blue eyes. Then I easily imagined him with some extra weight, his body trim now, but somehow suggestive of an endomorph yet to come. "He looks like you," I said and Martin laughed. "He does, I mean, you know, if he was a little heavier."

"Yeah, like Daddy looks like George Bush," Martin said.

"He does!" I said, and Daddy did. Kind of tall and thin with no butt and a silly grin. I could just hear the new vice-president saying goofy things to his kids like, "Keep your eye on the ball."

Thank God I didn't think anybody in my family looked like Ronald Reagan. I hated him already—uncharacteristically totally mistrusted him with his snake oil hair and that fake smile—his mouth, I thought, less like a human mouth, more like a gash someone had struck with a hatchet into the face of a wax figure. "He could sell your Mama's sex services to your Daddy," one of the cooks at the restaurant where I worked observed that depressing night last November when the polls quickly proclaimed Reagan the next president of the United States.

Luckily, too, Reagan wasn't in my odd dream that night. Otherwise, I might have aspirated on my own vomit while I slept in my brother's guest bed. In my dream I was sitting in my parents' living room in Memphis with my brother and my father—only it wasn't Martin and Daddy, it was Bill Clinton and George Bush. Bush, my father, was not the vice-president, but the president. Bill, my brother, was arguing with my father, trying to convince him that he was dead and it was his turn to be president. Finally Bush, my father, turned to me and said, "Case, am I dead?"

I said, "Yeah, Daddy, you are."

He shrugged and said to my brother, Bill, "Okay, you win." Then he laid down on the couch with his hands clasped above his waist.

Bill turned to me and said, "Thanks Casey. You know, as awful as it feels, it reaches a point where they just have to get out of the way so you can get on with it."

I awoke the next morning not feeling very refreshed. I had a deep sunburn along the whole left side of my body. I told Martin my dream and he pointed out across a wide field that flanked his house. "See that?" he said. "That's the West. That's where you're going to get on with it." Martin failed to understand that this dream did not represent to me all that was positive about being motherless, or fatherless, or, God forbid, somehow responsible for your parent's death. I climbed into my car, my brother basking in vicarious pleasure. As I pulled out he waved vigorously, shouting, "You're gonna *die* when you see the Rockies!"

I CONFESS

Kris and I lied to ourselves during the six years we were together, and our denial systems were in perfect harmony. But when we knew the truth, we were compulsive confessors.

In our apartment, that first year together, on most nights I melted easily against Kris, my body conforming to hers as she wrapped her thick arms around me and pressed her ample breasts into my back. But when her lips would graze my neck, or her finger would wander below my waist, I would freeze with inexplicable terror and resistance. It quickly became obvious that ignoring her was not an acceptable defense—and, already, both of us were afraid to talk openly of problems in our relationship.

"I'm getting a migraine," I would say—and soon, Kris learned the game and I didn't have to say anything.

Like the mother of an infant, she would read my body—a clenched fist, a craned neck, a sigh, a barely perceptible shiver. "You're getting a migraine," she would whisper, returning to her soothing, sexless touch. Most of the time, the headache would really come. *Somehow,* after all, I should be punished for my lies.

Our relationship was like wet sand. Every time a hole appeared, something rushed in to fill it. There was constant chatter, lots of laughter, and, always, the blank canvas of our infinite future together upon which we painted our fantasies.

When I arrived home on the morning after Alex's birthday, there was no denying the truth I had to tell. It was sticky around my neck and ears and soaked into my Levi's. Kris didn't get up when I came in, and I didn't join her in our king-sized bed. I grabbed a quilt from the hall closet and ordered the dogs off the couch. I didn't sleep. My hair reeked of cigarette smoke, my hands of Alex—and the smell excited me and reminded me that last night I had placed the item on top of my precarious life that was certain to bring the whole stack tumbling down.

When Kris got up, I was in a stuperous state on the couch. She stood over me and I looked up and felt, in one instant, all the fear I had ever felt when caught being bad by my parents, my teachers, God, and Jesus Christ—and somehow I knew the punishment was going to be more severe than anything those folks could have dreamed of meting out. For a brief moment I saw myself, eight years old, glancing furtively over my shoulder as I carved "FUCK" into the trunk of the huge oak that stood in the far corner of the school playground. I can't remember how my teacher knew I did it—perhaps I compulsively confessed—more likely, I was caught red-handed. At any rate, when my mother read the note I came home with, I recall her yelling at me, then throwing her hands up in disgust and saying, "If you're going to do shit like that, for God's sake, don't get caught!"

From then on, when I was compelled to do something sure to shame the Lord, my mother, or my country, I was always careful to cover my back. Still, I often chose to tell my mother of my misadventures, because she was so tolerant, for the most part, and somehow, not telling anyone ruined the fun. My delusion that Kris loved me like my mother had was about to come to a screeching halt.

"Too bad you don't have your degree yet," Kris said. "You would have made a lot of money last night."

I couldn't look at her as I moved toward my rocking chair. "She's not my client."

"Alex?"

"We terminated last week."

Kris' eyes widened and her mouth dropped as she sat on the edge of the overstuffed rocker opposite me. Then, she made it easy, which had always been her tendency. "Did you . . . ?"

During our six years together, Kris gained and then lost weight, but she never lost her impressive strength. On that morning she bolted from the chair and charged through the house, slamming doors until paint chips from the walls and frames flew through the air. Our sturdily-constructed house shuddered beneath the blows from her fists. The dogs watched until their fear propelled them out the back door and into the yard, perceiving accurately, as did I, that our house had become as dangerous as Mt. St. Helens' red zone had once been.

I sat silently because nothing I said was going to be heard over the roar of Kris' pain. I shook. The Halcion I had taken at Alex's had long since worn off and I was too frightened to move to get my Valium. I dropped my head to my chest and stared vacantly at the irregular streaks and splotches of white, baby blue, and navy blue that covered my button-flies, now soaked with cum of a woman who was not my wife. "A bleach accident," I had told Alex, explaining the look of my Levi's.

"I think they look cool," she said.

I wasn't lying—but these jeans were the farthest thing from cool. These jeans were marked forever by the bleach they had to be soaked in, back in '85, to remove all traces of the deadly virus that had killed our first puppy. Thinking of Shade did what all the craziness of the last twelve hours couldn't. Large, scalding tears dripped from my eyes, adding their dampness to my mottled denims.

When Kris' initial reaction had played itself out, we began two months of torment and negotiations that ultimately led to her writing a suicide note on a chilly night in October.

CRISIS WORK

Kris and I established an uneasy peace that was in effect for the week between Alex's birthday and my graduation. I promised not to see or talk to Alex, both of which I did without telling Kris. I had crossed the line—the old rules didn't seem to matter anymore—and I was surprised how much easier it was to commit other wrongs once the first transgression was done. Still, there was a constant and unshakable sense of impending disaster, which made me even better able to justify continuing this madness—suspecting my penance for this momentary thrill was going to be eternal anyway. When Kris was at work, I made phone calls, and the conversations all went something like this:

Alex: God, I'm so glad you called. I need to hear your voice. I want to see you.

Casey: I wish I could see you, too. I don't know if I can.

Ever again?

I don't know.

I'll kill myself.

Don't even say that.

Sorry. I won't really. I won't have to, I'll just die.

I love the sounds you make when you . . .

I want to make love to you back.
I haven't washed my pants.
Promise me, next time, I can make love to you.
I don't make promises.
Please?
No, that's not true. I do make promises—I just don't keep them.
Tell me you love me. Lie if you have to.
(Silence.)
How's Kris?
Devastated.
I'm sorry.
I've gotta go.

The night before my graduation, I was at the crisis center where I had been working part-time. Alone in the cozy house that had been converted into a political women's workplace, finishing up some work in the living room, I heard a distant roar. Like an animal, I had already learned to tell the difference between the sound of Alex's car and everybody else's. I watched her come up the darkened steps and wondered how she found me. This was a confidential location where women who had been battered, raped, and otherwise abused could come for solace in an atmosphere of safety. Others were denied access. I suspected Alex had been doing more than driving by my house.

When I opened the door, she pushed past me and said, "Come here, please." She walked briskly up the stairs toward my office. I grabbed the back of her shirt once but she tore my hand away. My office lights were off, but the bay window allowed the streetlamp's glow to dimly illuminate the room. She turned her back to the glass and sat on the window seat, leaning back and moving her arm which was draped across her stomach. I gasped when I saw the murky stain bleeding out from the neat slash in her starched white shirt.

"Alex," I said, kneeling, taking her hands, the right one tacky with blood. Her face was streaked with dried tears and her breathing was shallow. "We gotta get you to the hospital." I pulled her shirt from her pants and lifted it carefully to expose the wound.

As I inspected the gash below the ribs on her left side, she mumbled, "He took all my money. The fucker took all my money."

I relaxed a little when I saw the cut was no longer bleeding. "Alex, baby, tell me what happened." She pulled me next to her and draped her legs across my lap, wrapped her arms around my neck and nuzzled her face into my shoulder. I rocked her and told her it'd be okay, I'd take care of her, don't worry, the money doesn't matter, you're safe here, he can't find you here. I'm glad you found me.

Woman in trouble. My job. Justified.

I laid her back on the window seat and wadded up some work clothes I'd left in my office, arranging them under her head. I went to the bathroom and got some towels and alcohol from the medicine chest, came back and opened her shirt and began cleaning the cut. She gasped at the sting and gripped my forearms, her eyes closed, lips parted. I was dying to see her come again.

"You might need stitches. This is a crime—we've got to report this."

"No!"

"Alex . . ."

She squeezed me tighter. "Casey?" Her dark blue eyes looked wet and terrified. "I was somewhere I shouldn't have been."

"What? Where were you?"

"I was way out north. Just sitting next to these old abandoned warehouses. Thinking about you."

"Aw, Alex," I said, touched and dismayed. Her wound was clean and appeared to not be too deep. "What did he cut you with?"

"I don't know. A knife."

"A knife?"

"Maybe a straight razor."

"You might need a tetanus shot."

"No, I don't."

"If the blade was rusty—"

"It wasn't, it was clean."

"How do you know that for sure?"

"I don't . . . I don't want to get a shot. I don't need to."

She smiled, then turned her face away, closing her eyes. "You're all I need."

Her breathing was even and I watched her for a few moments. Her hand was resting on my thigh. I brushed the hair away from her face. She started to open her eyes, her lips. I drew my palm gently down her face. "Shhh," I said. "Don't say anything. Don't look at me." She obeyed. "I have this dream about you. You are sleeping, in a bed, in a car, and I make love to you and you come but you don't wake up."

"What does that mean, doctor?"

I leaned down and licked her ear. "I guess if you're not really there, my guilt is assuaged."

She peeked at me and her eyes crinkled as a thin band of white teeth showed behind her tiny smile. "Did you have to go to college to learn words like that?"

Never for a moment did I think Alex was lacking in intelligence. In some ways, I knew, she was a lot smarter than I—in some ways that, probably, were more important in life than others. But suddenly, the nearly twelve-year gulf in our ages yawned mightily and I thought, *Who is this child I'm about to make love to?* I unbuckled her belt and pulled her pants to the floor. She had no underwear on. She raised her left knee and her right leg opened and dangled from the window seat. I spread her lips with my thumbs. She smelled like denim and leather—tasted like fear and spun sugar.

She made love to me on a twin bed in the next room. When I was naked, she ran her hands across my ribs. "I didn't think you would be this thin."

"I wasn't until a month ago."

She looked panicked. "You don't have AIDS do you?"

I pushed her hands away. "No, I don't have AIDS. But if you're worried, this can wait until—"

"I'm not worried about me. I'm worried about you! I don't care what happens to me, but if I ever have to say good-bye to you, I'll die." She kissed and licked my lips and tongue and eyes and nose. "If you had AIDS, I'd shoot myself up with your blood." For the rest of our time together that night, she held me, rocked me in her arms saying now and then, "Please don't die. Please don't die."

WITHOUT EVEN THINKING

―

Your biggest problem is you don't ever think *before doing something!*

If you would just think *before doing something stupid. . . .*

I shouted these words to the Mojave and there was no echo. My voice simply flew into the darkness, never to return. Variations of these comments, I explained to the desert, were made to me many times in my life.

In second grade, I took my little friend Joey out into the backyard. Joey was painfully slow, obedient as a guard dog, and he had this perfectly round head whose top was perpetually shaved. I picked up my old wooden tennis racket and explained the neat trick I had discovered. "If I hit you on the head with the middle part, it doesn't hurt at all," I said. He bent forward to let me demonstrate. I whacked him repeatedly, the netting bouncing, Joey laughing, until my small arms grew tired and my aim faltered. I watched with alarm when, after a loud crack, Joey toppled over on his back in the tall grass that Daddy had, as usual, neglected to cut. I flung the racket deep into the weeds and took off.

Several hours later, as the Harper family gathered for dinner, there was a knock on the door and Joey's mother asked mine if any of us had seen her son lately. A french fry lodged in my throat, crowded by a lump of panic. My confessional tendencies welled and I mumbled, "He's out back."

Just as they all rushed outside, Joey was coming to, dazed but apparently not permanently damaged—although, in Joey's case, it would have been hard to tell. I tried to make it to my bedroom before Mama caught me. I didn't succeed. We stood in the hallway. She screamed at me, punctuating her attack with the line that would become so familiar: "What the *hell* is the *matter* with you? Can't you ever *think*?" I quaked with fear. Maybe I'd found something that would make her stop loving me. She ended her assault with the warning, "Don't you ever, *ever* hit anybody in the goddamn *head*!" Then, she struck me for the first and only time in my life—not hard but her hammy hand flew from her side and, oddly enough, she delivered a well-placed slap right to the side of my head.

I remembered, but I didn't learn.

By tenth grade, the bad boys were my buddies and one day, in Spanish class, I coerced them into throwing their textbooks out the third-story window. Boredom, by this time, was my biggest problem and my greatest motivator. A new movie, *Harold and Maude*, had shown me that I wasn't the only kid compelled to do weird things to escape the horror of a dull life. The Spanish teacher saw nothing, but the Civics teacher below our classroom on the ground floor did, and she came up to tell. I still don't know how Mrs. Watson knew it was me, but as I settled in for my first day of detention, she stood before me, hand on hip, and said, "God gave you *brains* so you could *think* before doing something *stupid.*"

Kris probably would never have known about Alex's and my crisis line tryst had it not been for the hickey on my collarbone. I hadn't even noticed it, but, of course, I was not *thinking* very straight at the time, whereas Kris' marked attention to detail had actually sharpened over the past week.

I rocked violently and she sat on the couch staring at me. "Why?" she said.

"I don't know."

"What's the matter with you?"

"I don't know." She stared incredulously at me, like I had suddenly become autistic, which is sort of how I felt. Finally I added meekly, "At least I told you."

"I don't want you to *tell* me. I WANT YOU NOT TO DO IT!"

"I can't control myself. You know what I mean?"

Kris erupted. "Ya know whut I mean?" she mocked me. "What the fuck is that shit, your rat's-ass imitation of some fucking teenage boy? Is that how little Alex talks? What is she anyway, about twelve?" This tirade pissed me off but I was too exhausted to show it. "You're not even trying to control yourself," she continued. "WHY AREN'T YOU EVEN TRYING TO CONTROL YOURSELF?"

"Maybe I am."

"What? What?"

"Maybe I can, but I don't want to." I knew there was no right answer.

Kris flew off the couch. "What the fuck is *that* supposed to mean? What, you're doing this to me, to yourself, even to Alex just because, just because . . . This isn't doing anybody any good, you know. And now, what, you're trying to tell me you're doing it on purpose just because you want to, just because it feels good? What is this, like, third grade, like sticking erasers up your nose? Well guess what? That's stupid! Only stupid people and third-graders do things just because they feel good without even *thinking*."

There it was again. Need I say I didn't even hear the rest of her sentence. I gave her a wan smile, but she didn't get the humor. "Would it make you feel better to hit me upside the head?" She didn't get that either.

"I hate you," she said.

I went to Alex and we drove around Portland for hours. She asked me as I dropped her off, "Do you think we'll ever see each other again?"

I stared at her and said in my therapist's lingo, "If I give myself permission to *think* about it, no, we won't." She got it, and we kissed each other goodbye.

LIGHTS OUT

I successfully fought the effects of my Halcion. I took another and promised myself this time I would let it work. The renters were coming at ten the next morning. I had to be on the road early. But I was reluctant to surrender that last night to sleep. I thought of Gary Gilmore, how, the night before they shot him to death in Utah, they plied him with uppers so he could enjoy every moment he had left. That's how I felt, although "enjoy" was not really what I had in mind. From my rocking chair, I prodded my sleeping bag with my toe.

"I think nobody bought the chair because you were sitting in it the whole time," Allie had said as the garage sale waned.

"Oh," I said, the $65 cardboard price tag flapping behind my head.

There was no distracting noise in our empty house on that quiet street except a cacophony of voices that spoke their muffled taunts through the drug-induced cloud in my head. One voice sang over and over: *When the going gets tough, you give up.*

Finally, to silence it, I sang softly aloud the opening line of "Stairway to Heaven." But my voice, not great to begin with, sounded simply awful.

I glanced at the telephone on the floor. It was still operable. Kris insisted I keep it so until I left the house for good. "You never know what might happen at the last minute," she said. I couldn't disagree. But I also couldn't think of anyone to call, anyone I would even remotely feel like talking to.

I stepped out onto the porch. The April night was cool and someone else may have found it refreshing, but I smelled that sweet and sour Portland odor that drifted from a lumber mill across the Columbia when the winds were right, a smell like something large and meaty decomposing. I peered through the hazy light of the streetlamps, at the darkened houses of our sleeping neighbors. *Portland is a morgue,* I thought. *Our precious, perfect house is my refrigerated drawer.*

I wondered, did I make this hard or did it just get hard? Don't I always pick the easiest way? That's what one voice kept telling me. I remembered sitting alone with my brother and my mother's corpse that night in the funeral home, eliminating all possibilities but one, moving to Portland, Oregon, with no fore or afterthought. I sat there in that place whose stock-in-trade is altering the most profound reality the living encounter—where the stench of rotting flesh, the patchwork of accident trauma and surgical scarring, the odd tints and sunkeness of disease are artfully disguised with magical fluids, heavy make-up, crisp clothing, and cut flowers. Somebody even told me they wrap disposable diapers around dead babies' bottoms to give them the bulging look of life.

No wonder it was so easy for me to turn my back on the agony of saying goodbye to someone who wasn't ever supposed to die, to forget the sights and smells and sounds of her dying. To choose the peaceful bliss of a long road trip, the oblivion of a strange town and unknown people—that seemed infinitely easier than standing racked with grief on my mother's freshly dug grave.

My decision to go to Portland was so wrong and now, tomorrow, I was going to do the same thing again, backward, and hope for a different result.

I sat in that cavernous house where there was no sound, bare walls, empty halls, a bombed-out shell. An empty shell . . . the Pacific. I knew I was going to miss the Pacific. I cocked my ear and listened to the ocean in that house, in my head—imagined myself on a jagged cliff, and I said my name once. Again, louder. And I heard it again without saying it. In our house, an echo. I saw a flash of Harley with her mountain goat agility scaling the sheer cliff walls surrounding the ocean and I burst into tears. I want my Great Dane. Where's my Great Dane? I want my mother. Memphis. They're all in Memphis. All the love that was real and unconditional is in Memphis.

Go on Halcion, I prayed. *Work, please work.*

As my eyelids drooped, I pictured myself in Portland busily building an elaborate stage set so authentic it is almost indistinguishable from the reality waiting in the wings for me to finish the last act. And now, the curtain is falling. I wondered, will anyone or anything I know be there in the darkness I am about to enter? If not, will I have the courage to face the emptiness alone, or will I trick myself into building a set again?

I reached up and rubbed the upper curve of my right ear. Something small and hard stuck to my fingertip. I looked at it, and it was a rye seed. I couldn't even remember the last time I ate, much less the last time I ate rye bread. What started as a laugh froze into rictus. My humiliation was complete.

———

Unlike Gary Gilmore, I did sleep a bit. In the morning I gathered my sleeping bag, one pillow, my toothbrush and toothpaste, one towel, and my black bag of drugs and stuffed them in the small remaining space on the front floor of my truck. Then, I went back inside to say goodbye to the house.

Ghost laughter rang from the bedroom as I disturbed Kris' nighttime reading—snapping my fingers, peeking around the door frame, singing "The Way You Make Me Feel," in Michael Jackson's high, wispy voice. I missed my playmate. Down the hall, the memory faded and there was Harley at four months, getting her height but not yet her weight, her huge paws preceding her gangly body, her blue eyes catching the light from the setting sun. In the bathroom, I leaned on the cabinet and gazed out the shutterless windows at the tall cedar in the center of the big backyard, at the three foot patch of dirt around its base that had long since surrendered its grass to three sets of dog paws. I saw Griff, head held high, prancing proudly with a small tree limb twice his size clamped firmly in his jaws.

In the kitchen I heard a sigh and felt melancholy cocoa eyes behind me. It was four-month-old Shade, dying on the bed of old T-shirts we had made for him so our first puppy would bond to our scents.

At the front door, I pressed my lips against the wooden frame and, with one last glance behind me, I said goodbye. I stepped outside, locked the door, and dropped the keys through the mail slot for the renters who would be inhabiting our home.

It was April 15, 1990.

SOPHIE LEARNS A LESSON

I left my brother behind me in a cloud of Arkansas dust and headed toward Missouri. At lunchtime I wasn't hungry, but my back was sore and tired from driving and I was getting sleepy, so I pulled into a lot beneath a sign that said "Sophie's Diner" and I got out for a stretch and a cup of coffee. Inside, I couldn't stop thinking about my dream—especially the image of my father, even though he was George Bush, lying in that death pose on the couch. My mind kept trying to click back to memories of my real dead parent and I struggled to resist it. Staring at Sophie's logo on the plastic-covered menu at my table, I thought about my childhood best friend and finally conjured up a memory I could live with.

I was eight and my father took Sophie, who was six, and me to a public swimming pool. Sophie couldn't swim and she was afraid of the water, so she sat in a lounge chair and watched as my father and I played. As time passed, I noticed Sophie looking terribly forlorn, and concern for her was taking the joy out of my day, so I joined her poolside and begged her to get in. I promised her everything. I'll hold you,

you can hang onto my shoulders, we'll stay in the wading pool, but nothing worked. Finally, my father, who my friend adored, sat down next to us. "Daddy," I said, "if Sophie gets in the pool *you* can make sure she's safe, can't you?"

My father laid his hand gently on Sophie's arm and she looked at him with teary eyes and a pouting bottom lip. "Case," he said, "why don't you go get some Cokes and let me talk to Soph for a minute."

I don't know what he said, but when I returned he was standing in water up to his waist and Sophie was crouching on the side of the pool with her toes dangling over the edge. I sat quietly and watched as Daddy held out his arms and she jumped into them. He caught her before her head went under water, then carried her to the edge and set her down. They did this a dozen times. Sophie was shrieking ecstatically and could barely wait to scramble to her feet and take another leap each time Daddy put her back on the side.

On the last jump, I saw my father standing there with his strong arms outstretched and his jack-o-lantern smile and, as Sophie's small body sailed through the air, I saw Daddy wrap his arms around his hairy chest and watch as my friend plunged four feet to the bottom of the pool. I jumped up and ran to the edge and Daddy ignored my screams as Sophie bobbed to the surface, spewing water and gasping for air. Her eyes were filled with terror and she was too disoriented to see my father. After she thrashed for a moment, he gathered her in his arms and carried her out of the pool.

She was sobbing, but she must have also been listening as Daddy explained: "See, Soph, most of the time somebody'll be there to catch you, but every once in a while, they won't— and that's when you find out if you're a person who's gonna sink or swim." Sophie lost her hydrophobia that day, and she and I spent many hot summer afternoons over the next five years playing together at the public swimming pool.

Not long after I left Sophie's Diner, I crossed the state line into Missouri and gave up trying not to think about my mother. I also shed my inhibitions and started talking to myself. "Mama stood in the pool and caught me for twenty-two years," I said. "For the last two she was too sick to get in the pool, so I sat in the lounge chair beside her." I looked out at the unfamiliar state whizzing past my windows. "So, now there's nobody on the side and there's nobody in the pool. Time to jump in, Case, and see what happens."

I navigated the interstate loops and exits of Kansas City— the first major city I hit on my journey west—perfectly. Stiff and starving, I pulled into a diner in Sunflower, Kansas and, although it was close to six in the evening, I ordered coffee, bacon, hash browns, toast, and eggs—sunnyside up. I told the voice in my head that questioned whether the eggs would be done like Mama did them to shut up. When my food arrived, I ate every bite. My confidence knew no bounds.

I took a large cup of coffee to go and started on my way across Kansas. "Kansas is the most boring state in the country," Martin had warned me. "Drink a ton of coffee and drive through it all night, if you can. That way, you'll get to see the Rockies at sunrise."

I drove for an hour and a half before the sun set. I found the landscape in the waning daylight exceedingly eerie. This open, flat expanse went on and on in every direction, as far as I could see. I had always been claustrophobic—but this was too much the other extreme. In Kansas, I felt exposed and unprotected. Nobody wants to be somewhere where there's no place to hide, should one need to hide for some reason. In Kansas, even if you laid flat on your belly, somebody would see you. Kansas, I observed, would be perfect for housing the entire American prison population. Escapees would be caught in seconds. The license plates would be "Kansas—The Penal State."

I was passing through Salina as the sun set and a steady rain began to fall, and my musings led me to thinking about serial killers.

CRIMES OF HORROR

I landed my first job, babysitting, when I was eleven years old. My charge was a six-month-old boy—the son of a couple who lived on our street. Peter was a great baby, didn't cry much, and the job was relatively boring—except for the first time I was on duty when he pooped in his diaper and I gagged so badly I had to call my mother to come down and change him for me.

One of my mother's favorite pasttimes was buying and reading books from The New and Used Book Exchange. One day, with a babysitting job lined up for the weekend, I asked her to get me a couple books to read. I liked mysteries and horror stories, and so did she. I trusted her taste and was rarely disappointed. She brought me a stack ten high—mostly tattered and yellowed tales of ghosts, murder, and intrigue—but one was brand new and I pulled it from the rest, becoming engrossed in it immediately. By the time Saturday came and I had said goodnight to the Alders and Peter was snug in his crib, I was halfway through *The Boston Strangler*.

The first problem I noticed was that, as night fell, I was nervous about leaving the den and going alone into the kitchen for a Coke. The second problem was my growing fear of sitting in the rocking chair, whose back faced the open hallway. I moved to the couch, its back flush with the wall. When I heard a small peep and a whimper from Peter and realized I was afraid to go into his dark room to check on him, I figured it was time to call my mother.

"Hey Mama," I said on the phone. "Can you come over? Just for a while. I've got some questions for you." When she arrived she fussed over Peter for a few minutes, careful not to wake him, and drilled me about whether I fed him and changed him before putting him down. I let her go on and on. My sole purpose was keeping her there without revealing why. I didn't care what we talked about. We talked about school and church and what we were having the next day for Sunday dinner. We talked about the Beatles, the Vietnam War, and President Johnson. The conversation started slacking off and Mama seemed tired and ready to leave. "Oh, Mama," I said, pulling out my ace. "The questions."

"Oh, what questions?"

"I've got a few questions. . . . There are some words, uh . . ." I picked up the book. "A few words in this book. I don't know exactly what they mean."

"What are they?"

"Well," I said, flipping through the pages I had dog-eared. "Uh, let's see, ummm—'masturbate,' 'semen,' and 'ejaculate,'"

I looked up to see my mother blanching and wide-eyed. "Casey! Gimme that book!"

She never did tell me what the words meant, but she did give me back the book. By the time I finished it I had figured out enough to be perhaps the most paranoid eleven-year-old in Memphis, Tennessee.

The following Christmas, my sister gave me two books. One was a collection called *Crimes of Horror* in which were the first pictures I ever saw of a murder victim at the scene—Sam Sheppard's wife. It also contained a photo of a dead body on an autopsy table, its fatal ax wounds washed clean. The other book was *The Complete Jack the Ripper.*

In 1969, the Manson murders occurred and I clipped and memorized every newspaper and magazine story. In 1970, I was in ninth grade. For my book report, I delivered a presentation I called: *Jack the Ripper, the Boston Strangler, and Charles Manson: A Trilogy of Horror.* My stunned English teacher sent a note home to my mother. At the meeting in the principal's office, I sat silently as my mother shrugged and explained to the befuddled school authorities: "If she was a boy I might be concerned. But she's a girl. What harm can it do?"

THE START OF THE END

It was much too hot and humid for mid-April in northwestern Oregon. I had both windows of my unairconditioned Toyota truck rolled down as I headed south on I-5, which made listening to tapes impossible.

I couldn't relax at all.

I nibbled my fingernails. I furtively glanced into the rearview mirror every few seconds, regardless of the fact that the entire view was blocked by boxes. I looked at my watch every five minutes. I tried to think of songs to sing but couldn't. I had been to Eugene before, so these first miles were boring and nothing came to mind except horrible thoughts and unanswerable questions. It occurred to me: *I am insane.* In my mind I saw Portland, which I knew, and Memphis, which I knew, and nothing in between because I knew nothing about the places I would be stopping in. I kept thinking: *Why am I driving for seven days to get to the same place I just left?*

I stared at my fingers gripped around the steering wheel. I saw the ones on my right hand, over and over, dropping my keys irretrievably through the mail slot, locking me out of my own house. Not even fifty miles out of Portland, and the monotonous patience of the road was altering my perception of reality. The bones in my arm disappeared and my rubbery limb easily slipped through the mail slot, my fingers curling around the cold metal keys. Once, I recalled, I could sleep without drugs—and I believed everything in my dreams could come true.

———

I had the wolf and castle dream many times after I moved to Portland. At first, I was alone in the castle—but soon Mama showed up and, in the beginning, she was still alive. I awoke each time hiccuping with glee, only to remember moments later, again and again, that she had died. One night in my dream, she appeared waxy and dressed in her green gown, and I knew she was dead. She encouraged me to leave the castle; but, when I did, I found myself surrounded by slobbering, snarling wolves with glowing ruby eyes. I ran back inside and begged her to make them go away, but for the longest time she just stood there pale and silent. Finally, in 1983, she opened her arms to me and I rushed into them and rested my head on her breast with my hands around her back. There was a sickening, sweet smell and my hands ran across something tacky and viscous and I looked down to discover she was decomposing.

The last time I had the dream was during the time that Kris and I were living in our apartment together, before the dogs, before the house. By then, Mama was horribly rotted. Flaps of blackened flesh hung from her cheeks and chin, her hands looked like overripe banana peels. Her sparse hair was mussed and her green gown sported great patches of fuzzy gray mold. I tried to muster the courage to face the wolves. I couldn't, so I turned to my mother once more for help. This time, she raised her decaying arm and gestured toward a cedar chest I had never noticed before. I opened it, and it was full of pots of cooked Kraft Macaroni and Cheese. Knowing instinctively what to do, I threw the bright orange food around the grounds. The wolves writhed and howled, baring their teeth and shoving their tails between their legs, and they slinked in fear off into the woods.

Kris, who knew of my recurring dream, held me that night when I awoke and told her of this new development. "What do you think it means?" she said.

I thought about it, then let loose a befuddled giggle. "I think you're the macaroni and cheese."

She laughed and kissed the top of my head. "I would be honored to be your macaroni and cheese."

I'd found my safe person—now all I needed was the castle. It would take six years for me to wish I had given myself over to the wolves rather than succumb to the soporific delusion that comfort food can cure cancer.

OUT OF OREGON

It took me close to a hundred and fifty years to get to Eugene. The sun was high and hot and covered with fuzzy, gray clouds. The temperature was nearly ninety; the humidity, one hundred percent. Why had it taken me nine years to realize how suffocating this state is? My head was practically shaved to ward off my having to find a new hairdresser for as long as possible; and, even in my thin T-shirt, gym shorts, and Nikes with no socks, I was still sweating copiously.

Just outside Eugene I remembered Kris stressing the importance of fluids, so I stopped at a gas station/ mini-mart and bought a quart of Gatorade and a bag of Nacho Cheese Doritos. On the way to my truck, I asked a greasy guy I thought was the attendant if they had a restroom. He scratched his porcine belly and said, "A men's room or a ladies' room?"

"Oh, shut up, asshole," I muttered, and trudged off to the side of the building as his Mountain Dew can came whizzing past my head. Back on the road, I nursed my drink, ate about ten chips and half of a Linzer torte from Marlena's gift box, which made my chest burn. Less than a day into my trip, I broke a promise I made to myself and swallowed a Valium with a big gulp of Gatorade. *Fuck it,* I thought, as the evergreen blanket of the Willamette Valley segued into the tall trees of the Umpqua National Forest. *Who needs the anxiety?* I figured if worse came to worse, I could stop in Southern California for a month at the Betty Ford Clinic.

Asshole's comment caused me to consciously think about being a dyke—something I don't do very much, except when jerks who seem to exist only to make our lives miserable force me to. Like the mangy guy in the parking lot back when Kris first moved to Portland—the guy who cursed violently while his little son looked on because I took "his" parking place. "That's a pretty disgusting way to talk in front of your kid," I said.

To which he brilliantly responded, "At least I can *have* kids, you fucking queer!"

And the woman at the dry cleaner's . . . Her big sign said: *Dress Shirts, One Dollar.* I lay my three Oxford cloths across her counter. "That'll be six dollars," she said, and I pointed to the sign. "That price is for *men's* shirts," she explained.

"These *are* men's shirts."

She looked shocked and frightened and, desperate to crack the conundrum that was me, she tried to explain her pricing. But, she couldn't figure out for sure whether I was a man or a woman, and she even appeared to be suspicious of my shirts themselves—so, rather than force her deeper into her sudden psychosis, I snatched the overpriced receipt from her hand. "But, but . . ." she said, cupping her hand over her mouth as she burst into tears. "I'm just so confused," she wailed as I left the building.

No wonder when Kris and I found each other we clung together like kelp on driftwood. The Valium worked, and I was able to remember painlessly how we went from being strangers to homeowners in a year and a half.

Kris and I survived a brutal winter whose strong, bitter winds whistled through the substantial cracks in our underinsulated apartment on Hawthorne. We burned a full cord of cherry wood in our fireplace to keep warm. Kris busied herself making minor repairs that cost nothing more than her time— and she dreamed about what she could do to a place of our own. I made pots of homemade vegetable soup and hot rolls, four-alarm chili and cornbread and, finally, outdoors, there came the promise of spring.

Already in our first year, the sands had shifted. I had developed a sexual dysfunction that neither of us could bring ourselves to confront. Sometimes I found myself thinking, *I love you too much to have sex with you* —but I never said this to Kris because it made absolutely no sense. Our relationship back then had a hole the size of a two-bedroom bungalow. It was only fitting that, since the missing sand was in my hand, I should be the one to find our home. I was driving down forty-seventh street, halfway between Hawthorne and Division, and there it was with its fireplace and fenced yard and "For Sale" sign out front.

We met the sellers' realtor who turned out to be the most persistent man we had ever known. He optimistically moved on when the first lender balked at our dearth of credit, Kris' short Portland employment records, our lack of savings or a down payment. He forged ahead again when the second lender executed a legal act of discrimination that went something like this:

Straight White Banker (Clearing his throat): The problem is the family *instability here, do you know what I mean?*

The Realtor: No sir, I'm afraid I don't.

I think you'd have to agree this, uh, arrangement *is a bit unorthodox, shall we say.*

Two people buying a house together?

Two girls *buying a house together.*

You got a problem with girls?

Lender number three said yes, and, by early August, we had a mortgage and a new defense mechanism—distraction.

Southern Oregon was cloudless, arid, and sandy brown. Mt. Shasta rose before me with its promise that soon I would be out of Oregon, and nobody could make me go back. I ate a few more chips, a cinnamon bun, and finished the Gatorade. As the sun set, I paid thirty dollars to enjoy the comforts of air-conditioning, cable T.V., a big, firm bed, and a clean bathroom at the Catalina Motel just off I-5 South in Redding, California.

KILLER ON THE ROAD

As I drove through the blinding rain of that dark Kansas night, my last conscious thought about serial killers was, *Oh wow, in a week I'm going to be in the Pacific Northwest, where Ted Bundy happened!* I don't know what made me think I could make it all the way to Denver on this leg of the trip, but it was past midnight and I was still in Kansas and I hadn't seen any lights, even of the smallest town, in ages. Sheets of rain and a gusty wind battered my little brown car and I was beginning to see phantom flickers and furtive movements in my peripheral vision. The car was stuffy. The rain was so violent I couldn't crack my window for air, and I was sleepy.

The choice was simple. Keep driving and risk having an accident, or pull over for a while and risk, what? Despite my heightened awareness of the dangers of being a woman in the world, I really didn't know what the risks were. I couldn't see anything. I didn't know what was out there. And, for the first time in my life, there wasn't a soul I could turn to for advice.

"Wouldn't it be funny if you had a phone in the car?" I asked myself aloud. I pulled over. My doors were locked. I decided I was willing to take the risks, whatever they might be.

My back seat was so packed I couldn't recline the front one. I slumped down and extended my legs as far as I could over onto the passenger's side. The first time I started to lose consciousness, I distinctly heard my mother's voice. *Casey?*

"Mama?" I opened my eyes. "Look, if you're around, I could use some help. Is this okay? Am I going to be okay?" I didn't hear anything else. No cars had passed me since I stopped.

The second time I started to doze off, I saw a thin, winding funnel cloud twisting across the barren Kansas countryside. Then, I was in a nursery full of babies in incubators and they were all screaming and I couldn't take care of any of them because I couldn't take care of all of them. I jerked awake.

The third time, I actually achieved a state of sleep and, according to my watch, was out for fifteen minutes. In my dream, I was sitting in my car with the window down at a gas station, and I heard a young man say, "Hey, Portland,"—like that was my name. I looked out the window and it was the attendant I met as I left Memphis—the one who'd moved there from Portland—only he was caked with grease and had a gash in his forehead from which the blood had been washed. He grinned and said, with a backwoods country accent, "You gonna die out there."

I dragged myself awake and my head lolled toward my right shoulder. I heard a click to my left, then another, and I saw out the driver's window a young man staring through the glass on this road, in the middle of this black Kansas night. Rivulets of rain dripped from his hair, nose, and jaw. He was tapping on my window with a heavy high-school class ring and mouthing words I couldn't hear. I was paralyzed with fear for a second. Then I noticed a sound of lowing that emanated from the very center of my chest. My trembling hand moved in slow motion toward the ignition. I willed my frozen fingers to turn the key and I sped off, chanting, "Oh shit, oh shit," until my thundering heart quieted.

Perhaps my brother had imbued me with unrealistic expectations of the Rockies, or maybe I just wasn't capable of appreciating them—but I paid little attention to anything around me as I arrived in Denver at seven a.m. I straggled into the first motel I saw, the Triple D. I approached the desk clerk, a chubby woman with graying hair swept into a loose bun. Before I had a chance to speak, she arched her eyebrows and said, "Oh honey, are you okay?" Her kindness broke my heart so badly I didn't even have to affect a hangdog look.

"Is there any way I can get a room this early?"

"Oh, honey, of course." She patted my hand and flipped through her registry book. She handed me a key and I went to my room, collapsed fully-clothed on the bed, and didn't wake up until eight that night.

METAPHORICALLY CHALLENGED

I stayed at the Triple D for two days. I needed the rest. I was disturbed by my lack of awe in the midst of the Rockies, wondered how I could possibly be so unimpressed, having spent all my life on the insipid Mississippi Delta. In Denver, the agoraphobia I experienced in the infinite sweep of Kansas gave way to the more familiar claustrophobia from being in this place ringed by mountains that I would remember best as blue-gray monoliths in the dying light of a summer day. "The Rockies are so big they make their own weather," my brother had told me. I had no idea what he was talking about. Certainly he didn't mean that literally, did he? I sat in a coffee shop on a main Denver street eating a buttered cinnamon-raisin bagel, staring west at the Rocky Mountains, concentrating not on what my body was doing there in Colorado, but on why my mind was feeling so disoriented.

———

From the day I was born, when my mother and sister said, "I love you," and meant just that, I have always tended to take things literally. From these two important females, I learned to trust what people say. It would be years before I recognized how perilous that can be.

I had at least one opportunity to discover much earlier in life how disruptive, if not dangerous, failing to understand the deeper meaning could be—an opportunity, unfortunately, lost to hilarity. I was seven and my parents had invited the pastor and his wife over for dinner. My mother and grandmother were busily preparing a feast in the kitchen and, as usual, I was underfoot. So they gave me a chore, to set the table. We rarely entertained dinner guests and I was aware this was a very special occasion, so when I asked, my mother said, "Yes, use the special plates and silver and napkins."

The guests arrived as I was putting the finishing touches on the dining room table. Daddy stayed with them in the living room chatting while Mama filled the serving dishes—and nobody noticed until they all approached the table that, to the left of every dinner plate, was a thick, absorbent Kotex. Many a night, as I kept my mother company during her bath, I would point to the top of the bathroom closet at the big, pink boxes and ask, "What are those?"

"Those are the special napkins," she would say.

My father was more metaphorical than euphemistic and was, to my mind, equally unintelligible. Often he would take me to his favorite place, a baseball diamond, and he would wrap one arm around my shoulders, look out over the vast deserted field, make a broad sweep with his free hand, and say, "Case, you'll always be successful if you just remember three things. Keep your eye on the ball. Concentrate. And follow through." Because I failed to understand and he neglected to explain the metaphor, I paid little attention because, from a very young age, I was not particularly career-minded, and I certainly had no interest in playing professional baseball. So, while he talked, I would bask in the summer breeze, scrutinize the big, fluffy clouds, and simply enjoy the male warmth of his heavy arm around my body.

Whether it was a project abandoned, a story unfinished, or a promise unkept, I was always in trouble with someone who expected the follow-through. When their hounding became unbearable and I would ask my father for advice, he would suggest I ask my mother to bail me out because it always worked for him. And it always worked for me. My father taught me two other lessons. He hadn't a nurturing bone in his body, and he taught me how to get my needs met if you haven't a nurturing bone in your body. But, most importantly, my father taught me to seize the day. I guess at some point I was old enough to understand his metaphors because, when he suggested, "Don't ever buy unripe bananas because you may not be around when they are ripe enough to eat," I knew exactly what he meant.

———

I stopped thinking when I noticed my eyes had adjusted to an unnatural darkness in this Denver coffee shop. I peered out the window to see the cottony clouds had been swept away by eerie black thunderheads that rolled over the mountain peaks and rained down huge, icy drops onto the steaming asphalt streets. I left the coffee shop and sought shelter under an awning and thought: *It's hot down here and cold up there. How can this be? I don't think I know anything.* Soon, I would make my first ascent into real mountains, and I had no idea what was up there. Under the awning, as I shivered in the frigid wind and rain of a hot July day in Denver, Colorado, I pressed my hands against the brick windowsill that retained warmth from the summer sun, and I clearly thought, for the first time: *I have no idea where I am, where I'm going, or what I'm doing.*

FRAYED

—

The motel room in Redding was humid inside for reasons I couldn't figure, and, already, just walking from my truck up to the second floor, I heard something that really bothered me. I think it's like they say, when you lose one sense, another becomes more developed to compensate. Like, if you're deaf, or "hearing impaired," as I was instructed by the crisis line bigwigs to call it, your sense of smell or sight or whatever becomes more acute.

Hearing impaired. I'll never forget one humiliating experience brought on by my buying into the complex semantics of the politically correct. I was doing my job at the crisis line, interviewing a woman for a volunteer position who had brought along her interpreter. To break the ice and show my infinite sensitivity, I said as I perused her application, "So, I see you are hearing impaired."

She threw her head back in great, silent laughter and signed wildly. Her interpreter also chuckled and said aloud for my unimpaired ears, "Well, *that's* an understatement if I've ever seen one!" Then, her amused hands added, "I'm deaf as a doorknob!" And they both laughed some more.

I was not laughing when I related this story later to my boss and coworkers. "So, what the fuck are you supposed to say when they make *fun* of the euphemisms?"

"*They*," my friends explained, emphasizing that word to further highlight my privileged position as a physically un-challenged middle-class white person, "can say anything they want to. It's like, African-Americans use the 'n' word amongst themselves, but the Goddess knows *we* don't!"

I said nothing, and thought: *Thank God I'm a lesbian— a.k.a., a big fucking queer lesbo dyke—otherwise, I would have to wander out into a field of tall weeds and shoot myself.*

———

I was in a humid room in Redding, California, and I was insane. Though the seeds of this psychosis were sown when my mother died and I pretended she didn't, though its buds had been popping out here and there for the past nine years, only in the past six months had I lost the strength to suppress the emergence of its brilliant blooms. To compensate for my lost mind, all of my senses fired, sparking thought associations that led to recollections of one particular side trip I took along the Portland road that brought me, finally, here, to the Catalina on I-5 South.

On the way up to my room, I heard the screeching cry of an infant which seemed to be coming from the motel's trash cans. Instead of investigating, I remembered I was in Califor-nia where the serial killers have a penchant for leaving torsos in the dumpsters. I scurried up to the relative safety of my rented room. From inside, I heard the plaintive wail again. With the deadbolt thrown and the chain drawn and the win-dows latched, I had the courage to peek through the heavy curtains and, there by the metal cans, were two cats fucking.

I took two Halcions and crawled into bed, curled up into the fetal position, and covered my head with the scratchy blanket. Behind my closed eyelids, I saw a vision of a big plate of brown rice topped with strips of tender chicken breastmeat, plump green peas, and chunks of fresh carrots in a thick, tangy cream sauce. I recognized Judith's Chicken a la King, and my mouth watered.

MOTHERS AND BABIES

The first chink in my wall of denial appeared four months after I arrived in Portland, in November of 1981, when I had my first migraine. My mother had migraines all her life—her last, just three days before she died—and I was convinced she came to me one night with this gift so I would remember her regardless of how far I traveled to forget, so I would feel the pain in my body I should have felt in my soul when she died.

The day preceding that night was a good one. I worked my shift, sat afterward and talked with my new friends. Made some long distance calls to old friends. I was writing prolifically in my journal for the first time in three years and had sat at my typewriter until my fingers cramped. I was not sleepy but decided to go to bed and think. I turned out the light, rolled onto my side with my face to the bedroom door, and closed my eyes. Immediately, I got the spins, which concerned me because I hadn't been drinking. When I tried to open my eyes, I couldn't. When I tried to move my arm to turn on the bedside light, I couldn't. I lay frozen, frightened, and breathing shallowly when I distinctly heard my sister's voice in my doorway. "Casey?" The specter of death I thought I had successfully obliterated rushed in. Clara was teaching in Manchester, England, where, at that time, there was a serial killer at work, the "Yorkshire Ripper." I feared my sister was dead. I willed myself to move, and still couldn't.

Then, "Casey?" my grandmother said, also from the doorway. Grandma was devastated by Mama's death and hurt that I'd left so soon after—and I thought she had died, but still, I couldn't move.

There are dead people in my room, and I can't move.

Finally, I heard Mama. "Casey." It wasn't a question. My eyes opened. She looked good. She had on make-up and her hair was done and she was wearing the green gown we buried her in. "Casey." This time she spoke a little louder. The moonlight through the thin, drawn curtains illuminated her cornflower blue eyes. She extended her right hand and took a step toward my bed.

I couldn't speak, couldn't move.

She took another step closer. Her brow furrowed and she cocked her head slightly, an expression of concern and comfort, but my fear rose to a level that, finally, ignited my paralyzed synapses. I bolted upright, and her face fell in sadness. I barked in a low-pitched voice that did not sound human, "I'm sorry!" When I turned on the light, she was gone. I was not ready to see my dead mother in my apartment in Portland, Oregon.

The next morning I awoke with a stuffy feeling in the left side of my face that, within two hours, turned into a fiery stiletto embedded behind my eye that lasted for two days. The following February, I called in sick with a migraine for the twelfth time in three months and crawled back into my bed to pray that this beast would either leave me or kill me. Thirty minutes later, I was jolted from a pain-induced stupor by someone pounding on my door.

It was my boss, and she looked very, very mad.

I opened the door. It was raining hard and Judith was standing there, her wavy brown hair dripping, her eyes molten, her teeth clenched for verbal assault. I held my hand over my left eye, the one that felt like it was going to be forced out of my skull by the bellowing migrainous monster behind it. I stood aside as Judith charged into my kitchen.

"What the fuck do you think you're doing?" she screamed, glaring at me. I couldn't look at her even if I wanted to. The light scorched my eyes. "I have a business to run. I'm sorry if you're sick, but you can't keep calling in and expect me to just cover your ass like this." She snapped her thick fingers and the sound, to me, was like the report of a shotgun. "I've *tried* to be nice, I've *tried* to compensate for you, but I can't continue this way. You need to decide . . ." She yammered on, following me into the living room where I sagged to the couch. I pulled up my knees and dragged a quilt over myself, shivering, never saying a word. Finally, my boss left. I didn't stir. I fell into a fretful sleep and had my wolf and castle dream for the first time.

I woke up a couple of hours later, still in excruciating pain, and I peeked over the quilt to see night had fallen. The apartment was awash in twilight shadows. I felt like I wasn't alone. When I became conscious enough, I remembered that I hadn't locked the door after Judith left. If she left. Was she still in my house? I didn't know. I moved slightly, then heard a faint command. "Shhhh." A hand gently touched my hip beneath the blanket. I peered through the shadows at my mother. I wasn't afraid this time—death would have been a relief at the moment, if that's where she wanted to take me. Besides, I realized as my heart leapt with relief, she wasn't dead—wasn't wearing her burial gown. And best of all, she was fat. Mama was here with me, joyously, undeniably covered with layers and layers of health, just as she'd always been before . . . before . . . I stared into the dimness and swallowed hard as a head of damp, wavy hair moved into my line of vision. Judith took my icy hands and knelt beside the couch. "I'm so sorry," she said. "I'm such a bitch. I don't know why. You don't deserve it, and I'm sorry."

"It's okay," I whispered. *I want my mother.*

The moonlight shimmered in her tears. She squeezed my hands. "I wish there was something I could do to make the pain stop." Her caring made me feel like crying, but I couldn't. I knew that was the worst thing I could do while in the throes of a migraine. So I lowered my head below the quilt to shut out the sight of her and her tenderness. She ran her fingers through my hair. "It may not be worth much after I was such an asshole," she said, "but I brought you some chicken soup and a surprise. Please see me to the door. You won't be safe here with the door unlocked all night."

I got up and did as she asked. On the way out, she showed me the jar of soup and a big Valentine's heart full of choco-late-covered cherries. I reached for the candy. She pulled it away and smiled. "Don't eat that until you've had some soup," she said, thrusting the jar at me. She noticed my expression as I gazed at the two big hairy-looking balls floating in it. She laughed and rumpled my hair. "My little goy," she said. "Those are motzah balls—they're good for you, too. You gentiles are so deprived."

When she left, I threw the furry balls away, ate a few spoonfuls of soup and six chocolates, then went to bed for the night.

———

Judith's place was a little espresso/juice bar painted in lavender and earth tones, accented with lush hanging ferns and women's artwork. The mighty triumvirate of Holly Near, Chris Williamson, and Meg Christian softly sang their hear-me-roar tunes from speakers discretely mounted in the bar's four corners. Up until then, women's music to me had meant Pat Benatar, Blondie, and Grace Jones. Had Judith's business been a person, it would have attracted grandmothers prone to pinching cherubic children's cheeks. Had she opened in 1980 anywhere in the United States other than Portland, Oregon, she would have folded when the start-up cash ran out. As it was, Judith's was constantly bursting with trendy yuppies and their little boomettes and lots of dykes and some gay men who appreciated the accepting atmosphere.

Judith ruled her successful bar with an iron fist. Most of her employees felt little for her but fear, and I was no exception. Fortunately, she was a day person and I worked nights; but, when we had contact, she treated me like everybody else—screaming, criticizing, condescending. The story was, this powerful, portly dyke had chewed up and spit out every lover she had ever had.

My boss called me back into the office the day after she came to my house. I figured she was going to fire me. Instead, she made me night manager. In my apartment the night before her eyes had resembled ugly little Raisenettes—in the light, I noticed they were more Goober-like, larger and a smoother milky chocolate. Her heavy face was much more attractive when she softened her voice and the redness ebbed and the protruding veins of anger disappeared from her neck.

I became suspicious that evening when Judith, who claimed she was always asleep by nine o'clock, hung around until closing. When everyone but the last dishwasher was gone and I was counting the night's take, Judith leaned against the wall behind me and said, "You're a real stud, aren't you?"

I was shocked. No one had ever called me a stud before. I felt an uneasy twitch as the thought occurred to me that my thirty-seven-year-old boss was coming on to me. I glanced at her standing there in her heavy sweater that strained to conceal her girth, and I felt my ribs heave, rippling my starched shirt. I hooked my thumb into the waist of my jeans, pressed my other hand against my flat stomach, and thought: *She thinks I'm handsome. She wants to fuck me. Oh, whoa.*

Judith stared at me and I looked away. To recapture my attention, she said something that proved to me once and for all that Portland was a place for adventure and difference. "I'm pregnant," Judith said, lightly touching the front of her sweater.

————

By March my headaches were killing me. None lasted less than forty-eight hours, and they came to visit at least twice a week. Judith was not only no longer angry at me for calling in sick, she was displaying generosity that seemed limitless. Her offers and deliveries of cash, wholesome food and fresh-squeezed juice, medical advice, ice packs, aspirin, and heating pads came almost daily. If my brain had not been so clouded by pain, I might have been able to ask myself: *Who could possibly be interested in taking care of a mess like me?* If I had been a little more worldly, I could have asked: *How am I going to pay her back when the debt comes due?*

On our first date, we saw *My Dinner with Andre*, which had been highly touted as the artistic film of 1982. We both hated it and somehow believed that made us girlfriend material. After the movie, Judith stopped at a Plaid Pantry so I could pick up some cigarettes; then we headed out the Sunset Highway to her house in West Slope. A recently reformed smoker, she hoisted all the windows and teased me about the fumes on my breath. When we made love, I marveled at her tight, swollen belly and laughed when the baby inside landed a well-placed kick to the bridge of my nose. As I lay in Judith's beefy, warm arms afterward, I mustered the courage to ask the question that had been on my mind since I first found out my lesbian boss was pregnant.

"Who, by the way," I said, stroking her stomach, "is her, uh, father?" Judith's amniocentesis had indicated the baby was a girl.

"I don't know."

My first thought was rape, and I was horrified. "Oh, uh . . ." I didn't know how to say it. "You mean you didn't, this wasn't, uh, on, uh, purpose?

Judith laughed and hugged me close. "Oh, it was on purpose. About as on purpose as it gets!" Portland was about to reveal another of its exotic secrets. "The sperm was from a donor." She proceeded to introduce me to artificial insemination.

"Do you know what he looks like?"

"Tall, blond, handsome, and smart," she said. "He's a med student. That's all I know."

We made love again. Afterwards, Judith sat propped against the pillows and I lay snuggled in her arms. I walked my fingers back and forth across her stomach, occasionally raising one, *tap tap tap*, and said, "Hey little girl. Is there a little girl in there?" I asked Judith, "Have you decided what you're going to name her?"

Judith pursed her lips. "Well, I like Jessica, but that's getting to be one of those names everybody picks."

"Yeah."

"I think I'm going to name her Penn."

"Pin?"

She slapped my head. "Not pin. Penn."

"Pin."

"You Southerners."

"What does pin mean?"

"*Penn,*" she said, trying to make some distinction between the two words my Tennessee ear refused to hear, "is where I got my M.B.A."

The next morning, as I was leaving, Judith stopped me at the door and kissed me. "You're really sweet," she said, tapping my shirt pocket and adding, "although I wouldn't mind if you'd lose the addiction." I shrugged and giggled. "Casey," she said. "I'd like you to be here when I have my baby."

"Here?"

"I've got a midwife. I'm having her at home."

"And you want . . ."

"You to be here."

"Okay."

"Think about it. You don't have to answer right now."

But I did.

———

We were the only lesbian couple in our birthing class, but no one even blinked as I performed the coaching exercises right along with the other expectant fathers. Having encountered the end of the world when my mother died, I was now unwilling or unable to take anything very seriously. Judith's pregnancy was no exception. Whether I was careening down a mountainside in the middle of the night in Utah, exploring the allegedly inaccessible ruins of the Toutle River bottoms on Mt. St. Helens, or flirting with death on the Pacific Coast rocks during a stormy high tide, I had adopted the belief that either I was indestructible or that it didn't matter if I wasn't. *A baby*, I would think as I swaggered down a Portland street, adopting some macho teenage boy attitude. *I'm gonna have a baby.* I felt potent and tough and a little rebellious, although my biological contribution was exactly zero.

By May, I was general manager at the bar and doing a decent job of delegating responsibility to others as I continued to battle my migraines and Judith's due date neared. Because there was no ambiguity about the moment of conception, the baby, if she decided to arrive on time, would be born on June 15, 1982, the first anniversary of my mother's death.

I wore a beeper so I'd be the second to know when the labor started. I bought mountains of food with Judith's money and prepared it for her at her house every night. Judith and I had not made love since April, and we never would again. She said coming made her nauseous. Otherwise, she treated me with kindness and affection. She had a lovely voice and would sit on the couch with me on the floor between her feet, playing with my hair, rubbing my shoulders, singing me Billie Holliday tunes.

As the fifteenth neared, then passed, Judith got larger and lethargic and moodier, often calling me to come to her house, then asking me to please leave when I arrived. Sometimes she wanted me to touch her, sometimes it made her skin crawl. I ran her tub full of water and couldn't ever seem to get the temperature just right. Commiserating with my friend Eddy over a beer one night, I said, "The last thing I ever thought I'd understand is what a guy with a pregnant wife feels like." The macho thrill was gone.

Late in the afternoon on June 21, Judith called me at work. "It's time for you to come home," she said, and I raced out to her house. We lounged in bed together and watched *The Graduate* on television. Judith plowed through a huge bowl of fresh Queen Anne cherries. She hated the contractions. "This hurts like bloody hell," she would say, tossing on the bed, getting up and trundling through the house, bolting into the bathroom and slamming the door. She slept for a few hours and I read in the living room. At two a.m., she woke up screaming and I ran to her. She used my body, heftier now that Portland had helped my mind shed its stress, to haul herself up out of the bed. "I gotta go to the bathroom," she grunted.

Forty-five minutes later she emerged, sweaty and distraught. She grabbed a wad of cash from her wallet and thrust it into my hand. "Go to the Plaid Pantry and get me some prune juice. I'm constipated."

"Judith," I said, "you're in labor."

"Yeah, dumbass, I'm in labor, and I'M CONSTIPATED. Now go!" She shoved me out the door.

"Remind me not to have any more kids," I mumbled as I walked to the car. I had never so badly wished for a flat chest and a penis as I did that night when I walked into a convenience store at three a.m. and bought two gallons of prune juice. I wanted to look at the male clerk and shrug, "The wife's having a baby," and know that between us guys he understood. When I got back, Judith was sleeping again and I didn't wake her.

The midwife, Helen, arrived at eleven the next morning, deemed Judith insufficiently dilated, and promised to return around six. By the time she came back, Judith had been in labor for twenty-four hours. She was dilated to capacity and we all assumed the baby would come soon. Helen stuck a stethoscope in my ears and let me listen to the astounding whoosh of the baby's rapid heartbeat. I had donned my most comfortable clothing—a pair of industrial green hospital scrubs, a baggy black T-shirt, and black Chucks.

Between six and eight p.m., Judith stayed in the bathtub. Finally, Helen insisted she come into the bedroom. Judith was, to understate things, snappish. She sat on the bed, laid on the bed, sat in the chair, stood at the window, sat on the floor, paced the floor, complained about the light, demanded we lower the shades, complained about the darkness until we raised the shades. She was starving, but the midwife wouldn't let her eat anything but ice.

Judith's contractions were just moments apart. She was stark naked and on the floor, panting and pushing, when she suddenly stopped and glared at me with glassy eyes. "Get out of here!" she bellowed, and I left quickly.

Thirty minutes later, Helen came into the living room and said, "Judith wants you back."

"What's the matter with her?"

Helen laughed. "She's having a baby, sweetie." Judith, who had a phobia about hospitals, later told me my pants were making her sick.

When I reentered the bedroom, Judith was sprawled on the floor, her legs askew. For a second, I had the appalling vision of a murder victim in a book I owned. The sun was setting and the room was pink and shadowy, and these two women were on the floor and the sounds in the room were grunts and monosyllabic commands.

For some reason, I felt the overwhelming presence of death and wondered why that might be, here in this room where a new life was emerging. I crouched down and peered past Helen and saw Judith's genitals stretched unbelievably wide around a bulbous pink ball. "What's that?!"

The midwife laughed. "That's her head!"

The next thing I knew, Helen's hand was shaking as she flipped on the overhead light.

"I hate that light!" Judith shrieked, but the midwife, for the first time, completely ignored her protestations. Helen dropped the stethoscope and began wildly lubricating her hands and arms to the elbows. I melted into the wall.

"There's no heartbeat," she gasped. "Judith, get up, squat, NOW—get her out of there!" Judith squatted. "Give her your arms!" Helen shouted at me. I knelt down in front of Judith and she grabbed my arms and pulled and strained until I thought she would dismember me before, finally, shoving me violently away, slamming my back into the closet door. I scurried away like someone escaping a nest of rattlesnakes, and Helen slid beneath Judith and began doing something with her greased hands that I preferred not to watch. Judith kicked her away, too.

Suddenly, there was a deafening roar and Judith collapsed onto her back. In the harsh light I saw the baby, puny and blue, trailing a shredded cord, lying motionless in a huge clot of blood that covered the floor and Judith's legs. The midwife lunged for the limp baby, scooped her up and laid her on her back on the bed and began mouth-to-mouth. "Get the oxygen!" Helen screamed at me between two puffs of breath.

"Where is it?" I said, shaking and panting. It was supposed to be in the house. This was supposed to be a perfect birth.

"It's in the trunk," she said, and threw a ring of a dozen keys at me.

"Which key?" My voice was cracking with terror.

"Goddamn it, I don't know. Just get the oxygen!"

The front of Judith's house had no lights and night had fallen. I couldn't see anything and my hand was frozen with fear, the same way it felt that night the serial killer was looking in my car in Kansas. I was crying, thinking, *her brain, no oxygen, get the oxygen.* I tried one key and it didn't work. Another. Didn't work. And another. *She can't breathe. How long can she go without air? Which keys have I tried? I can't keep track.* I believe it was the fourth key that opened the trunk. I ran back inside with the metal container.

Helen grabbed the tank. "She's pinking up," she announced as life was being pumped back into the baby. She looked stone dead to me, gray and still. *This woman's crazy,* I thought. I glanced at Judith, so determined to give birth in the comfort of her own home without the bright lights and sterile surroundings of a hospital. She was lying on the floor, her eyes open but glazed and staring, blood caked from her waist down. She looked as dead as her daughter.

"Call the hospital, get an ambulance!" Helen shouted.

"What hospital?" I shrieked. Later I would note how slapstick humorous this charade would have been were it not for the fact of this innocent newborn dying of ineptitude on the bed.

"*The* hospital, on the hill," Helen barked. Now, that helped. There was a hospital on stand-by, I knew that. I didn't know its name. Its name and number were supposed to be by the phone, in this house, but they weren't.

"What's the number?" My voice had deteriorated into a hoarse, hopeless whine.

"Goddamn it, I don't know. It's the University Hospital, Oregon Science, uh University Health, Hospital—LOOK IN THE PHONE BOOK!"

I probably ran to the kitchen but I felt like I was lumbering through the deepest Cascade snow. I grabbed the yellow pages and tore them open. Hospitals. H. There. The first thing I saw was one minuscule line of fine print in the middle of the page. Oregon Health Sciences University. I called the number and, within fifteen minutes, the ambulance attendants had wrapped Judith in blankets with Penn on her chest, strapped them to a stretcher, and driven away, with the midwife, into the night.

I sat at the kitchen table and successfully fielded two phone calls, one from an acquaintance, the other from Judith's brother. "Everybody's fine," I assured them both. Incapable of sitting still, I wandered into the bedroom that now looked exactly like a murder scene with an overturned lamp and the sheets dragged off the bed and a massive area of clumped and spattered blood on the carpet and wall. Signs of a struggle.

The phone jangled and I slammed the bedroom door shut, running to answer it. It was Judith's best friend, Jerri, and my steely resolve shattered as I wailed the truth into the receiver. "Meet us at the hospital," she said.

"How do I get there?"

"Call a cab."

It had started raining and had cooled considerably as it is wont to do in Oregon, even in the summer. I stood trembling in my thin scrubs and T-shirt in the dark waiting for the taxi to arrive. When I saw the yellow light, I ran to the curb and jumped in, breathless. "Take me to the hospital on the hill as fast as you can!"

The young, bearded driver smiled and saluted. "Sure thing, Doc!" As he stepped on the gas and roared away from the house he added, "Guess you got a baby to deliver." I didn't bother to answer. He got lost navigating the complicated loops and curves of the West Hills and a ten-minute trip turned into forty-five. When we pulled up to emergency he apologized. "God, I'm so sorry. I hope everything's okay. This one's on me."

Which was good. I had left the house without a penny.

———

There were rhythmic beeps and flickering red lights of life-sustaining machinery—spontaneous clatters of equipment picked up, used, discarded. There was the austere gleam of white-blue fluorescent tubes and the mushy beat of busy nurses' industrial-strength shoes on linoleum floors. I stood in a holding area. Visitors were a select few in medium-risk where the babies had a fighting chance of survival with expeditious aid in their first hours of life. I had just left Judith who was, with the help of Demerol, nodding off in a room down the hall. She was packed with cotton and swaddled in enormous sanitary pads to protect her and her bedding from the blood that still oozed from her hemorrhaged womb. I promised her I would check on Penn. Already, there was no place else I wanted to be.

I entered the room full of babies encased in clear plastic boxes, clad in my mask, cap, and gown. A motherly nurse led me through the maze of baby boxes with her warm hand gently cradling my quivering elbow. She explained that my name was on "the list," meaning I was welcome here to see this baby any time day or night. I felt like the most honored person in the world. The nurse stopped at a box by the window, patted my arm, and said, "Look for as long as you want."

Penn was on her back, arms and legs sprawled, fists clinched. Naked, except for her impossibly small diaper. She was rosy pink, her eyes and lips closed peacefully. She was not moving except for her heartbeat thumping beneath the translucent skin of her bony chest. Sound asleep, still she begged to be touched. I pressed my palms against the plastic barrier between us. "Hey baby, it's Casey." She tensed her thighs and scrunched her face and her lips moved in a sucking motion as her toes splayed, then curled. I shouted for a nurse.

One came and smiled. "She's fine, just dreaming."

"Why's that thing on her heart?" I asked.

"She's hooked to a monitor, so we can be sure everything's working right!" the nurse said, a little too cheerily, I thought.

"And the things on her head?"

The nurse looked somber. "Well, sometimes when a baby has trouble . . . when they don't get enough oxygen, there can be problems. There aren't any signs of . . . problems, but, we're just monitoring her brain for the first day or so to make sure all the activity is normal." She saw I was disturbed and patted my arm. "I'm sure she's going to be fine." Penn had settled back into a dreamless sleep.

"Can I touch her?"

"Tomorrow," the nurse said.

I stared at the baby until I was too tired to stand up. Then I left, shedding my sterile garb in a hamper by the door.

———

I never really slept that night, scooting around on a cheap plastic sofa, trying to find a position that was conducive to resting, always half-aware of the bleary-eyed men who shared the harshly-lit waiting room with me. I couldn't help wondering, even in this time of tremendous stress, what they must think. The scrubs may have given me some air of legitimacy, but I was sure the ratty T-shirt and soiled sneakers undermined that. Maybe they thought I was a homeless person who had found a dry place for the night. *No, we had a baby at home and a couple things went wrong, so the baby's in medium-risk and my lover's in a room down the hall packed in sanitary pads and I'm just waiting here until morning so I can go visit both of them.*

At 6:30 a.m. I gave up trying to keep my eyes closed, got up, and went to the nursery. Before I could suit up, one of the graveyard nurses stopped me, explaining they were changing shifts and I should come back after seven. This nurse, Jenny, was a tiny woman, and I looked over her head through a series of glass partitions, desks, and equipment—but I couldn't see what I was looking for. "Is Penn okay?" I said.

"She's fine."

"Is her brain okay?"

Jenny smiled. "Nothing's showing up on the EEG at all, nothing unusual, that is. Don't worry, everything will be fine."

I wandered down the hall and stuck my head into Judith's room. She was sleeping on her back, a white thermal blanket stretched over her, her normal heaviness disguising the fact there was no baby in there any more. I felt a lump in my throat, pressed my fist against my heart, stared for a moment, then quietly turned to leave.

"Honey?" Judith said.

I turned back and went to her bed. She reached for my hand, her bloodless face luminous in the silver dawn that peeked through the blinds. I sat carefully on the bedside and she pulled her arms from under the covers, hugged me close to her, and pressed her lips against my neck. I started crying. "Don't cry," she said. "It's okay."

"I'm sorry."

"How's my baby?" she whispered.

I ached for her. She hadn't even really seen her baby. "Oh Judith, she's beautiful. She looks just like one of the seven dwarfs."

"Hey," Judith said, pretending offense.

"No, I mean, she's really cute. She's got a perfect body and her cheeks kinda press up under her eyes and in the middle is this little nose, sorta like the Pillsbury Doughboy." I thought I saw a flicker of genuine anxiety in Judith's eyes as I faltered in my attempt to describe her newborn. "She sleeps great!" I said.

I told her about the EEG and Judith seemed satisfied that all was well. "Can you help me to the bathroom?" she said. We squeezed into the small stall and Judith held onto my shoulders while I tugged down her underpants. She complained a little when the blood-soaked pads pinched her as they came unglued. I eased her down onto the toilet and asked if she wanted to be alone. "No," she said.

I knelt beside her until she started to pee. Then I stood and threw away the pads, got some fresh ones from the cabinet, pushed them into her underwear, and helped her up. I couldn't look at Judith's large, empty stomach. I kept thinking about my mother—the hole like a gunshot in her gut, the blood gushing from it in those last weeks of her life. *Nobody's dying here,* I kept saying in my head. *Nobody's dying.*

When Judith was back in bed, she squeezed my hands and looked at me with more love than I had ever seen from her, or ever would again. "Thank you, Casey. I don't know what either of us would have done without you." My heart soared and the lump in my throat returned. "I love you. I'm going to sleep now. Go be with Penn, okay?"

The whole first day they wouldn't let me touch the baby. All I could do was talk through the box surrounding her, try to make eye contact when she was awake, and watch her sleep, her lips sucking a phantom nipple. That afternoon, I wheeled Judith into the nursery to see her daughter. Then she was released with an order of a week's complete bed rest. Jerri, who had come back up that morning, drove us home. That night, Judith asked me to stay with her during the day and spend the evenings with Penn until they let the baby come home. And, for the next week, that's what I did. Within the month, Judith would convince me to move into her home—an offer I readily accepted because, after that first week, I couldn't imagine being separated from this new baby.

I arrived at the hospital at 10:30 p.m. on the second night of Penn's life. When I was tying my gown, I felt a poke in my ribs, turned around, and there was Jenny, grinning. "She's off the EEG," she said. "No reason she can't be a rocket scientist!"

"Everything's okay?"

"Not a blip."

I followed her into the nursery. The baby was awake, yawning, with her fists pressed against her ears. Jenny grabbed a pink blanket and threw it over my shoulder, then lowered the front panel of the plastic box and slipped her steady hands under Penn's head and bottom. I didn't react until a drop of saliva spilled over my lip and hit the floor. I blushed and closed my mouth. "Come here," Jenny said.

I followed her into a little room in which there was nothing except a wooden rocking chair. "Sit," Jenny said, glancing at the chair. She moved so close to me our knees touched. I held out my arms, palms up, fingers spread, and touched Penn for the first time. Jenny draped the blanket across Penn's body. Then she left the room and I started to rock. I slipped my right hand out from under Penn's diaper and laid it on her stomach and chest. She was toasty, much warmer than me, it seemed. I hoped she didn't have a fever. Her eyes were open, moving, straining to focus. Her head was perfectly cupped in my average-sized hand. She spoke first. "Huuhh," —just a tiny gust of air from her throat, then a peep.

I raised my eyebrows and cooed, "Hi little baby." Her eyes widened and her fist went to the side of her head and her finger got caught in her ear. I slipped my finger under her knuckles. Her hand curled and she tried, without good aim, to bring me to her mouth. Her lips sucked the air furiously. I touched her lips and she sucked my finger until her eyelids drooped. Then she was asleep, rocking in my arms. Whenever I tried to pull my finger out, she didn't wake up, just sucked harder. I have no idea whether it was minutes or hours before Jenny showed back up with a bottle.

"You get the honors," she said, sticking the bottle in front of me. "Her first meal."

I was horrified. "You haven't given her anything to eat yet?"

"Babies don't eat for the first day or two. Don't worry, we're not starving her."

"But she's sleeping."

"Well, she needs to eat. Let's wake her up." Jenny was so matter-of-fact, like taking care of this tiny human being was the easiest thing in the world.

"How do you wake up a newborn baby?"

Jenny took Penn into the bright lights of the nursery, held her upright, talked to her in a singsong voice. When she brought her back, Penn was awake. She placed her back on my lap, handed me the bottle, watched as I pushed the nipple against Penn's lips, and laughed as the newborn turned beet red and squirmed to move her face away. "Come on, baby, it's milk. Mmmmmm." Penn kicked her feet and flailed her arms and let out a squawk like a baby bird. Seizing the opportunity, I stuck the nipple into her open mouth. She screamed and gagged and broke into a hiccuping wail.

"Take it slow," Jenny said. "She doesn't know how to eat."

"Can she swallow?"

"Sure, she can swallow. She just doesn't know what the nipple is. Take your finger and rub her lips." I did. "Okay, now, when she relaxes, slip the nipple in and move your finger away. With a little luck, she won't notice." Penn took the nipple, clamped it between her gums, and stared at me. She wouldn't suck. "Be patient," Jenny said. After a few moments, Penn's jaws started working the nipple and she was eating.

When the first meal was over, Jenny took the half-empty bottle and dropped it into her smock pocket. She tossed a towel over my left shoulder. "Time for a burp!" I raised Penn up. Her chin dropped to the towel and I patted her back. Within seconds, she burped as loudly as a teenaged boy. "Very good, very good," Jenny said. I beamed, not sure if she was praising me or the baby.

Penn fell asleep on my shoulder, her face hot against my neck, and I dozed along with her. *I love this*, I thought. *This is so easy. We'll just eat together and sleep together and stare at each other and, I guess, when she's older, we'll talk.* An hour later, I was rudely awakened by a screaming baby and I quickly realized it was the one I was holding and I panicked. I bolted into the nursery and Jenny was nowhere to be found. "She's crying!" I blurted to the first nurse I saw. "She's crying!" The nurse smiled and nodded at me like this was the psychiatric ward. "What am I supposed to do?"

I was relieved to hear Jenny's voice behind me. She tugged my arm and we went to a table covered with crisp paper. "Put her down, right here." Jenny handed me a fresh diaper and I untaped the wet one. As soon as Penn's naked body felt the breeze, a perfect arc of pee hit me square in the chest.

"Oh shit," I said, jumping back. Jenny and two other nurses burst out laughing. "I thought only boys could do that!" As we cleaned Penn with a disposable damp-wipe, Jenny pointed to the baby's swollen genitals. I was a little embarrassed to stare, even more so to talk about them. Jenny explained that a girl's tissues are engorged from the mother's hormones, so, what is usually hidden is protruding, so, when she pees, it shoots out like a boy.

My mind was full to capacity. I felt like I'd learned more in the past two days than I had in the preceding twenty-five years. *What am I doing here in this hospital in Portland with a newborn baby who sort of belongs to me, talking with strangers about her sexual organs? Just over a year ago I buried my own mother; now I'm here being a mother to some other baby girl. In a hospital, in the West Hills, in Portland, Oregon.*

Things couldn't get any weirder, but they did.

Back in the dark room, I held a diapered and fed baby who still wouldn't stop crying. She wrenched her body, arched her back, beat her fists, desperately tried to communicate in a language I had once known, but had forgotten. "You know what would make her happy?" Jenny said, kneeling beside me. She told me about comfort nursing, then politely left the room.

I watched Penn crying, hiccuping violently, gagging, and sputtering. I thought about her mother at home, separated by birth trauma from the daughter she had carried so safely for nine months. I thought: *I've got twenty-five years on you, kiddo, and take it from me, the best nine months of your life are over.* Then I felt terrible. It was up to me to make this baby happy. *Not always,* I thought, *but sometimes somebody can give you what you need, and they do, maybe, even if they don't really know you.*

But I did know this baby. And I loved her already.

I unbuttoned my shirt and pulled the left side away from my chest. Penn stopped crying, looked up at me and, not breaking our gaze, dropped her head toward my breast. I guided my nipple into her soft, wet mouth and she sucked, staring into my eyes, until she fell asleep.

During that first week I learned things I never dreamed I would know. I learned what a gift it is to have two breasts—one to give the other, swollen and raw, a break. I felt the agony of seeing a large needle plunged into a baby's thigh smaller than my wrist, felt the referred pain of another as my own thigh ached with sympathy. I experienced the joy and horror of another human being's gaze that says: *You are my whole world.* And means it.

I learned how to attach a disposable diaper in such a way that it doesn't fall off. I came to understand the phenomena of projectile vomiting and the danger of microscopic but deadly fingernails. I learned how to read the deeper meaning behind a curled lip, a grunt, a sigh, varied decibel cries, this baby's eyes.

I emerged from my half-sleep in a pool of icy sweat in a strange motel in the Redding, California dawn. The cries of an infant pierced the silence. I sat up and tried to scream, but could only mutter, "She's crying, she's crying. . . ." But the nurses weren't there, and the baby wasn't there. No one was there but me, and two cats outside fucking behind the trash cans.

GOING DOWN IN HISTORY

I watched the sunrise light up the mountains—the Cascades they were called just a couple hundred miles back, now the Sierras—to the east of the town in California where I spent my first night. I never dreamed I'd be making this trip again, alone. Backward.

By eight o'clock I'd showered and collected my few possessions and hit the road. It was balmy already, so I had to keep my windows rolled down. No music again today. I settled into a comfortable sixty miles per hour and had this fantasy that somehow I had become famous, more likely infamous, or, most likely, this would be part of a psychiatric evaluation. At any rate, I spoke to an interviewer, my fantasy based on the optimistic assumption that I would actually live to tell anybody anything. I said, in response to imaginary questioning:

"My life was shot so full of holes I could no longer see the fabric. The hardest thing was saying goodbye to Penn. I didn't know if I would ever see her again. It's odd how you can do the most intimate things with another human being, then, one day, just say goodbye and walk out of her life forever.

"The last day I saw her she was almost eight. We went to Chuck E. Cheese and ate really awful pizza and she played games skillfully and amassed lots of free tokens. She jumped around in a room full of balls and climbed on colorful animal statues while I watched. We went to swing at sunset on the school playground by my house where a little boy disappeared the previous Halloween, only to be found two weeks later naked and strangled in a field in Vancouver. Now, his killer is waiting to be killed in kind, on the gallows, in Walla Walla. It's scary how quickly we can get ourselves into irreversible trouble.

"Our last stop was my house. It seemed to me Penn was trying to pretend like she didn't notice that the furniture was gone and the dining room was stacked with boxes. She was plenty old enough to realize this wasn't the same cozy home where we had carved pumpkins, opened holiday gifts, and watched two out of three puppies grow into big dogs. As we got ready to leave, she asked me if she could have something of mine from the few things that hadn't been sold. I said yes, and she chose my punching bag. Good girl.

"I stayed at Judith's for about an hour and it was obvious she was trying to pretend like nothing was out of the ordinary. We chatted about everything except the fact that I was leaving Portland, probably forever, in a week. Finally, there was nothing safe left to say. Penn followed me to the door. She had gotten so tall. She hugged me and I kissed the top of her head that wasn't too far below my chin. I tried hard but unsuccessfully not to cry. Penn looked up at me, her tearless emerald eyes expressing something more like worry than sorrow, something far beyond her years. She touched my cheek and said,

'It's okay, Casey.' I knelt and she buried her face against my neck and whispered, 'I love you.'"

———

I imagined that the Mojave is the father of many little deserts that have since moved to their own spaces in the western United States. Imagined that he knows how special being a parent is—that he will understand that I can't be a terrible person because I saved a baby's life, nurtured her through infancy, taught her some of the basics—new words and first steps. Can't we balance that with all the pain I've caused, all the wrongs I've done—call me a fallible human rather than a monster?

Then I remembered the stories, however apocryphal. Albert DeSalvo, by night, uses the powerful muscles in his arms and hands to massage his young daughter's legs, atrophied from polio, until, against all odds, she walks again. Albert DeSalvo, by day the Boston Strangler, stalks the streets, rings bells at random until a woman answers and he slips his powerful hands around her neck and strangles her until she is dead. And, on a frigid day, standing on the edge of the choppy Puget Sound, Ted Bundy hears a scream, dashes into the water and pulls a little girl to safety—a girl who, had she been fifteen years older that day, may have met an entirely different fate once in this killer's arms.

Okay, I shrugged. We can call it compulsion, obsession, loss of willpower. We can blame drugs and drink. But it is choice, isn't it? The good doesn't excuse us at all. In fact, it may make the bad we do that much worse.

I prayed for a moment that this desert would punish me. I wandered a few feet from my truck disturbing the silent sand with my feet. *Send a snake to strike my legs, Mojave—incapacitate me so I'll never leave here alive. Send a lightning bolt.* I have the audacity to think at least that's a little less humiliating than having some prison guard strap you shaved bald and hooded, wetting and shitting yourself, into an electrified wooden chair.

Kill me, Mojave, right now, if that's what I deserve. The desert did nothing, just waited for me to tell him more.

COLORADO DEAD

My virgin kidneys had never been pressed up against a driver's seat for so long before, and I couldn't ignore the ache back there. But, when I checked out of the Triple D on my third morning in Denver, I was otherwise rested and ready to resume my trip. Because I was a spontaneous and inexperienced traveler in completely foreign country, I had no knowledge of common tourist spots and, thus, visited almost none. But I did have a personal itinerary. Whenever possible, I planned to follow somebody else's trail—to stop here and there and try to read silent memories of disappearances and grisly finds. As the object of my obsession languished in the shadow of Ol' Sparky in a prison far way in Florida, I had entered Ted Bundy country.

High in the Rockies I saw a sign for Pike's Peak and stopped to look, remembering it from an old children's story about a goldminer there. While I ate an overpriced lunch at a tourist's cafeteria, I pored over my Triple A maps and was terribly disappointed that Aspen, Vail, Grand Junction, Owl Creek Road, Berthoud Pass, and the Wildwood Inn—all Bundy landmarks—were too far south to justify the side trip.

But I did drive through Golden where a hitchhiking teenager once had disappeared. Fifty miles west of Denver, I veered through Nederland where a high school girl vanished in April of 1975. I drove slowly along the isolated roads of Coal Creek Canyon, where her bludgeoned and strangled body was found eight days later. I pulled off the road and smoked a cigarette with my back to the cold, wet, and rugged rock. All around me were tall pines. I took that moment, in that place, to whisper into the chilly air to the Colorado dead: "Caryn, Julie, Denise, Melanie, Shelley. As horrible as it was for you, rest assured, they're giving him plenty of time to anticipate what's coming for him. Sleep in peace."

As I wound out of the Rockies and entered western Colorado, Memphis began to feel as dead to me as the papery skin that was beginning to peel from my sunburned left side. I noted with pleasure that this chameleon, finally, was free to grow a new skin of her own choosing. Everything ahead of me was new—and anything was possible.

I rolled across the flat land and a gentle rain began to fall. When it was done, I pulled over to marvel at a quadruple rainbow arched across the High Plains. *Over there*, I thought, as I stared due west and a warm, humid breeze ruffled my hair, *over there is Portland. Over there is the end of the rainbow.* I thought of *The Wizard of Oz* and was overcome with a resurgence of my belief, all but destroyed by Mama's death, in some superior cosmic power that orchestrates the universe, ensuring that everything happens for a reason. I knew in my soul at that moment that my choice of Portland was not an accident—that Oregon was where I was meant to be. I would have given anything that day for the Wicked Witch's crystal ball. Although, if that had been the case, I might well have defied the Higher Power and established residency in Dinosaur, Colorado, the next town I reached.

SOUTH

Northern California was luscious to look at. I took note of that just in case there came a day when I might be wanting to remember it to someone. I was feeling decent, although those fucking cats disturbed my sleep and gave me bad dreams. Time had lost its meaning for me, my circadian rhythm having long since surrendered to the Halcion's superior strength, so I enjoyed a big breakfast of Kentucky Fried Chicken and continued my descent through the Golden State.

A hundred miles later, I saw the first signs for San Francisco. I arched my travel-tired back, winced at its stiff soreness, and remembered back to '81 how, during that trip, my body transcended this pain somewhere around the third day. Then I indulged a little fantasy—*What if I took that next San Francisco exit and ended my trip tonight? But what would I do in San Francisco? I don't know anybody there. Oh, yes I do. . . .*

Everybody warned me about the dangers of going to Mt. St. Helens except South, so, when I decided to go, I asked her to come along.

The first time I saw South was the day I was filling out the application for my first Portland job. She was sitting across the employee table from me, eating a piece of dense chocolate cake filled with thick almond cream. She obviously was peeking, because when I wrote my place of birth she said, mimicking a Southern accent, "Memm-fus Ten-uh-say." I looked up at her and she winked. "Suth-un gurl."

Before I even knew her name, I knew South was the best looking woman I'd ever seen. She was two inches taller than me with a firm athletic body—square shoulders, tapered waist, and slim hips—flawless, tanned skin which already I knew was a rarity here where the perpetual rains left most Portlanders pale and pasty. South had dark brown hair with black eyebrows that met in the middle, and sparkling violet eyes. She befriended me immediately, and our casual flirting started soon after. With her name and my region of birth being the same, it is possible we would have believed we were destined to be together, had our relationship gotten that far.

On a cool, late September morning I packed chicken salad sandwiches, organic fruit from The Daily Grind, a big bag of Chee-tos, blueberry muffins, and a six-pack of Rainier beer—picked up South at her apartment which was four blocks from mine, and headed north toward the volcano. Once we were alone together we both became bashful, no flirting; but nothing could quell the excitement I felt being in the car with this stunning woman, embarking on a new Northwest adventure. Our sexual reticence did not spill over into our conversation— we talked and talked and learned a lot about each other that day.

Having passed Vancouver, we cut through the countryside passing roadside stands laden with Washington apples, fresh vegetables, and fat, bright pumpkins. As the Cascade peaks tend to do, St. Helens was nowhere one minute, then filling the horizon to our right the next. South steered for a moment while I stared at the decapitated mountain.

"I wish I'd seen it before."

"Oh, God," said South, "it was the most beautiful mountain—not the sharp point like Hood or the double bump like Rainier—just perfect, like a bowl turned upside down, covered with melted vanilla ice cream." South's voice was rich and soothing, no accent at all, and her lips barely moved when she talked.

"Where were you when it happened?"

"Oh," she laughed. "It was so bizarre. I was with my softball team. We practiced every Sunday morning at the diamond right there on the corner of 20th and Belmont, right by your place. We hadn't started playing yet—we were still unpacking our stuff, limbering up, putting on our shoes. The news didn't really say much at all the night before. I mean, it had erupted already a couple times and it doesn't seem like anybody thought it was going to end up doing what it did. I had just taken off my shoe to shake a rock out of it and I was squatting down, putting it back on. My glove was in my lap and my friend Janis was standing next to me swinging a bat with her catcher's mask on top of her head. All of a sudden . . . we didn't actually *hear* anything—it was more like we felt it. Of course, you can't see the mountain from that ball park, but we all looked to the north and there was this gigantic mushroom cloud rising over the houses. It was the weirdest thing. Nobody said anything. We all just picked up our equipment and walked away."

"Nobody said anything?"

"Nothing. We didn't even look at each other. Most of us thought it was a nuclear attack. I think we just didn't have anything to say. We just wanted to go home. A couple of us thought it was a meltdown at Hanford. Same difference."

"Hanford?" South told me about the controversial nuclear power plant across the Columbia River in Washington.

"I burst out laughing when I got home and turned on the television and found out it was *just* Mt. St. Helens. But nobody laughed for long. It was horrible. The mountain was demolished, people got killed—this journalist just, like, *combusted* in his car. And *then*, oh, the sky was black as night for weeks. We had to wear surgical masks outside because the ash was so thick in the air. It looks like dust or smoke but it's gritty and heavy—it ruined people's cars and ripped storm gutters off houses. It was a nightmare."

Everybody in Portland seemed to have a story to tell about the morning the volcano erupted in their backyard. Some of the tales, I suspected, were taller than others. I didn't know if South was exaggerating, not that it mattered. Just listening to her talk was good for me.

We drove in reverent silence for a moment. I glanced at the quiet giant, amazed at the damage her pent-up fury had done. I heard a giggle next to me. "What's so funny?"

"Judith's bar. Have you heard this story?" South said, her eyes sparkling with diabolical pleasure. "May 18th was opening day! Every dyke in town was talking about *our* bar. Judith got the word out in the community big-time that this was going to be, like, lesbian-only space or something. As you've noticed, that's not how it's turned out. But it was great PR. Anyway, that morning there was a line out the door a mile long waiting to get in, then boom! Everybody had to go home. Judith couldn't open for months because of the ash. I think part of the building might have been damaged. I shouldn't laugh, but you know how much I despise her."

"Why do you hate her so much?"

South sighed and shook her head. "Because she's a maniac." She was silent for a moment. "I think what's so creepy about it is, she can be so *nice* . . . not *nice*, exactly, but *generous*, with money and food, even with time off and stuff like that, you know? But then, it's like she lulls you into liking her, into almost trusting her, and then she just turns on you. She has those screaming fits and she lets you have it right in front of everybody and humiliates you—like when your mom or dad spanks you in front of your brothers and sisters, you know?"

I didn't know because my parents never did that—but I had a spontaneous image of somebody doing it to South and the crotch of my jeans tightened uncomfortably. I concentrated on pulling a cigarette from my pack and lighting it to dispel that vision. I was horrified that South would read my mind and be offended by my kinky sexual response to her innocent, and apt, analogy.

"She thinks she's smarter than everybody else," South continued. "If you don't know anything else about Judith, you know she got her bachelor's degree from UCLA and her fucking master's in business from the Wharton School. She mentions it constantly. I don't know. It's hard to explain. I just think Judith's the type of person who can't control herself, or, for some reason, doesn't think she has to. She seems to get some kind of sick satisfaction from pulling you in then ripping you to shreds. I hope I'm wrong, but I suspect you'll know pretty soon what I mean."

If I had known on that gorgeous September morning how prescient South's words were, I would have jumped in her lap like a kid being chased by the bogeyman and begged her not to let him get me.

As we approached the forests surrounding St. Helens, signs began popping up on the roadside. *Proceed with Caution. Warning: Dangerous Area. Official Access Only.* And finally, hung from sawhorses that formed a road block: *Red Zone: Do Not Enter.*

I looked at South, dismayed. We couldn't even see the mountain from where we sat on this dusty road. She winked at me.

"Let me drive."

An hour later, South had negotiated mud, mounds of ash, and access roads littered with scorched forest debris, and we stepped out to explore the Toutle River bottoms.

When Mt. St. Helens went, she didn't go alone. Ice blue water teemed with fish not so long ago in the riverbed we sat along to eat our lunch. Evergreens, never naked, lined the banks —deer and birds and rodents, bears, maybe some wolves or wildcats, myriad insects—all lived full, productive lives there. But on May 18, 1980, all of that disappeared, leaving only what we saw. A cracked riverbed caked with brown and gray sludge. Gigantic trees stripped bare as though God had trundled through this forest in a fury with a blow torch. Blackened sticks and tree limbs and trunks lay strewn haphazardly like some bored child's tinkertoys. But the eeriest aftereffect was the silence, the absolute absence of the clicking, chirping, rushing, galloping, howling sounds of life.

"How did this happen?"

South shrugged. "The heat from the blast was so intense it just incinerated everything. And everybody. I bet this is what nuclear war would look like."

"Probably so."

We packed away the remains of our lunch and wandered through the desolation until both of us felt we had seen enough. On the way back to the car I said, "What would happen to us if she went off again right now?"

South laughed. "We'd never know what hit us."

Mt. St. Helens was angry again the next day for some reason. She spewed another plume of steam and ash that stretched hundreds of feet into the sky, clearly visible from Portland—but no more of the dome was lost and there were no fatalities. Everything in the red zone that day was already dead.

———

South introduced me to the dyke bars, took me to the movies, to the Washington Park Zoo, up to Mt. Tabor at dusk to see the rising of the city lights. Our flirting continued at work. We drank, and when we danced our heat penetrated each others' clothes. Conjectures about our relationship flew wildly at work. In December, against South's wishes, Judith switched her to the day shift. We went out for a drink the next afternoon. "I hate that bitch," South said. "And I suppose she knows it."

"Why did she move you to days?"

"Because she knows that's exactly what I don't want." South sipped her gin and shot kernels of popcorn, one by one, across the room. "And, I think she's jealous."

"Jealous?"

"Yeah, of me—of you . . ."

"No way!"

"She's got the hots for you, Southern girl."

"Oh, you're full of shit." South shrugged and wouldn't look at me. I kicked her foot and she looked up. "I don't have the hots for her, you know."

"Hey," South said, "are you working tonight?"

"No."

"Let's do something cool."

"Such as . . ."

She took my hand and led me from the bar, took me to her house where she threw goosedown jackets, hiking boots, ski masks, and gloves into a duffel bag. We walked out to her car.

"Where are we going?"

"It's a surprise. Trust me?"

I did. I would have done anything South wanted.

We ascended Mt. Hood, climbing higher than the tops of the evergreens, and South parked in the lot at Timberline Lodge. "Does that look familiar?" she said, pointing to the rustic log building behind which Hood's snowy peak stood illuminated by the brilliant light of a full moon in a clear, starry sky.

It did, sort of. Maybe I'd seen it in a tourist book.

"That's the Overlook Hotel, in *The Shining*." South knew my affinity for horror.

"Oh, my fucking God," I said. She was right, and I was just about as excited as I can get. "Let's go!"

"Wait a minute, Tennessee," she said. I had no concept of the brutal cold outside our car.

It took South nearly a half hour to bundle us up enough to brave Mt. Hood's winter temperature. By the time the boots, socks, sweaters, jackets, gloves, and masks were on, the only body parts showing were noses and eyes. She pulled our jacket hoods up over the wool masks and tied them tightly at our necks. We got out and trudged through deep snow away from the lodge's lights until South took my arm. "Let's stop here."

"No, no," I said, gazing at the peak still a deceptive four thousand feet above us. "Let's go all the way."

South laughed. "It's further to the top than it looks. Let's not push our luck." Without warning, she grabbed me around the waist and tackled me into the snow. I jumped up to run away and she brought me down again. We were laughing and squealing like school girls—I was throwing snow in her face and she kept tripping me and pushing me down, tumbling along with me. Finally, we were exhausted and we lay panting in the snow. My chest and throat hurt. It took both of us a while to catch our breaths in the gossamer air.

"The wind chill up here can go to seventy below," South said, her voice muffled by the wool covering her mouth. "They say it can freeze the tears in your eyes."

"I wouldn't ever make you cry."

South sat up and pulled the wool below her chin, then reached out and lowered mine, too. We kissed in the moonlight until our faces were too frozen to move. In the hour it took us to get back to South's house, my body was already giving hints of the shrieking pain it was going to be in the next day. South taunted me as I moaned all the way up her apartment stairs. "Come on old lady."

"Hey, you're a year older than me." She was, but also infinitely more fit.

"Nobody'd believe that right now!"

"Oh shut up, jock," I groaned, watching her ass muscles grip and clench as she took the steps ahead of me two at a time.

In her bedroom, she turned up the heat and we stripped down to our long underwear. "Make yourself comfortable," she said. "I'll fix us a treat." She came back ten minutes later with two steaming hot toddys. We sat crosslegged on her bed and drank enough to thaw the remaining icicles in our lungs. South took my cup from me and, stretching across my lap, set it along with hers on the bedside table.

The sight of her tight ass was more than I could stand. I ran my hand up her thigh and gripped her right cheek cloaked in thick thermal. She lay across my lap and let me continue. When I slipped my fingers beneath her waistband she moaned and turned around, wrapping her legs around my hips. We kissed, pressing ourselves together.

South pushed me back against the pillows, knelt over me and pulled off her shirt, then moved down, tugging my underwear along with her. She turned her back to me, straddled my chest. When her sultry mouth touched my clit, I pulled her underwear down and was hit with her scent—fresh and salty and powerful as the Pacific. I watched her move while she made love to me. When I was threatening to come, she stopped and lifted her mouth away.

"Ahhh," I cried, clamping my hands over my abandoned crotch. She slapped them and pulled them away.

"No, no, no," she chided, squeezing my wrists together to restrain me. She opened her bedside drawer, extracting a smooth, peach-colored dildo, which she held in her right hand as her mouth resumed its work. When I flushed and shuddered, South drove her toy deep inside my cunt and I dragged long scratches across her ass. She collapsed across me, resting her head on my soaked pubic hair until my breathing regulated. Then she rolled over and we kissed with our eyes open.

I ran my fingers between her lips, lighting probing her vagina, spreading her moisture across her clit as she moaned and gazed in my eyes. "Oh, Casey," she said, parting her legs to encourage me deeper. I started to slip beneath her. She caught me by the ears, running her hands through my hair, kissing me. She stopped and picked up the dildo, glancing at it, then at me, then handed it to me. She turned her back to me, knelt, and leaned forward. I had never seen such a nice ass, perfect, save for the long welts I had put there moments before. "I want it up the butt," she whispered.

"Oh, yeah?" I said. "Well, there's only one thing I like better than a woman who asks for what she wants."

"Oh, what?" South's breathing was short, shallow.

"Giving it to her."

I ran my hands from her shoulders to the backs of her knees, then came back up, lingering on her cheeks, pulling them up and apart. South's lube lay in the open drawer. I coated my right fingers with it and slipped my left hand under her groin. "Come on up," I said, encouraging her ass higher. She moaned and arched her back, raised her hips. I slathered her crack, spread her open, danced my fingertip across her asshole, teasing its outer rim. She cried out and pushed back and I slapped her butt. "Greedy little girl," I said, then inserted one finger just an inch up, then another inch. I massaged her asshole in and out, toying with her clit with my other hand, until she started moving rhythmically. "Ready for it, girl?" I said. I removed my fingers and let her wait, empty, while I stroked the dildo with my oiled hand. "Spread your ass for me." She squirmed when I touched the slick, cool tip to her asshole, whimpered when I slowly inserted it deep inside of her. With long thrusts, she raised up high, and my fingers ran easily across her clit. "Good girl, good girl," I said softly as the strokes got harder and South pumped her ass to meet them. "Open all the way, open your ass—God I love fucking you in the ass." I lodged the dildo deep inside, then moved quickly beneath her, replacing my fingers with my mouth on her clit. When she came, it was with a fury that would have made St. Helens proud. Her pelvic bone slammed into my cheek. The next day, my black eye was only one of many sore spots my body sported—memories, all of them good, of my strenuous date with South and Mt. Hood.

———

"South's there," I said softly to myself. I took a dangerous last-minute right at the next San Francisco exit. The ache was so overwhelming, I pulled onto the shoulder, hit my hazards, and masturbated until I came back to my senses.

Back on I-5, I remembered that night so many eons ago, lying in South's arms thinking, *Oh God, please let this be Portland.* And it could have been, had Judith not fired her, had South not moved to San Francisco. But she did, and she did.

———

ECLIPSE

———

By dusk I had crossed the Utah state line and more mountains were in the distance. Without stopping, I fumbled with my maps and determined it was the Wasatch range. By nightfall, I was winding through the Uintas. The moon was bright and full. To my right as my car climbed the steep slopes I saw herds of hooved animals dashing up the inclines. Deer, antelope, goats, buffalo? I had no idea what they were. Few other cars passed me. I was alone in what, even at night, appeared to be the most awesome land on earth.

My high beams and the brilliant moonlight did little to increase my visibility as the highway curved sharply around the great jutting rocks of these mountains. My loaded Corolla chugged slowly on the ascent, then picked up speed as I reached more level ground. I knew I was at a high altitude because the walls of rock no longer extended up past my line of vision. They terminated just above me and met the sky. Or was that a body of water, black in the night? Or the undifferentiated trees of a forest?

It was ten p.m. I rubbed my eyes. I wasn't climbing any higher, but the night was getting darker. How was that possible? I became disoriented. Was I entering something? A tunnel? What would a tunnel be doing on top of a mountain? I glanced at the moon and saw a black cloud draped across it. *Rain. Oh, shit, please God don't let it rain. I don't know where I am.* I realized I was hitting seventy miles per hour and figured I was beginning my descent. It was still getting darker. But I was not in a forest. The cloud on the moon hadn't moved. Or had it? Was this the same cloud? I had the fantasy again about a car phone.

Hello, Martin?
Yeah?
The road's really steep and curvy.
You're in the Uintas.
But it's really dark.
It's nighttime.
Oh, okay, bye.
(Dial tone. Punch in long distance numbers.)
Hello, God?

My car went faster. I wanted to be checked into a motel somewhere, now. The shadows cast by the moonlight were gone and my headlights cut a severe glare through what seemed an immutable blanket of unnatural night. I went around another curve and glanced at the moon. A blackness darker than any storm cloud was overtaking it and would continue, I realized, until the shadow eclipsed its whole.

I was out of touch with the reality of newspapers and television. And I was out of touch with the reality of nature. Still, there's no way I could have known those creatures didn't scramble up the mountainsides as one every night, but only on those occasions when the earth's shadow is cast upon the moon, stimulating their primal instincts to seek safety from impending doom.

The eclipse was total for about an hour. During that time, I slowed considerably, superstitious in my own way, and prayed no one would tear up onto my rear end and knock me into a cinemaesque freefall off this mountainside to the land thousands of feet below. As the light resurged, I relaxed and resumed a high speed.

I flew around yet another curve, and a huge stag stood in the road in front of me. I crushed my brakes, coming to a stop just inches from this massive animal and my seat belt locked, cinching my ribs painfully.

I had never seen a real deer before outside of a zoo. He was staring at me. He didn't move. My lights shined in his tender brown eyes. I saw his nose tremble, catching my scent. I wondered what a car smells like to a stag. He had scratches and nicks on his broad antlers. Breaking out of my own hypnosis, I realized that we were both in grave danger should the next car come zipping around the curve behind me. I remembered what they say about deer and headlights, so I flipped mine off for a moment, then back on. He shook his head. "Bye handsome," I said, assuming he was ready to bolt away. But he leaned his huge head toward my hood and started sniffing it, then lifted one heavy hoof and rested it on my bumper. The Toyota sagged beneath his weight. Quickly deciding this horny stag mistook me for a hard-body doe, I honked my horn. He removed his hoof, looked at me, and cocked his head like, *Is that a no or a maybe?* I honked again and he dashed off into the darkness.

I drove on, not sure how many more miles it was until the next town but determined not to stop until I got there. The eclipse and the stag and the pain in my ribs gave me a powerful second wind. I turned up the music and sang for a while, sometimes sticking my finger in my ear to see if my voice sounded any good. It didn't, especially when it tried to harmonize with Dylan on "Mr. Tambourine Man." I quit singing and started thinking about my first lover, Reed, who had a lovely voice. Reed once sang this song to me, accompanying herself on six-string guitar, not long before we made love for the first time.

Reed was rich and well-traveled, and I remembered her coming back from somewhere in South America once where she claimed she had met a shaman and gone on what she called a Vision Quest. Reed said the people were what we would call primitive, but they had this whole ritual journey that was perfectly coordinated with certain stellar and planetary positionings and phases of the moon. She said the preparation included fasting and sexual abstinence, scalding steam baths and bloodletting. Reed did little of the latter—she said they were understanding of Americans' squeamishness—but she said the natives cut and pierced and otherwise mutilated their tongues and dicks and clits and noses and ears and nipples with sticks and stones, all of this to the sounds of drums and rattles and trumpets made from dead animal parts. Reed said they did all of this to "break the bonds of the flesh," whereupon they would ascend to heaven or plunge into hell. She said the best part was they ingested all kinds of hallucinogens, one, in particular, that came from fungus that grows on deer shit. I think that is why I thought of Reed and this story because I remember she said deer were symbolic to these people, representing the act of ritual self-sacrifice. I was just incapable at that lonely Utah moment of pondering how the sudden stag in the road might be meaningful to me.

It was almost midnight when I saw a big green highway sign. *Provo.* My exhaustion had no effect on the trivia center of my brain, and I knew this was where I wanted to spend the night. As I approached the little Mormon capitol, I passed a stretch of interstate awash in huge streaks of red paint. My city mind said, *Some paint truck must have lost its load.* Then I saw more paint and more, then, where it ended, the shattered carcass of a huge deer I had to swerve to miss.

Ribs aching, I checked into Provo's City Center Motel where, on a hot July night in 1976, Gary Gilmore touched his gun to the back of Ben Bushnell's head and pulled the trigger. I slept and didn't dare dream.

TED AND ME

—

I entered the San Joaquin Valley.

San Joaquin. I whispered the words aloud over and over, watching my lips move in the rear view mirror. Pretty words. They should roll off my tongue if I ever get the chance to say them to another human being. When I tired of this exercise, I lapsed into my default thought category.

I watched the road stretched in front of me and disappearing behind me. *When I leave California,* I thought, *I will have traversed, over the years, the I-5 corridor all the way north to Canada, south to Bakersfield—experienced for myself this long interstate*

*leg with its ghoulish nickname, The Super Slab, so well-traveled by
Ted Bundy, Ed Kemper, Randall Woodfield, Jerome Brudos, Angelo
Buono and Kenneth Bianchi, and the Green River Killer, whoever
he is. If I was a serial killer, I would hide the bodies and never want
to be caught. But I would be.*

I didn't even try to hide Alex from Kris, and maybe that
was my biggest mistake of all.

In those dreamy California hills and valleys, my interviewer reappeared in the seat next to me, and I said:

"Living with Kris was easy, relatively speaking. She was
compulsively organized which simplified life. There was a
time and a place for everything. Except sex. The sex thing, I
admit, was my fault. Well, it was my fault that we didn't have
any. It was her fault, I suppose, that she didn't dump me for
somebody a little more affectionate. Why didn't she? I think
Kris was more afraid of being alone than of being dissatisfied
forever and ever. Why didn't I want to have sex with her?
Somewhere I got the idea that sex is only safe if the person
you're doing it with doesn't know you at all. Anyway, I blew
it because I let her in on all my secrets. She even found a place
in our relationship for my murder obsession."

I chuckled.

"You know, I'd never read the book about Jerome Brudos,
so I picked it up at Powell's one summer day. I was sitting out
in the backyard reading it and it gave the address in Portland
where the first murder happened and the house was three
doors down from ours! It was this girl selling encyclopedias
door-to-door. Brudos' wife and kids were out and he invited
her in, feigning interest in her books, and he killed her. He
had a foot fetish, so he cut off her feet and stuck them in the
basement freezer, pulled them out now and then, dressed
them in hose and heels and masturbated on them. And he did
this just three doors down from us, well, twenty years earlier.
When Kris got home I shared this with her and she was horrified, of course, but she listened anyway.

"Kris knows me too well for me to have sex with her, if that makes any sense. This is a woman who bundles me up and takes me to the emergency room for a shot of Demerol when I have a migraine that won't go away, then sticks the antinausea suppositories they give me to take home up my ass. How can you be romantic with someone who cleans up your vomit? We're talking not an ounce of mystery left here, you know?

"In the winter of '88, Kris proposed a trip to Vancouver, B.C.—a last-ditch effort at revitalizing our love life. I had a migraine for the whole two days, during which we tried to make love once and, for some reason I can't remember, two minutes into it we both burst out laughing—so we got dressed and went out for Italian food.

"Back in the U.S., I begged her to make a side trip, and we did—across the Snoqualmie Pass, through the Washington town of Issaquah, deep into the forests on Taylor Mountain, finally stopping at Lake Sammamish. That time of year it was icy and desolate, not at all like it was on that hot July day in 1974 when thousands of people sunned on the shore, and sailboats, swimmers, and skiers clogged the lake.

"Kris stepped away from me and I stood with my hands thrust in my coat pockets, my face stinging from the brutal wind that swept across the choppy water. I glanced to my left at the deserted restrooms where Denise, fourteen years before, had met the man who would take her life. The day we were there, all was silent except for the light clicking of bare branches and the thumping of a sign, buffeted by the wind, that stood at the water's edge and said: *Caution: Dangerous Area.*

"I knelt and performed my private ritual, aware Kris was behind me, aware she knew of my obsession with the victims as well as the killers. And it was in Washington state that there were so many of the former. 'Lynda, Donna, Susan, Kathy, Georgeann, Brenda, Carol—I'm sorry if there are others and I don't know your names. You aren't forgotten,' I said. I opened my eyes and looked at the stark majesty of the land around me. In the sand I drew x's over and over and continued. 'Denise and Jan, I didn't know you, but I miss you. I'm here, where you were. If you're still here, go home. No one can ever hurt you again.'

"Two years later, I visited the apartment house in Seattle's University District that was Ted Bundy's home while he was immersed in killing the young women of Washington State. Ted had been dead for just over a year. Even though he was executed in Florida, the event topped the news for days in Oregon and Washington. Mostly what stuck in my mind, besides the change in him from cocky self-assurance to dry-mouthed terror, was the tape of his mother in Tacoma, on the telephone in her house, talking to her oldest son, telling him goodbye. Telling him and the world she still loved him and always will, no matter that he became a serial killer. Mama, I suspected, might be somewhere on the other side, waiting for dawn the next morning to take Ted under her wing. At Ted's apartment, I got out of my car and smoked a cigarette and still felt afraid, standing so close to where this most inexplicable human being once lived so long ago. 'Ted,' I whispered, 'I followed your trail all the way across the country. No one can explain you, least of all, I'm sure, you, so I won't ask. I think I mean it when I say I hope you can rest in peace, but please don't even think about coming back again as the man you were.'

"Alex, who was with me that night in Seattle, never got out of the car. When I climbed back in beside her she said, 'Where are we?' I said nothing, but thought, *it's none of your fucking business.* Alex was getting sex from me. It was imperative that I keep everything else to myself."

My interviewer said, "So, you didn't hide Alex from Kris because . . ."

"We didn't have any secrets."

"But another *lover?*"

I shrugged. "Yeah, well, I thought she would love me no matter what. I thought she would forgive me."

"Still think she will?"

"I have no idea." I paused a moment. "And, see, Kris didn't want me to hide her. Once she knew the basics. One night, she said to me, 'If you're going to keep fucking her, I want to meet her.' And this started Kris' and my bargaining: you can have this if I can have this, etc. So I brought Alex over, and Kris *liked* her, and the next thing I knew, I was coming home from work and finding these notes: *We went to get something to eat. Went to the bar. Went shopping. Back soon.* I let it go because any peace between them was peace for me. And that was true, briefly.

"By the time Kris left Portland they weren't speaking, though, right?" my interviewer said.

"Their fraternizing came to a sudden and bizarre halt. It was a warm night in September. Portland was having an unusual extended summer and the breeze that puffed through our open front door was muggy. Alex had arrived earlier and, as time passed, the silences grew and none of us felt comfortable, so I proposed we play with the Ouija board.

"I extinguished the lights and lit candles to set the mood. I noticed that the corners of Alex's mouth glistened with saliva, a sign of anxiety I hadn't seen from her since our tense early days of therapy. Kris sat in a stiff, stoic pose that sought to dismiss this as silly child's play, but I knew her nervousness often hid behind bravado. 'Is anybody here?' I asked the board, and nothing happened. 'Concentrate,' I said. We all closed our eyes and dropped our heads. 'What is your name?' There was no answer.

"We looked at each other and shrugged. 'I've got an idea,' said Alex. 'Has Casey lived before?' The plastic pointer inched toward yes. When it stopped we all looked up and, as is the usual Ouija scenario, denied moving it and accused the others of doing so. 'You ask it,' Alex said.

"'Has Kris lived before?' I said, and the piece moved to yes.

"'Has Alex lived before?' Kris said, and the piece moved to yes.

"'Whoa,' said Alex. We paused and shared a cigarette.

"'I want to know who's talking to us,' I said.

"'Ask it again,' Kris said.

"'Who are you?' I said, and the board said *Sam*. We shrugged and closed our eyes again and when I did, I experienced the feeling I had before seeing Mama in my first Portland apartment years ago—the spins, accompanied by an absolute paralysis of my muscles. I couldn't feel my fingers on the plastic piece and I lost all perception of Kris and Alex in the room. I couldn't open my eyes. As abruptly as it began, the spinning stopped and my eyes opened. I was standing on the deserted shore of Lake Sammamish in the dead of winter. The trees clicked in my ears. I stared out at the water, then felt afraid and whispered, 'Kris'—but she didn't answer me. My hands were in my coat pockets and my face was freezing and I felt like someone was behind me but I couldn't turn around.

"The winter's sounds became a woman's voice that said: *I will still love you even if . . . I don't know what I would've done without you. . . . All my life I've waited. . . . I never thought I'd find you. . . .* Then, a soft male voice right behind my ear said sweetly: *My arm's kinda banged up, think you could come over to my car and help me get my bike on the rack—it's just over here, behind the restrooms.*

"My heart pounded. I faintly heard in the distance Kris' voice calling my name. It became louder until my eyes opened and I was sitting dazed in our living room in Portland. The lights were on. Alex was shaking my leg and Kris was saying, 'Casey, Casey, are you okay?'

"I stared at Kris, my eyes glassy, and I managed a weak grin. 'Oh boy,' I said, 'I went somewhere.' Kris knew what I meant.

"'Where were you?'

"I cocked my head. 'I was at Lake Sammamish.'

"Kris shouted, 'Oh shit!' and jumped up, sending the Ouija board flying. Alex, not having any idea what any of this meant, leaped up, too. Kris pressed herself up against the wall. Both of them were shaking—Alex was halfway out the front door. I was standing in the middle of the room staring at Kris, who had her fist against her mouth.

"'What the fuck is the matter with you two?' I said.

"Kris slumped halfway down the wall and looked up at me. 'Casey, while you were gone,' she said, 'the board spelled out *Ted*.'

"Then the most bizarre thing of all happened. The only way I can explain it is that it was as if, at that moment, Kris saw one layer deeper than she had ever seen before—she saw my obsession as some sort of evil communion, as something *intentional*, and I think she believed my soul was as tainted as my heart. But still, she couldn't take it out on me, so she ordered Alex out of our house and never spoke to her again."

———

I was starving after finishing that interview, so I stopped at a Chico's in Fresno and had a couple tacos.

UTAH DEAD

—

After checking out of the City Center Motel in Provo, I visited the Great Salt Lake and had a good laugh at a guy shooting this most placid body of water imaginable with a video camera. I filled up my gas tank at a station just off the Lake, bought a map of Salt Lake City, and headed there for one of my tourist stops. I drove to 2725 W. 3500 South and stood at the site of Ted Bundy's first arrest.

I sidetracked through Midvale and Lehi—passed by Viewmont High School in Bountiful—remembered the dead girls' names attached to each place. I had sausage pizza for lunch in the Fashion Place Shopping Mall in Murray, then strolled past the Walden Books where the only victim who was known to have escaped from Bundy's death grip, and whose memory survived to identify him, had been standing when she first encountered the handsome stranger who called himself Officer Roseland and coerced her into his car. I wondered if Carol ever came back here.

Before continuing on toward Idaho, I stopped at American Fork Canyon where a body had been found in November 1975, and again I stood in its cool, quiet recesses. Suddenly, I saw Pastor Barker from my childhood church, standing in the pulpit in his flowing robes, his face too handsome, his body too taut for a man of God—or so I thought as a little girl with a big crush. I smiled, happy that he was here with me, with us, in this tragic place. I took the hint, bowed my head, and recited the Twenty-Third Psalm. "The Lord is my shepherd, I shall not want. . . . yea though I walk through the valley of the shadow of death, I will fear no evil . . . *Melissa, Laura, and Debby, maybe someday we'll meet.* . . . surely goodness and mercy shall follow me all the days of my life. . . . *Carol, wherever you are, stay sane and safe.*"

As I drove out of Utah and the great pale blue lake disappeared behind me, I rubbed my eyes and shook my head and wondered, *Why am I stopping at these places? Why am I doing this?* Then I answered myself: *Because I have to, because I want to, because all of this happened. I didn't make it up and I didn't do it and I don't have to explain myself to anybody.* I pulled myself up in the seat as I crossed another state line, eager to see how far I could get before stopping again for the night.

STRANGER

At Bakersfield, I faced the most complicated challenge of this whole trip and failed miserably. Somehow, instead of looping onto 40 East, I bypassed my assigned route and ended up back on I-5 South. But I didn't realize it until, after driving for over an hour through the San Bernardino mountains in a merciless rain, I topped a peak and saw spread below me millions of city lights. Something huge and sprawling. My night's destination having been the tiny desert town of Needles, it occurred to me that something was terribly wrong.

I careened into the parking lot of a rest stop and flipped frantically through my Trip-Tik, highly agitated by the rain that thrashed my windows and skewed my vision. I experienced a moment of vertigo, then realized I was turning the pages backward and, according to Triple-A, I was in Oklahoma. I leaped out of the truck, shivering in my shorts and T-shirt as I called Kris from a public phone. There was no answer.

I slammed the receiver down and leaned my head against the phone, closed my eyes, and my guts whipped first to the right, then the left—like I was on the Octopus at the Mid-South Fair, but I wasn't. I was at a phone booth, somewhere.

I tried to open my eyes and couldn't. *Oh God, no, not here, no dead people.* "Mama?" I whimpered, starting to cry, the tears forcing my eyelids open. I spun around and there was a shadowy figure at the curb surrounding this desolate rest stop. It was Rod Serling standing stiff and still, a thin line of smoke curling up from his cigarette which burned in defiance of the downpour, and he said through clenched teeth, lips barely moving, "Submitted for your approval . . ."

"Nooo," I growled, a deep, gutteral, animal sound. My right hand curled into a tight fist and, without even thinking, I reeled back toward the wall and slammed my knuckles into the rough brick. "No, no, no," I punched until my skin broke and blood trickled down to my fingertips. "I'm lost," I wailed, like a little child who's wandered too far from home. "I'm lost."

A heavy hand touched my shoulder and I heard a soft voice, "Yo, yo, mister . . ." I turned, my battered hand hanging by my side dripping fresh blood into deepening puddles of rain, and a handsome young African-American man was staring at me. "Oh, I'm sorry, uh, miss. Are you okay?"

"I'm lost."

He looked down at my hand. "You're hurt."

"I'm lost."

"Come here," he said. We dashed across the lot to his car and I jumped into the passenger seat. He pulled a T-shirt from the back and wrapped it around my hand. "You heading to L.A.?" he said.

"L.A.? Is this L.A.!?"

He grinned and nodded his head toward the windshield. "Well, over there."

"I'm going to Memphis."

"Memphis! Man, you *are* lost!" He accurately read horror on my face. "Hey, hey, it's okay . . ." He patted the makeshift bandage on my hand.

"I'm coming from Oregon. I fucked up at Bakersfield."

"So you need to get back to 40 East?"

Suddenly terrified, I blurted, "I've never gotten into a stranger's car before!" Then I thought, *Oh shit, I shouldn't have said that.* Then I remembered at the crisis line they said if you have a suspected suicide on the phone, ask them directly, "Are you thinking about killing yourself?"—because your saying it isn't going to give them ideas they didn't already have. So I thought, *I'm in a car with a black man I don't know—there goes my racism! Fuck racism. I'm in a strange man's car in Southern California and it doesn't matter what color he is.*

An image of my feet in this guy's freezer emerged and I took the crisis line's advice. "You're not gonna kill me are you?" I saw my fright reflected tenfold in his face as his eyes widened and his lip quivered and his hand reached for the door handle. I felt better immediately, realizing he wanted to get out of the car as badly as I did.

When our terror subsided, we sat straight in our seats peering through the rain on the windshield. "I'm Winston, by the way," he said, not looking at me.

"Casey."

"What's in Memphis?" he said.

"A smaller problem than the one I left in Oregon. At least that's what I'm telling myself, but . . ."

Winston started to giggle and it made me smile. "What's so funny?"

He still didn't look at me, just stared straight ahead and said, "Did you ever see that Pee Wee Herman movie, where he's sitting in the dinosaur with that lady, Simone, and he says, 'Everybody I know has a big *but*—let's talk about your big *but*.'"

"Yeah, I remember that." We burst out laughing.

"That was funny as shit."

"Yeah," I said, "cause it's true."

"Yeah." We stared in silence for a moment.

"So, Winston, let's talk about *your* big *but*." We both laughed again.

When we were silent, wiping tears from our eyes, Winston said, "I got HIV."

The fractured reality of my insanity instantaneously mended and my whole life receded into a shadowy background as I turned in my seat to face him. "Oh, Winston," is all I could think to say.

He picked at his fingernail, then spread his strong hands across his thighs, leaning his head back. "Yeah, well . . . I'm not gay. And I don't do drugs. I don't even drink. I got it from a girl." His hands nervously massaged his legs. "I'm twenty-seven. I'm a paralegal. I wanted to be a lawyer, but . . ."

He laughed for a second and I smiled, then I realized he was crying—quaking, masculine sobbing that sounded jerky, out of practice—and though I hadn't held a man in many years, I didn't think twice before slipping my hands across his arms. He wadded the sides of my T-shirt in his fists. I closed my eyes and felt and smelled my best friend from Memphis, Tim—I was dancing in his muscular arms, my head resting on his hard, flat chest. He smelled of some musky male cologne and seventies' disco sweat, his red hair curling wildly from the heat. I would have believed no one that carefree night in 1978 who told me that five years later I would be wiring flowers to Memphis for Tim's funeral.

I was soaked with Winston's tears. When he felt like talking again, he said, "Thanks. Whoa, shit." He leaned back in his seat and I stayed facing him. "See, Pee Wee was right. Everybody does have a big *but*." He chuckled and swallowed hard.

"It's just that some people's are so much bigger than others."

Winston shrugged. "Well, yes and no. I mean, whatever your bad shit is, you have to deal with it alone. Knowing somebody else has it worse doesn't make you feel any better."

"I guess."

"Hey, we've got to get you back to 40."

He pulled a paper and pen from the glove compartment and while he wrote I said, "Winston, do you have a number? Like maybe where I could call you when I get to Memphis?"

"Oh sure." He added it to the bottom of the page. "This is my mom in L.A. I'm gonna be staying with her a while, or she'll know where to find me." He handed me the paper.

"Winston? Thanks for the first aid, and for the dry place to be for a while, and for the directions—thanks. I'm glad it was you who was here."

"Thank *you*, Casey, for the talk." There was an awkward moment of silence. Then Winston said, "Isn't it weird how sometimes a stranger can make you feel better than anybody else?"

He gave me a giant hug and I stepped out of his car, dashed to my truck, and headed east.

ELVIS SAYS

I played color association games with the new states I traversed on my long trip west that had nothing to do with reality but were attached to mostly forgotten memories or myths. I saw Arkansas as red—red clay, red blood dripping from wild boar tusks. Missouri was blue—blue rivers and Mark Twain's eyes. Kansas was black and gray, the colors of the sky as it bore down on Dorothy and Toto—and Colorado was brown—big, tall rocks. Utah was honey gold, some Mormon promise from a past life. And Idaho was white, potatoes maybe, or just the blankness of not knowing enough about this state to free associate.

I was surprised at the rich landscape of Idaho—stretches of flat land but always, it seemed, ringed in the distance by the deep slate blue-gray of mountains—or maybe it was just my imaginary perception of the sky itself. As I traveled north and west on this next to the last day of my journey, Idaho was verdant, lush forests and great valleys and the Snake River wound through canyons of spectacular depth and breadth. Just because of the name, I got out of my car at Hell's Canyon and wandered as far as I dared.

I stopped in Horse Shoe Bend for dinner—a fabulous nostalgic feast of salt pork and collard greens, sweet corn, broiled buttered new potatoes, fresh tangy beets, cornbread, peach cobbler, and a frosty mug of cold whole milk. The waitress was extremely friendly and I enjoyed talking with her. It seemed like eons since I'd talked with anybody except myself, and, in fact, my voice sounded sheer when I answered her first question.

"You on a trip?"

"Yes," I hissed, wondering how she knew, forgetting my left-sided sunburn/tan and the way my short hair stood permanently up and to the right.

"Where you headed?"

"I'm moving to Portland, Oregon."

"Really! I've never been there. Heard it's beautiful. Where you movin' from?"

"Memphis."

"Really! You ever meet Elvis?"

"No, not really."

"Seen Graceland?"

"Yeah."

"Oh, my," she said, wistfully, sitting in the booth across from me and touching my arm. "I'd die to see Graceland. I'm goin' someday, when I get enough money. Just pack up my Bug and drive right down."

A shudder ran up my spine at the thought of taking this trip backward. "A 'coon just walked across your grave," my mother used to say when I experienced one of those sudden chills. *How's that possible if you're not already dead?* I always thought, taking things literally, as usual.

"Hey," the waitress said, "do you believe in, you know,"— she made an eerie sound and her fingers tickled the air between us. I cocked my head. "You know, in spooky stuff, like tellin' the future?"

I thought for a moment. "Sometimes I do—yeah, I guess I'd say I do. Why?"

She squeezed my arm and broke into a huge smile. Her teeth were pointy stubs with nicotine stains. "I got somebody you'll *love*. Look, you go out the front doors here, okay, and when you pull out of the lot, take a right. The next street is Gulph. Take a right, then go about half a mile, then there's a street called Prosper and take a left and you'll see, first house on the right, there's a little sign in the window. That's a fortune teller lady and you just ring her bell and she'll tell your future."

"Hmmm. Okay." I giggled.

"You *gotta* go. Shoot, I bet she can tell you what'll happen in Portland. Wouldn't you like to know, cause then if it's bad you can go back to Memphis right now."

"It'd have to be pretty bad!"

She squeezed my arm. "Oh, come on, what've you got to lose? When are you gonna be back in Horse Shoe Bend, Idaho? It's now or never, like they say."

I gave her a ten for a five dollar meal and she kissed me on the cheek and wished me the best of luck. I idled at the exit of the parking lot for a moment and studied my map. A left would take me back to the highway. I looked at my watch. *You could be in Oregon by nightfall*, said a voice in my head that sounded suspiciously like Mama. *Seize the day*, said my father, and I took a right.

The house was neatly painted wood with well-tended impatiens lining a path behind an unlocked wrought iron gate. I walked to the front door without hesitating. When a woman answered I said, perhaps a bit formally, "The waitress at Billie's suggested I come see you." The kitchen was just inside the front door and the cooking aroma was so pungent my full stomach growled. "I hope I'm not interrupting your supper," I said.

"Oh, no, no." The woman led me into a back room that harbored the mingled old-lady smells of rouge and deep heating rub. As she offered me a chair I snapped out of perceiving and my first thought since entering this stranger's house was, *What if she's a serial killer?* But of course she wasn't.

It was difficult to discern the woman's age, especially in the glow of low-wattage tungsten light. I guessed early 70s. She had sparkling hazel eyes rimmed by fine crow's feet and pencil-thin lips accentuated by laugh lines that didn't disappear when she wasn't smiling. She tidied the table that separated us and didn't ask me anything, and I got the weird impression that this must be what it's like to see a prostitute who knows exactly what you've come for. The only sound in the house was static whispers from a television in the next room.

"Now," she said, finally satisfied that the table was in order. She laid her palms flat on the dark oak. "What is it you'd like to know?"

I told her I was moving to Portland, then stopped short when a deep male voice began singing the *National Anthem* with perfect pitch. My eyes widened and the woman's stiff shoulders sagged. She rolled her eyes.

"I'm sorry," she said. "That's Harriet."

My mouth hung open as the woman stood and bustled away. In the room just off ours I heard her say, "Harriet, stop it. We've got company." I thought of the two odd little old ladies in *Arsenic and Old Lace*, and my upper lip started to sweat.

Harriet boomed, "O'er the ramparts we watched were so gallantly streaming!"

"Harriet!" my hostess barked.

"AND THE ROCKETS RED GLARE!"

The woman laughed.

"THE BOMBS BURSTING IN AIR!"

"Goodnight Harriet."

"GAVE PROOF—" There was a loud squawk, then silence.

The woman rejoined me at the table. "I'm sorry," she said. "That was Harriet. I inherited her when my mother died and I'm sure she'll outlive me. Parrots can do that, you know. Anyway, every time President Reagan comes on the T.V.,

Harriet gets all patriotic! Now, where were we? Oh, yes, I've got the perfect vehicle for you."

She reached into a bag at her feet and pulled out a heavy ashtray the bottom of which sported a painting of a porky Elvis in his white sequined jumpsuit. "Greetings from Graceland" it said over his head. "Now," the woman said, placing the ashtray on the table top with its bottom up. "The only thing I must know before we start is, you know he's dead."

"Elvis?"

"Yes. You believe he's dead."

"Yeah, I believe he's dead."

"Okay, well, I have to ask because some people don't believe he's dead, and he won't respond to people who think he's still alive. He's very interested in us down here, and sometimes he speaks to me through this ashtray, if you're the right person."

"Okay." I shrugged. "What makes you think I'm the right person?"

"I guess because you're from Memphis."

"Oh." I frowned. "Hey, I didn't tell you I was from Memphis."

"You didn't? Oh. Well, I'm good with accents."

"Right."

"Now," she said. "You're moving to Portland and you came from Memphis. That's a long way. And you're young."

"Twenty-four."

"A baby. Do you have family or friends in Portland?"

"No."

"Anybody?"

"No."

She laughed. "I don't need Elvis to tell me you're a brave girl!" I shrugged and looked shyly down. "Well, let's see if Elvis can help you out."

"Do I need to do anything?"

"Just sit quietly. It's no sense in asking any questions. Elvis doesn't answer specific questions; he just tells what he wants to. Just relax. I'll have my eyes closed."

"Okay." I couldn't believe I was doing this.

The woman closed her eyes, placed her left hand in her lap and her right on the upturned bottom of the ashtray, and began pushing the heavy glass in circular motions. She emitted a low, steady hum throughout when she wasn't speaking. The initial hum went on for about five minutes and I found myself getting sleepy. Finally, she began speaking in her own voice but with no inflection.

"Elvis says: *Portland's between the devil and the deep blue sea.*

"Elvis says: *You aren't alone. Somebody you thought you left behind in Memphis has tagged along with you.*

"Elvis says: *Three times in Portland you will be denied. One will deny you life. One will deny you breath. One will deny you death.*

"Elvis says: *When it's time to leave, you won't miss it.*

"Elvis says: *Portland's gonna let you go without a fight.*

"Elvis says: *Don't be afraid. If it feels too hot or too cold, it's not. It's just right.*

"Elvis says: *In Oregon lean all you want. Somebody's holding onto your pants.*"

The ashtray had started making tighter and faster circles toward the end and, when she finished, the woman pulled her hand away like the glass was hot. She slumped in her chair, her gray hair caught in the sweat on her face. "Whew!" she said, opening her eyes.

"Wow," I muttered. She smiled. "I wish I could remember what he said." She pulled her hand from her lap. In it, she held a piece of paper upon which she had scribbled the words she had spoken. She handed it to me. "Wow, thanks. I wish I could've asked questions."

"I know, I'm sorry. He just won't answer them and, sometimes if you ask, he goes away."

"What do you think this means?"

"Um, I don't know what he said." She reached for the paper and read it. "Hm, I don't know. Well, it doesn't look like things are gonna be all wine and roses, but what ever is? He always makes some Biblical reference, this denial business. He was a real Christian, you know. Overall, though, it sounds positive, I think. Don't you?"

"I don't know." I took the paper back and rose to leave. "Well, I should hit the road and make some time before I need to sleep. How much do I owe you?"

"Twenty dollars."

I gave her the twenty and she saw me to the door. On the porch, after a pleasantry about the weather, the woman peered at me and said, "Elvis said something at the end, not out loud—he said to me, 'Tell her I saw her, too.' Does that make any sense to you?"

I squinted into the clear sky and lied. "Not that I know of."

I didn't turn on my tape player as I left Horse Shoe Bend. In the quiet Idaho darkness I thought about that day, August 14, 1977, when I was at Graceland shooting videotape for a student production. As I stood at the gates chatting with Elvis' uncle, his radio crackled and he ordered me to shut off the camera. I did, and stepped back as the gates parted automatically and a sleek, black limo glided down the winding drive toward us. The car stopped at the entrance, waited a moment to pull into the traffic, and I peered inside and saw, first, a pretty little blond girl who looked just like her father, then, sitting next to her, a man with black hair and bushy sideburns, a turned-up collar and dark glasses. Elvis' head was bulbous, his neck grotesquely swollen. He turned slowly and stared at me for a long moment on that summer afternoon, two days before he died alone in Graceland on his bathroom floor.

RULES AND CHAOS

Winston stayed in my head for a good hundred miles after I left the rest stop. *Every once in a while,* I thought, *something really real happens.*

That was the problem with Kris. Nothing real was happening in our lives—and that was not coincidental. We *worked* to make sure nothing real happened. We surrounded ourselves with things to block our vision—all those appliances, the house, even our dogs became part of our desolate moonscape. Except Shade. He was supposed to be the perfect son. We chose him carefully, paid a fortune for him, and Kris worked diligently training him. Then he died suddenly and horribly at four months of Parvovirus—an unseen congenital immune deficiency having rendered his puppy booster shots totally ineffective.

Even then, we coped with our grief by quickly purchasing Griffin. Okay, that was my doing. Kris didn't think Shade was replaceable. I'll never forget that day I was looking for Lab puppies in the paper and Kris got so mad, shouting, "What would you have done if after your mom died somebody looked through a newspaper and said, 'Hey, here are some new moms, let's get one.'"

What a dumb question, I thought. *I'd go get one, of course.* Then, five months later, just in case the hole wasn't completely filled, we bought a Great Dane.

Like chipmunks, we stored food in our basement. Kris never bought anything full price, and she stocked up at sales. I took fourteen grocery bags of canned and dry goods and paper products to a battered women's shelter before I left Portland. When I was packing them up, I remembered Daddy telling me that he didn't have to buy a roll of toilet paper for two years after Mama died. She was a smart shopper, too.

I remembered this note I wrote Kris. It was 1987 and I called it "Kris' Time of the Flu." Breathing room in the Hartley household had been usurped by rules exquisitely choreographed by Brantley, less precisely followed by Harper. One night, when Kris was sick, I decided to give up trying. I wrote:

One day Kris got the flu and Casey tried to cheer her up. First Casey did the laundry without reading the Tide box and Kris complained there were soap specks in the sheets. Then Casey mailed all the car contest envelopes at the same time, and that turned Kris into a bedbound worry wart. So Casey went to the store and got some much-needed items such as drinking straws and dinner rolls, and, in the process, she compulsively flung a package of Oreo Double Stuf into her shopping cart—much to Kris' dismay because these are among her favorite cookies and she is trying to lose weight. Besides, nothing tastes very good right now in this, her time of the flu. Now I've got to get the laundry dry so Kris can lie comfortably on the couch and complain about the reek of Clorox while we eat, hopefully-not-lumpy mashed potatoes and watch Friday the Thirteenth, *unless Kris doesn't like this show, in which case we will watch* The Karate Kid. *But one thing is for sure—Kris controls the remote no matter how sick she is and we most decidedly will not watch the commercials.*

Obviously, we found many things to fuss about other than our non-existent sex life.

I think that's what drove Kris so crazy about Alex. I mean, besides the obvious. Kris was in a perpetual state of vicarious anxiety over the chaos she saw in us—driven crazy by my unpredictable behavior that defied any rules. But that didn't stop her from trying to impose some order. Kris demanded once, after yanking my shirt below my collarbone, that I not allow Alex to give me hickeys where other people could see them.

And, of course, Kris only saw a glimpse of the madness my vagabond lover brought into our home.

Alex arrived at our house that autumn morning after Kris left for Memphis, and she didn't leave until January. She came with few belongings, no money, no desire or willingness to help with any of the mundane chores of homemaking. She played Nintendo with obsessive zeal until the computerized music rattled in my blank brain. The sex dwindled, and, in true karmic fashion, the disinterest was not coming from me.

"I can't get it up around domesticity," Alex said as I sat across the room behind her and she frantically tried to get the Mario brother in the painter's pants through a room where little fish with big mouths try to gobble him up. I would stare for hours at the back of her head and entertain fantasies of putting a bullet through her skull, which kept me from having to think about how much I hated her for reminding me of me.

Only my terror at losing the little I had left kept me from throwing her out. Alex, I discovered by that bleak winter of 1989/90, collected people the way my mother collected china figurines of animal families. And her shelf, like my mother's, was very full. Unlike my mother, however, Alex didn't care if the pieces were cracked, chipped, glued back together to re-semble their original form, or even totally shattered with parts missing.

Alex was Swiss cheese, and she kept many people in the icebox to fill the empty spaces that made her feel airy, ethereal, insecure. For a brief moment in time, I was her favorite. Twice I came home and found her bleeding, offering little explanation except that she had always been accident prone. When she got her fourth tattoo—a blue-black jackal on her collarbone—and her second piercing (bellybutton)—she explained to me why she did it on the ride home. "I just couldn't feel anything anymore, and that's a scary feeling."

Those wounds got her three days of intensive care at my house. "I love you," I would say at these times, and she would return the lie.

Alex forgot Halloween was my birthday. As November waned, she announced, "I don't do Thanksgiving," and she took off for four days with an ex-lover to a cozy bed and breakfast on the beach at Yachats. On Thanksgiving evening, I was walking home from Mt. Tabor with the dogs and I saw an elderly couple getting into a car, their arms laden with casserole dishes, and I longed for the comfort I had thrown away. I cried until I strained the muscles in my back and throat.

Christmas came and Alex said, "If I ever decide to kill myself again, it'll be at Christmas time." She played Nintendo continuously for three days and I got a migraine. I asked Alex to drive me to the emergency room for a shot of Demerol and she refused. I drove ten miles across the interstate to the hospital and convinced a nurse that a friend was waiting in the car. I willed myself to concentrate on the road as the pain disappeared, followed by the warm wash of oblivion. I made it home, uprooting one of our rhododendron bushes as I sailed into the driveway.

Just after Christmas, Kris, who had vacillated over the past month about returning to Portland, always finally deciding she needed a little more recovery time, called with the news she had been offered a job in the field she had chosen as an undergraduate and had ceased pursuing when she met me. For one of the few times in my life, I rose above my dependency and greedy need. I didn't know if I could stand Alex much longer, and I knew what Kris' taking a professional position in Memphis meant.

"I don't know whether I should take it or not," she said.

"Are you nuts? It would be ridiculous for you to give up an opportunity like that to come back here."

"But what about Portland, us?"

"Take the job!"

And she did.

A week later, Alex announced that she couldn't stand Portland another minute and was moving to Burien, just south of Seattle with the ex with whom she had spent Thanksgiving. Without giving a second thought to me, us, she was gone a week later.

I humiliated myself, having reached the point where sucking on a dirty dishrag was preferable to being left gaping and empty.

The problem at this point was Alex and I were both each others' Ringo trinkets—the difference was, she had kept her big bag of gumballs and other prizes. I still had my bag, too, but the only things in it were blue and yellow and white pills. I cried on the phone with Kris and begged her to come back to Portland, but there was no turning back for her and she stood her ground. "Come to Memphis," she said.

I cried on the phone with Alex and begged her to come back to Portland, and she said she was scared and lonely and missed me so much she was barely able to function. "Come to Burien," she said.

I drove to Burien in early March to see if that, or Seattle, was a place I might like to live. Alex and I clung to each other like the junkies we were—desperately hanging onto anything that looked like relief, however temporary. She said she loved me, said we were soulmates. On my last night in town she didn't say anything because she spent it with a new woman she had met. I left her house before dawn and drove back to Portland. We never even said goodbye. A week later, Kris had my Trip-Tik prepared.

REVELATIONS

I stopped speaking and, when I did, I realized how loud my voice had been.

How can you be so quiet, Mojave? Why won't you say something to me? You talked to Charlie—and one of your brothers talked to Jesus. I'm not lying—everything I've told you so far is the truth. Maybe it's that I'm a woman, huh? You don't talk to women. Maybe this desert communion stuff is some male-bonding thing. Oh well, too bad.

I was rambling like this when suddenly there was a stirring—the first breeze of the evening—then a quick gust, like the awkward blow of a baby extinguishing the candle on his first birthday cake. Three tumbleweeds, or whatever you call them, crashed into my ankles. I hopped back up on the hood of my truck and they fell off my feet. The desert was perfectly still again.

Okay, okay. Maybe some of it has been a lie. Maybe she wasn't as perfect as I pretended she was.

I sighed and lay back on my hood, knees up, arms extended straight out, and I stared at the sky. There were eighty million stars in my line of vision. I picked one out—the one that is the bottom left corner of the Big Dipper. I named it Mojave, and I told it my best kept secret.

"My mother is very, very fat, and she's lying on the bed elevating her puffy legs and resting her feet. They're misshapen from the extra work her weight makes for them. She's wearing a floral print housedress with a lacy beige slip underneath. Her legs and feet are bare and they smell of the nylons she peeled off when she came home from work tonight. Mama hates to work and I tell myself that someday I'll make so much money she won't have to anymore.

"Before Mama came home from work, I spent an hour with my friend Jeff in his front yard. There's a huge Poplar tree there with low limbs. I don't have on a shirt. Mama doesn't care if I don't wear a shirt, but she'd kill my sister if she took hers off in front of the neighbors. Jeff strips his shirt off, too. It's late afternoon, but it's August and the sun stays high forever in Memphis in the summer, and it feels good beating against our tanned trunks. We run to the tree and leap up to grab the lowest limb. We grip it underhanded. We start chinning and our sweat makes my hair curly and it glitters on Jeff's head beneath his crewcut. Jeff thinks this is great fun. When he's had enough, he falls to the ground and lies on his back kicking his heels and laughing and panting. But I stay on the tree, grunting until the veins in my neck and head throb, until my palms are raw against the white bark. When I have to let go, I feel sad because I failed to chin longer. Later tonight, I'll check my arm muscles again to see if they've grown at all. And I'll be back on the tree tomorrow. Building up my strength is hard work, but it's worth it to see the pleasure on Mama's face when, each night, I am capable of rubbing her feet longer without getting tired.

"Mama's feet remind me of something my brother told me he saw in a science book about why there are mountains and earthquakes. Big planks of skin have drifted up from the ball of her foot to create a short, sharp shelf beneath her big toe. Her nails are yellow and thick and I tell her they look like a rhino's toes. She has corns on her little toes that are big knots that glow red hot around the edges like a coal in the barbecue grill, and in the very center they look like a popcorn kernel.

"My favorite part of this is the Jergen's lotion which I think smells like the white stuff inside a chocolate-covered cherry. I squirt it directly onto her fiery feet and she moans with delight. I rub and rub, never missing a spot. I love to look at how her second toes rest perfectly in the indentations in the sides of her big toes. Her heels are hard and cracked like a dried up riverbed. I rub each foot and believe that if I do this every night, someday Mama's feet will look normal and they won't hurt anymore.

"I am eight and becoming discouraged. Mama is fatter and her feet have not improved at all. I ask her one day if she could have only one food for the rest of her life, what would it be. She says spaghetti—and I develop this new fantasy of Mama growing thinner on a desert island surrounded by spaghetti with which she had become bored. I don't have any idea how much it would cost to purchase a desert island and get her there.

"I am ten and beginning to get angry at my mother. I have realized that her feet are only the tip of the iceberg. The family is falling apart. Daddy won't get a real job. Everybody hates everybody else except me. They all come to me to confide their secrets and ask advice. Like I really know the answers. They all joke that I'm like Lucy when she's the psychiatrist in the *Peanuts* cartoon, and I joke, too, but I don't really think it's very funny. I could buy Mama that island if I got a nickel every time one of them told me something I really didn't want to hear.

"But the worst thing is, Mama keeps changing the rules. A couple years ago she said she'd leave Daddy, 'the bum', as she calls him, when I got to junior high. Well, I'm in seventh grade now and she says she'll leave him when I get to high school. I started first grade a year early and I make straight A's, but I can't move any faster.

"In the meantime, her hemorrhoids have gotten worse and I ask her why she doesn't get them taken out and she says because it's the most painful operation in the whole world. On a rainy, cold Saturday afternoon I get this idea. I talk Daddy into taking me to the big library downtown, but, of course, I don't tell him what for. When we get there he lets me go into the stacks by myself which part of me thinks is cool—the other part knows it's because he never wanted the responsibility of having children and he's never taken any. He stays in the outer lobby smoking a cigar since Mama won't let him smoke in the house.

"Even though I know he's far out of sight, my palms are clammy and my heart races as I squat in a corner with the book and look up *hemorrhoids*. I learned how to spell the word correctly off the Preparation H tube in the medicine chest. There are awful pictures of dark, puckered holes. First they have red clusters on them that look like holly berries; then they have rows of black stitches all around them. I try not to linger over the pictures because, even though Daddy can't see me, I know what I'm doing is dirty and I'd get in trouble if I got caught. The words, though, I devour. I don't think about how I'll explain to my mother where I got my knowledge of hemorrhoid surgery. All I can think about is this great gift I will give her of detailed information about the operation and the peace of mind she'll have knowing the discomfort will be worth getting rid of this pain she moans and sighs about almost every day.

"When I tell her what I know, she is soaking in a hot tub which, she says just like the commercials, 'relieves the itch and reduces the pain and swelling.' She gives me her wan and defeated smile, and she doesn't question how I know so much about this subject. She pats my hand. 'Maybe when you get out of high school I could think about doing something like that,' she says.

"I'm twelve and taller, 5'2", and stronger, having forsaken the Poplar tree for dumbbells that I lift as many times as I can every night. I can rub Mama's feet for hours, but I do it mechanically because by now I'm pretty certain it's not going to make a damn bit of difference. I'm smart enough to figure out hemorrhoid surgery, but I'm apparently not smart enough to figure out how to get older fast enough to save her ass, no pun intended. I have a calendar on my bedroom wall. Each month has a different type of dog on it and my birthday month, October, has my favorite dog, a Great Dane. I'd give anything to have a Great Dane, but Mama says we couldn't have anything that big in the house. So, I have two goals now for when I'm grown—one is to meet the Boston Strangler, in prison of course, and the other is to have a Great Dane. Anyway, I mark the days off this calendar and sometimes I flip ahead and wonder if there is any day this year when I'll be old enough to make Mama well and happy.

"Sometimes I wish my brother who is seventeen and my sister who is fifteen cared about my mother as much as I do because they may be old enough to do something I can't. Then I remember, Mama's pretty clear that nobody else's age matters except mine. This might sound stupid, but just recently for the first time it occurred to me that if I was dead Mama wouldn't have to wait for me to grow up to get better. Unfortunately, I don't know the first thing about how somebody goes about killing herself, and I don't even know how to look that up in the library.

"And now for the big confession. I'm not going to say exactly how many times, but let it suffice to say that on *numerous* occasions for a while now I have been going over to David's at night. David is my brother's best friend who is eighteen and going to college this fall. Anyway, we sit together in his carport behind his VW and we smoke joints. He says his dope is laced with angel dust which is incredible shit that makes the whole fucking world look completely different than it really is. Which is a relief. I mean, I can deal with reality most of the time, but everybody deserves some time off. That's my theory.

"David cracks me up. When we smoke he can't stop playing with his nose and he says no matter what he does it feels like it's full of boogers. He gives me Camels, too, and I know this may sound ridiculous, but whether it's a joint or a regular cigarette hanging between my lips, I feel like an adult when I'm doing it. Then, when I get ripped, it's even better. I look up and down our street and everything looks different. Things look wider, longer, bigger, brighter, and, while David fiddles with his nose, I start laughing uncontrollably and usually I feel like I'm going to wet my pants so I grab my crotch, but I don't feel the least bit embarrassed in front of him. I look at the sky and there are so many stars. I see the Dippers and Orion's belt and the moon and Venus and I feel like I did when I was a kid and Mama would read me bedtime stories about children who had great adventures. Sometimes I guess they were dreaming because they went places where there were mountains and oceans and deserts and where anything was possible. That was when I was really little, before I started noticing how much pain Mama was in all the time.

"Also, when we smoke and I start to come down, I crawl into bed and I feel like I did when I was really, really little and had earaches. Mama gave me this stuff called paregoric—and *that* was a feeling I never dreamed I'd have again. You feel totally warm and safe, no matter what's happening in the real world around you.

"Lots of nights lately I've been too stoned to rub Mama's feet. Once I tried when I was high and I hallucinated that her feet were massive slabs of jagged rock and I was climbing up them and I thought I saw my palms bleeding.

"I am a senior in high school and Mama has come up with a new milestone for me. 'When you get a job . . .' So, I get a job. 'When you're out on your own . . .' So, I work full time all summer and get an apartment. Then, in August, she says, 'When you get your college degree,' so I enroll at Memphis State on probationary status because there's not enough time for me to take the SAT's.

"By this time, you know, I think I've actually forgotten about her butt and her head—did I forget to mention she also had these horrible migraine headaches which I *never* figured out how to fix—and her miserable marriage. I am just doing this stuff like a robot. She could say, 'When you jump off the fucking bridge,' and I would start planning the plunge.

"I'm a second-semester junior in college and Mama's got this cough that won't go away from a bout of the flu she had a couple months ago. She says her legs ache all the time and she doesn't feel like eating. She's lost weight everywhere except in her belly. She refuses to see a doctor. I beg her to go, but most of my energy is being expended on my girlfriend and my senior thesis.

"On the day I officially graduate from Memphis State, although I don't attend the ceremony, my mother is in an operating room losing her rectum, colon, and reproductive organs to cancer. It occurs to me, after her surgery when the doctor is discussing her prognosis with us, that if I had graduated a semester earlier, the cancer may not have spread into her liver.

"Eighteen months later, when I am twenty-four, my mother loses the only battle of her life that I believe was truly unwinnable.

"My mother died," I said. The Mojave listened.

"My mother is dead. Stone, cold, fucking dead. Has been for almost nine years. Can you believe that? The biggest problem is that my mother lied to me all along. She told me she'd get better when I grew up, but really she didn't want me to grow up. But I did because I didn't get this paradox of hers—and when I did, wham, she fucking died on me."

I ran my fingers through my hair, sat up and pressed my palms against my cold truck hood, and kicked dirty sand and small rocks around with my feet. I looked back up at the moon and stars, stretched my neck and rolled my shoulders. For just a moment, I thought I knew what it would feel like to just be there, on the road, not chasing an impossible dream, not escaping from the scene of a crime—just another speck that belongs here with everything else. "Mojave," I whispered. "Mojave, Mojave. I love your name."

The desert was silent. I hung my head. "Thank you for listening." I wasn't sure how to say goodbye, so for a moment I didn't. "Memphis," I said. "I have no idea. . . ." I shrugged and managed a cynical snort. "Maybe because something else I love is dying and going back there is the only way I can save it. The problem is, I don't know if she wants me to be a grown up or a little kid either."

I pulled my keys from my pocket and opened my truck, draping my forearms across the top of the door. "I'll tell you one thing I've learned though. You spend your whole life racing toward a finish line, but when you get there, you know, there's nothing there. You're just finished."

I climbed in, started the ignition, and began pawing through my box of tapes. In the silence barely broken by the truck's quiet idle, I heard a bark, a yip, a moan. *Oh no*, I thought, *there's a lost dog out there.* Then there was a plaintive howl, and another, and the patient coyotes took their turns speaking.

"Goodbye, Mojave Desert," I said, pulling onto the highway and leaving a cloud of sandy dust behind me. I had no idea when I'd come to a town I could stop in for the night, but I wasn't afraid anymore. I knew this desert I was driving through wouldn't let anything happen to me.

REMEMBERING ELVIS IN IDAHO

I spent the night in Cambridge, Idaho—could've made it across the Oregon border, but I wanted the first glimpse of my new state to come in the light of day. I stopped at a convenience store and bought a bag of sour cream and onion potato chips, a liter of Sunkist orange soda, and a package of chocolate Hostess cupcakes, checked into a tiny motel inexplicably called the Boss Windsor, and lounged shoeless and shirtless on the sofa bed devouring my junk food and watching MTV.

By the time I was stuffed and bored it was almost midnight, so I turned off the light and tried to sleep. But I couldn't stop thinking. First I thought, *I wonder if there's any kind of job that would pay me to travel around the country by car, setting my own schedule?* I was so happy, so detached from anything I had ever known, good or bad—I wondered if there was any way to hang onto this feeling. Suspected there wasn't. Knew enjoying it while it lasted was imperative. I counted all the states I had been in during my whole life. Illinois, one. I guess we had to pass through Kentucky to get there. Two. Tennessee, of course. Florida—we must have passed through, maybe, Alabama and Georgia. Six. Mississippi, Louisiana, Arkansas. Nine. Okay, and since last week—Missouri, Kansas, Colorado, Utah, and Idaho. Fourteen. Tomorrow it'll be fifteen. Not bad for a kid who had spent her first twenty-four years in Memphis. I flipped onto my other side, then onto my stomach, then onto my back. I stuck one foot out from under the covers. I rested one hand on my crotch, gave a fleeting thought to masturbating, but my mind wouldn't focus.

I thought about the psychic and her Elvis ashtray. Then I reached over the side of the bed and pulled the paper she had given me out of my pants' pocket. I flipped on the light and sprawled on my back, holding the paper over my face. Part of me couldn't believe this happened; part of me had trouble dismissing its validity. The Elvis stuff seemed ludicrous, like *National Enquirer* material. But who am I to say Elvis isn't out there somewhere, waiting for the right person, the right moment, to poke holes in the plastic we wrap around ourselves and call reality?

"Tell her I saw her, too," Elvis had allegedly said. How could that woman possibly have known enough to make that up? Good guess? I don't know. He did turn his face toward me that day at Graceland. I imagine he did see me, not that I was anybody that mattered to him then.

I examined the paper on which the psychic had scribbled Elvis' message. I grabbed a piece of note paper and a pencil from the bedside table. *I've got an idea. I'll write down what I think this means now, and I'll keep it with the Elvis paper and every few years in Portland I'll pull it out and see if I'm right, see if he's right, see if I know enough to interpret it better.*

I skimmed through his predictions.

"Portland's between the devil and the deep blue sea."

I wrote: *I think this is sort of a joke—like a reference to the Pacific Ocean and maybe the devil is the hell I left behind me in Memphis.*

"You aren't alone. Somebody you thought you left behind in Memphis has tagged along with you."

Obvious first thought, Mama. I heard her voice in Kansas; maybe I'll get to see her in Portland. I'd love that. Mama's the only dead person I can imagine not being afraid of.

"Three times in Portland you will be denied. One will deny you life. One will deny you breath. One will deny you death."

Hmmm. Three lovers maybe. The first two sound pretty tight. Maybe the last one will somehow save my life, literally or, I hope, figuratively.

"When it's time to leave, you won't miss it."

Obviously, I'm not going to be in Portland for the rest of my life, or . . . I'm going to die there, maybe that's what he means by not missing it when I leave . . . because I won't exist anymore. Uh-oh.

"Portland's gonna let you go without a fight."

Maybe when I leave it won't be a hard decision—or maybe if it's death, it'll be an easy one.

"Don't be afraid. If it feels too hot or too cold, it's not. It's just right."

Sounds like what I was thinking earlier—that Portland's where I'm supposed to be and whatever happens there, good or bad, is what's supposed to happen.

"In Oregon, lean all you want. Somebody's there holding onto your pants."

I have no idea. Sounds like somebody will take care of me. A lover? Is the 'pants' reference a sexual one? Or maybe it refers not to someone but to some thing that will catch me if I fall. Mama did it all my life so far. Is it possible there is someone else who could take her place?

I scratched at the bottom of my page "July"—I had no idea what the actual date was—"1981."

I slept straight through the night with the pencil in my hand and the bedside light on.

ONE BRIGHT DAY IN THE MIDDLE OF THE NIGHT

I drove for an hour and a half still in Idaho, knowing soon I would be crossing into Oregon. My state. I had no conception of the width of this last state, of the miles and miles I would have to travel before reaching Portland in its far west corner. All I could think was green. Green, like the Emerald City, like the Enchanted Forest.

As soon as I could, after I crossed the state line, I stopped for gas. Got out and stretched and sucked in the freshest air, then strolled to the pump and froze when I heard a voice behind me. "What the hail duh you think yer doin'?"

Man, I thought, *rednecks sound the same no matter where you go.* "Need to fill 'er up," I said in my best imitation of casual old boy.

He squinted, then took the nozzle from me and held out his hand for my keys to unlock the gas cap. I struggled to think of something to say, knowing gas costs more if you let them pump it, too polite to let him know I knew. As the gas began to flow he said, "Where you from anyhow?"

"Tennessee," I said.

"Shit," he said, digging a dirty fingernail into his flaky scalp. "I din't think they even had *cars* in Tennessee."

A less sarcastic attendant several hundred miles later would tell me there is no self-serve gas in Oregon.

But long before that, I was still pissed at being ripped off at the gas pump, so when I stopped for breakfast in Enterprise I easily rationalized not mentioning to the waitress that she'd forgotten to add the sales tax. When the waitress where I later ate my lunch made the same mistake, I decided making a habit of stealing small change was not the way to start my new life on the West Coast. I pointed out her error and discovered there is no sales tax in Oregon, either.

What an exotic state.

But it wasn't green. I drove and drove and all around me were the empty spaces and wind-blown sand dunes—starkly dissected by the Columbia River and its low, brown jagged banks—of eastern Oregon. I had another one of those yearnings for a car phone.

Hey, Martin. I thought it was mountains and ocean.

It is.

I'm in a fucking desert!

Keep driving.

I-84 cut a straight path through this state, giving me lots of time on auto pilot to enjoy my new surroundings, time to think about whatever popped into my mind.

I thought about Tom Phillips, my buddy at Memphis State who was ten years my senior, a shell-shocked Vietnam vet, a brilliant playwright when he could shake off his ghosts long enough to sit at the typewriter for any length of time. He read weird books about modern physics that I couldn't make heads or tails of, but which became the board from which many of our midnight conversations sprang. One night, Phillips attempted to explain to me the faulty logic of the concepts of space and time which, he claimed, modern physicists had disproved.

Phillips spoke in a truncated *rat-a-tat-tat* style that was probably some combination of his New York City upbringing and his West Point training. He also basically never sat down. "Manmade constructs," he said, punctuating the stupidity of our beliefs with violent slaps to the sides of his balding head. "Linear,"—he extended his arm straight out, "just because we agree they are." I struggled to follow him mentally and physically. "Past, present, future—we made it up. It makes sense. The best sense. Really everything is happening all the time. See, time. There is no time. We don't even have the right words. And space. Same. Delusional."

I don't know if I really got it, but I did understand everything may be nothing like we think it is because what we think is real is only real because we call it reality. It occurred to me that sometimes things that seem to make the most sense make no sense—and other things that seem to make no sense make the most sense of all.

I remembered an old rhyme my grandfather used to say to me. We'd be out in the carport—more likely than not the rich odor of chocolate or coconut or caramel frosting mingled with batter rising in the oven would be wafting out from the kitchen—some grandkid's birthday cake in progress. Because of whatever was going on in the kitchen, I had to be aggressively distracted by somebody, otherwise all I could do was hang on Grandma and beg her to hurry up and finish.

Grandpa rocked in his chair and chanted:
One bright day in the middle of the night
Two dead boys got up to fight
Back to back they faced each other
Drew their swords and shot each other
Deaf policeman heard the noise
Came and shot the two dead boys
If you don't believe this lie is true
Ask the blind man, he saw it too.

I wondered if that rhyme was written before physics discredited our sense of normal reality and, if it was, who wrote it, and how did they know what to say?

I remembered the look of shock on most everyone's face—even ol' "Seize the Day" Harland's—when I told them I was moving to Portland. No one seemed able to find one iota of logic in my decision, including myself. For some reason, I just believed that the crazier it looked, the more sense it made—and there was no way I could explain myself to anybody, so I didn't even try. And then I remembered just the other day, how the frigid Rockies' rain chilled the hot summer sidewalks in Denver.

Phillips spent many nights trembling and sweating, pacing my floor—scared to go home alone, overwhelmed by memories of the war, sharing his secret horrors with me, his stories as brutal, sharp, and fragmented as shrapnel. He told me real tales of firebombed children, raped and dismembered women, and men, both enemy and ally, killed with knives and bullets. One time Phillips, caught off-guard and unarmed, thrust his thumbs deep into the sockets of a man's eyes. When his stories had exhausted us both, his thoughts rose above the carnage. One night, wrapped in my heaviest blankets to ward off chills that were coming from within, he tried to explain his interpretation of particle physics.

"Matter," he said, "solid things, don't exist. That chair, it's particles we can't see. They're energy congregated here, now. We agree to call this a chair. The energy is moving so fast we can't see it move. Solid," he said, shaking the chair vigorously, "—but—it could scatter, if something were to happen. Just—poof!"

I understood because I saw this theory in action in Phillips himself. So fast and furious, so tenuous.

I peered at the straight road ahead of me. Things were getting greener, the gorge walls were rising, and it looked like the cloudless sky was soon to become history as I saw, in the distance, a billowy puff on the horizon. Several miles later, I was puzzled because the puff hadn't moved, and I thought of the cloud across the moon in the Uintas that turned out to be the shadow of eclipse.

A few more miles and I was convinced this wasn't a cloud at all. Then I couldn't keep my eyes off of it, dying to know what this thing was going to turn out to be. But even when it became obvious what it was, it was so far past any vision I had in my wildest dreams that I was forced to squeal off the highway, laying two long tracks of smoking rubber behind me.

I stumbled out of my car and stood panting, my hand laid over my heart as though I were preparing to recite the Pledge of Allegiance. I didn't know this was Mt. Hood, but I knew it was a mountain—a towering, snowy mountain that topped its closest competitors, some tall evergreens on rolling hills, by thousands of feet. It looked painted on the cloudless blue canvas backdrop that was the sky—perfect, like a child's drawing, like a Platonic form that really didn't exist here on earth. But it apparently did, and it was looming right in front of me. From where I stood, its eastern face climaxed on top to a flawless point, the whole exquisite structure a perfect triangle, its bottom three-quarters a steely blue-gray, its top quarter streaked with white snow like icing artistically dribbled on a dessert in the glossy pages of a fine food magazine.

I didn't fully appreciate Mt. Hood's size until my loaded Corolla started chugging up its foothills—no small potatoes themselves—although, regardless of how deep into the hills I traveled and how close I got to this volcano—Mt. Hood continued to tower over the rest of the Cascade range.

I stopped in The Dalles for dinner around six and Mt. Hood loomed so large and so close I found myself feeling a little paranoid, especially when I thought about Phillips explaining how congregated particles of energy could, theoretically, fly apart. What a fucking nightmare that would be if Mt. Hood decided to unravel while I sat there in a little Asian restaurant eating Vietnamese spring rolls and drinking iced tea with heavy cream and sugar.

LITTLE BOY

It was well after midnight and I saw a cluster of lights in the distance—a real-life oasis—and I straggled into Lancaster, California where Judy Garland was born, according to a plaque on the wall at the Four Arms Motel. It was the first motel I saw and I walked in, desert-dusty and disheveled. "I'd like to get a room."

The clerk scratched his bald head. "Sorry buddy, can't rent to anyone under eighteen." I stared blankly at him and he shrugged. "Sorry son, rules are rules."

In a weary monotone, barely moving my lips, I said, "I'm thirty-three and I'm a woman."

The man reacted like someone just told him he was on *Candid Camera.* He shuffled his feet, turned half circles, thrust his hands in his pockets, and diverted his eyes from mine muttering, "Oh man, o-oh man! I'm sorry, sweetheart, I thought you were a little boy, I mean, a teenager, you know, pulling my leg. I'm sure sorry."

I smiled and nodded repeatedly wanting to say *It's okay, just give me the goddamn room before I lose consciousness right here in your lobby.* Then I noticed he was peering at me with squinty eyes. "I believe you about your sex persuasion," he said, "but you're no thirty-three. You over eighteen?"

I pulled my wallet from my back pocket and slid my driver's license across the counter. He picked it up and held it arm's length from his face. "Dang!" he said. "1956. Dang!"

I plodded past the pool toward the stairs that led up to my second-floor room and, along the walkway, an effeminate man passed and whispered, "Hey, sweetie." I groaned and dragged myself upstairs, unlocked my door, and fell on my bed. *Oh well,* I thought, *it's probably safer if people think I'm a boy.*

I closed my eyes and flinched at the memory of that night in Portland, after Alex left for Washington. It took four Percodans to knock me out, and still I only slept for a few hours—woke up at three a.m. ravenous, pulled on my sweats and drove to Carrow's on 82nd, fantasizing about a big plate of sausage and eggs and toast and grape jelly.

As I pulled off 82nd into the parking lot, an old Chevy rust bucket backed out and I stopped just short of hitting it, my reflexes amazingly quick for someone so full of narcotics, and I lightly tapped my horn. Although I'm capable of being just as big of a road asshole as anybody, on this night I was feeling too high, too free of pain, and I honestly just wanted to alert the driver to my presence and avoid an accident.

I parked my truck and stepped out onto the lot. Before I could close the door, I smelled the stench of old alcohol and saw this skinny, red-eyed man with wispy dirty hair standing on the other side of my door. "What's your fucking problem *little boy?*" he growled. I said nothing. Didn't move. "You got a fucking *problem* with me *little boy?*" I turned slowly, lifted my right foot to get back in the truck, and he kicked my door, slamming it against my left thigh. I moved away from the truck and he kicked the door shut. "Come on, little baby *pencil* dick," he said, clenching and raising his fists. "Come on and show me what a big man you are." I was dumbstruck. I was thinking, *I'm not a boy,* but was afraid to say it, afraid if I did he'd go homophobe on me, rape me or kill me. But my muteness inflamed him more and he grabbed my shirt and threw me against the truck, banging my back and shoulders, screaming, "What's your fucking problem little boy? Is little dicky gonna wet his pants?" All these other words strung together: *pussy, asshole, baby dick*—and always his refrain: *little boy, little boy.* He was twisting my shirt in his fists beneath my jaws and a heavy ring on his finger banged my lip, cutting it on my teeth.

I realized this guy wasn't going to be able to resist beating the living shit out of me, so in a tiny voice I said, "I'm not a boy." This dirty, stinking man's mouth dropped open and he let go of me, stared for a moment, then simply walked away, back to his Chevy. I got in my truck and pulled toward the exit, saw him standing by his door fumbling with his keys, fifteen feet from me, and we made eye contact. I stopped with my engine idling, rolled down my window and he stared at me, mouth open, as I snarled, "You rotten filthy son of a dick asshole." He bolted for me and I squealed out of the parking lot, the sounds of his high-pitched screams disappearing in the distance. *So,* I thought, as I dropped off to sleep hungry and sore but safe at home, *I know what they do to women. Now I know what they do to each other.*

Before bedtime in Lancaster I took the bandage off my hand and stared at the bright red abrasions that were already turning blue around the edges. *This will scar,* I thought and smiled. *I won't forget him.* But, just in case, I stuffed Winston's bloody T-shirt into my bag. I had taken to sleeping with my black bag of pills, and it rested on the pillow beside me, my fingers curled in its straps.

In the little Mojave desert town of Lancaster, California, I dreamed I was sitting in a chair in the North Portland counseling center where I got my training, where I met Alex. Only I was the client and I was tied to the chair and my therapist was my fourth grade teacher, Mrs. Tasker. She was pacing in front of me, occasionally spinning on her heels and snapping a question at me, her face just inches from mine. After each question I barked a response.

How would you feel if somebody poured India ink down your blouse?

I wouldn't be caught dead wearing a blouse *in the first place.*

How would you feel if somebody laughed when you vomited in the lunch room?

I wouldn't puke in the lunch room because I wouldn't eat that greasy crap they serve in there.

How would you feel if you devoted your whole life to somebody and they just decided one day to up and leave?

I didn't just up and leave—I grew up. I was going off to graduate school.

How would you feel if somebody you loved didn't love you?

I did love Kris.

How would you feel if somebody you trusted betrayed that trust without even giving it a second thought?

Alex started it.

After each of my answers Mrs. Tasker struck me hard across the face, except for after the graduate school comment, when she slapped me twice, the second time for Penn.

In my dream, I knew Mrs. Tasker could beat me bloody and I wasn't going to answer her questions right. And I knew that no matter how badly my face hurt when she was done, my Percodan would take the pain away.

ASK ABOUT MA

The Dalles is a quaint town that snuggles cozy on the sleepy giant Mt. Hood's east face. It is primarily populated with people I wasn't yet, in 1981, politically correct enough to call Native Americans. Once I was able to take my eyes off Mt. Hood, which seemed to appear everywhere I turned, I ambled into a souvenir shop whose sign said *Authentic Indian Relics, Jewelry, Beads, Clothing. Ask about Ma.*

I bought an arrowhead on which was etched Hood's perfect peak from a middle-aged woman with long, black braided hair and a round friendly face. "What about Ma?" I said, and her eyes widened.

"You're a traveler."

"Yeah."

"From?"

"Memphis. Tennessee." I added the state because now I was so far from home. "I'm moving to Portland."

"Great city. I got my bachelor's degree at Portland State." She was silent.

"So, what about Ma?"

"Oh, yeah," she giggled, standing up and putting her hand shyly over her mouth. "I don't mean to laugh, it's not really funny." She beckoned me to follow her into a back room that was furnished like a studio apartment. "She's not my Ma. Actually, she was my Gramma." She led me past the studio to a smaller room in which there was nothing but a bed. She pointed toward the paneled west wall and I saw on it the shadow of an adult that seemed to have been drawn with charcoal.

The proprietor's ebony eyes twinkled and she pointed to her feet. "There was a chair right here, where Gramma used to sit when she was alive. She died right here. See this?" She lightly touched the shadow on the wall with her fingertips. "Come here, touch it." I touched the black silhouette and glanced at my clean fingers. "It doesn't come off. It happened in 1944. I was eight. Pa was still alive, and he and Ma and I and my little brother were in the front of the store and Gramma was back here, rocking in her chair like always. We heard a great *whoosh*." She gestured broadly with her arms for emphasis. "Then, a crackling and popping, and Pa screamed, 'Somethin's on fire!' We all ran back to Gramma, and when we got here what was left of her chair was a pile of smoking ashes on the floor, and what was left of her was this shadow on the wall."

"You're kidding!"

"I kid you not. Pa said he had seen it once before, when he was a boy. It happened to another old lady in Fossil where he grew up. Spontaneous combustion, that's what Pa said it was. Pa told us it doesn't hurt, and I believed him when I was a girl, but now . . . well, it's hard to say, seeing that nobody lives to tell about it."

I nodded and thanked her for the tour, then headed out on my last leg west to Portland thinking, *Ma's particles flew apart is what happened.*

The sun was setting as I arrived on the outskirts of Portland. The first thing I saw was the mountain to my right bathed in red and pink and orange. Nobody had to tell me that this one, still standing high over the land surrounding it in spite of its sheared top, was Mt. St. Helens.

"I'm here, Portland," I whispered. My mind struggled to find words to explain how my heart felt—something like relief, like crossing the finish line after a long, grueling race—something like accomplishment. *I'm here,* I thought. *I decided to do it, I did it, and now I'm here to prove it.* I didn't have any past experiences to compare this feeling to. I could only guess that driving these last short miles into Portland must be what it feels like to finally walk across the stage, in cap and gown, and receive your diploma. Something, having graduated twice, I had never done.

In 1974, I didn't attend my high school graduation because, on the night of the ceremony, I was busy tending to my sister who had taken some really bad acid and was afraid to tell anybody but me. I arrived at her apartment at four in the afternoon, and as eight o'clock got nearer, it became apparent I wouldn't be able to leave for a long time. I left Clara plastered face first against the kitchen wall just long enough to run to the bedroom and call my mother.

I dialed without thinking and, in a burst of inspiration only possible in true crisis, I calmly explained that Clara had been reading her *Riverside Shakespeare* in bed and had dozed, dropping it on her face. I said I thought she'd be okay but we were nursing her black eye and waiting to make a decision regarding the emergency room. Clara had been estranged from the family since moving out three years ago, so it wasn't difficult to convince Mama she needn't come to help.

No occasion was too important for Mama not to be able to find some justification for not attending it, especially when the intended attendee was me. "Oh honey, don't worry about it," she said, her voice lilting with affection. "Those ceremonies are just a bunch of boring crap anyway. Thirty seconds you're in the spotlight and the rest is sitting there watching everybody else's kids. Just take care of your sister and I'll see you tomorrow."

Clara was still on the wall when I got back to the kitchen, and she spent the evening doing fascinating things such as blanketing the kitchen table with thin slices of Plumrose cooked ham and staring into the aquarium insisting she could see bright orange trails marking the paths the fish were taking, had taken, would ever take.

In August of 1979, while my undergraduate classmates were parading across the stage of the Mid-South Coliseum accepting their sheepskins, I was sitting outside the operating room at Baptist Hospital waiting for my mother to emerge from cancer surgery that was supposed to last four hours but had dragged on to fourteen.

———

This is the follow through, I thought. *This is success, at last.*

I followed the interstate signs to the Portland airport. The owner of the restaurant where I last worked in Memphis was the public relations director for the Holiday Inn chain and he had extended to me the unlimited use of free room and board while I searched for an apartment. The airport Holiday Inn would be my first home in Portland, and I would stay there for two weeks.

THE RATTLESNAKE FAMILY

———

So this is what a real desert looks like, I thought in the light of day as I rolled out of Lancaster toward Arizona—endless expanses of desolate flat land, not like the fluffy dune country of eastern Oregon I first saw so long ago. Squat brown and yellow and pink prickly foliage strewn about, tall strong-armed cacti like you see on the logos of Mexican fast food restaurants. And a relentless, beating sun.

My most primitive anxiety had resurfaced some time between yesterday's tacos and this morning. I had avoided trying to figure out where to assign blame since my relationship with Kris began to slide. Was it her mindlessly filling our holes or me? But now I had to think, *is it a coincidence that my old fear of eating has come roaring back the night after I eliminated another by jumping into a stranger's car?* I feared that, for the rest of my trip, all I would be able to eat was eggs, sunnyside up. Somehow, despite my childhood paranoia, they had become my comfort food of the road. At least, I figured, they're a little more nutritious than Kerouac's apple pie and ice cream. I could manage toast, too. Eating toast is like breathing—effortless, unless you're really dying. I could even put grape jelly on it, as long as it came in individual plastic packages as opposed to out of a jar that other people have stuck their spoons into.

There were so few towns on this leg. For every mile of I-40 that disappeared behind me, a hundred empty, shimmering others appeared ahead. Finally, I zipped through Needles and was in Arizona. A whole lengthy state, and most of Oregon, now separated me from Portland.

My breakfast eggs had long since abandoned me and I stopped for more at the first Stuckey's I saw. I took the Syrofoam container to go—my complimentary anxiety about eating in public having also been resurrected—and I penetrated the next stretch of desolation for five miles. Then I pulled off the shoulder and got out of my truck to eat alone.

This desert said nothing to me. I heard a rushing noise, like water, then a hissing and rattling—and, like many times before, my city ears played a little trick and told me it was music, some kind of synthesized music from the windowless chambers of a recording studio. But I guess I hadn't lived in the wild, wild west for nine years and not learned something, because almost as quickly as the delusion entered my mind, I looked ahead and to my right and saw sliding through the sand from around a rock, two large rattlesnakes followed by a small one, their tails erect and vibrating.

I pulled my feet up and tucked them under my thighs and remembered Daddy's crazy story about the snake in the road jumping up into our car on our trip to Ft. Lauderdale. I realized I never found out for sure if such a thing was even possible. Right then, I hoped not. I also remembered how often I wished, on my trip out to Portland nine years ago, that I had a car phone—and I found myself wishing that again. Which is funny because, by 1990, of course, people really had car phones, but I was not one of them. How reassuring it would be to have called Daddy and asked him about the snake, although chances are he still would have given me some screwy answer that wouldn't have put my mind to rest.

When I finished my meal, I lay back on the hood of my truck and pulled up my shirt to enjoy the deep solar heat. I wanted to close my eyes, but lately, when I did so without taking a Halcion first, I was assaulted by a kaleidoscopic array of distorted and bloodied human faces that I almost recognized. Instead, I turned my head to the left, my eyes scanning the empty land for something innocuous on which to focus so I could steal a few moments of rest.

I couldn't relax because I saw something in the sand— something small and shiny that stood out against its dusty brown backdrop. I cased the area surrounding the truck, and when I was satisfied the rattlers were gone, I hopped down, peeking quickly at the undercarriage before going any farther.

The trinket was a metallic blue bottle cap. I turned it over and underneath it said *Paradise!* "Paradise," I muttered. "Paradise?" I started to laugh, looking out across this barren wasteland around me, dull and lifeless as yesterday's newspaper—

and I dared by the light of day to taunt this sullen desert. "I've seen paradise," I said with contempt, "and it doesn't look anything like you."

Returning to the hood of my truck, I successfully closed my eyes and dreamed about Mt. Rainier.

———

A month after I had arrived in Portland, I was running low on money and feeling lonely, so I started applying for jobs, landing one at Judith's juice bar after a four-day search. Soon I would meet people named Blue and South, Persephone, Puck, and Almond. Although I'd also know Joans and Bills and even a Mary or two, the weird in Portland outweighed my twenty-four-year concept of the norm.

After a brief interview, Judith asked me if I could start tomorrow and I asked her if I could wait a week.

"Where is that accent from?" she said.

"Memphis, Tennessee."

"Oh, God, a Southern girl. There's something about Southern girls," she said, slightly flirtatiously, and agreed to my starting a week later. That would be the last time she'd say anything nice to me for the next six months.

Knowing I had job security, I made a trip the next day to Mt. Rainier, following vague directions provided by my brother until they petered out, by which time I had seen the mountain's impressive double-humped dome several times peeking out above the rest of the Cascade Range. I tried to reach it by keeping an eye on it and got lost, but every time I was on the verge of giving up, a snowy point would pop up again, although it looked different each time and I started fearing there were lots of mountains around there and who knew which one was Rainier.

Finally, I swerved off the highway into the dusty front yard of a farmhouse. I opened my door and had one leg out when I heard snarling and saw a huge German shepherd bounding toward me. I pulled my leg back in and slammed the door, and an old man stuck his head out of the house and squinted at me. The dog was standing with his front paws on my car door, snapping his yellow teeth at my closed window. The man continued to stare at me, so I slid over and rolled down my passenger window, stuck my head out, and yelled, "I'm lost!"—and the dog came tearing over so I pulled my head in and rolled up that window, bolted back to the driver's side and cracked the window and yelled, "Help me! I'm lost!"—and the dog came tearing back.

Finally the man called the animal away and sauntered out to my car. I cracked the window again and he stuck his face close. Near tears but trying to be cool I said, "I'm trying to find the mountain."

"What mountain?"

"Mt. Rainier."

He gave me directions and I made it to Rainier within the hour. As I drove up the most massive volcano in the continental United States, I followed signs that said "Paradise," with arrows pointing in various directions, not knowing if Paradise was a specific destination or merely descriptive of the forest that dressed the mountain's sides.

There were waterfalls, some still frozen from the past winter. Signs constantly cautioned me to watch for deer—and once, when I was stopped behind another car, a doe and her two fawns walked casually up to my open window.

Paradise, it turned out, was the inn built just above timberline. I parked in its lot and followed the footsteps of other tourists and hikers who set out on the steep paths—some barren, some snowy, some slick with glacial ice—that were clearly delineated on the rock that was Rainier's topmost six thousand feet.

The farther up I climbed the fewer people I saw, but I was too hypnotized by the view and the fact that I was climbing a volcano to notice. I had no understanding of, no respect for, the danger of attempting to scale this thing—me in my worn sneakers, jeans, and sweatshirt—no backpack and certainly no plans for how I would negotiate any surprises this geological wonder might toss my way.

I especially didn't anticipate the surprise I got.

I had slipped across a wide sheet of ice, ripping my fingernails on the rough rock that rose up ten feet on my right. I made my way around its ragged turns to find a vast green meadow dotted with summer flowers. I stood staring at a moose who casually munched the grass fifteen feet in front of me as a cold, gentle breeze ruffled my hair. After a moment, the animal stopped eating and jerked his head up, looking off in front of us toward another rocky ridge, then resumed eating.

Then I heard what he must have heard before—and he heard it again, too, and looked back up in the same direction. I was at 8,000 feet on a volcano, and when I heard the deep, low hum, I thought, *a motor.* I suppose I expected next to see a golf cart driven by an old man in plaid pants, but, of course, I didn't. I just heard the hum again and noticed the moose was very alert and had abandoned his lunch.

Mmmmmmmm, we heard again, and suddenly the moose's dark eyes widened and he bolted off, across the meadow, deftly up the mountain with his hooves beating perfect time. I was immediately overcome by an odor like the dirtiest, mangiest hound and his several dead companions. I remembered Martin the mountaineer telling me once that if you're ever in a pristine forest or on a secluded mountain trail and you encounter the worst smell imaginable, there is a bear very close by.

I knew I couldn't scale this peak like the moose did, but in my otherwise best imitation of him I turned and fled back the way I had come, hoping the bear wouldn't be there, slipping several times on the ice, skinning my palms and knees and spraining my wrist.

In bed that night, packed in ice and coated with Neosporin but safe in the eagle's nest, I wondered if I would ever be able to use the few things I did know to extrapolate the dangers inherent in everything else.

————

In my dream, I was standing on the glacial peak of Mt. Rainier thinking, *I have a home in Portland, Oregon. I have a job. Nothing bad has happened and I hope I can keep it like that.*

Suddenly, I heard a distant rumble that became a steady roar as it got closer and closer to me. In my dream, I didn't know much about avalanches yet, but my animal instinct told me this mountain was coming apart. I bolted up and every vertebrae in my bony spine screamed from sleeping on the hood of my truck. The Arizona sky had blackened ominously and I hurried back onto I-40.

The sinister storm clouds continued to rumble but shed no rain as my foot pressed hard on the gas pedal, trying to put this hostile desert behind me as quickly as possible. To ease my anxiety, I attempted to recapture the good memories of Mt. Rainier. How many times I went up there and so enjoyed my solitude and her beauty. My thought associations led me to recall another of those mystical Pacific Northwest place names—Nisqually Falls—that breathtaking, precipitous area on Rainier where once I sat alone happily munching the wholesome lunch I had packed for myself.

But I wasn't alone. Later I learned, on that peaceful day a body lay just yards from where I ate—a body that evidence showed was revisited many times by its killer whose grisly, prolific work began on the banks of the Green River.

My mind gave up searching its parched corners for pleasant memories and I reconnected, for a second, with the young girl who wouldn't speak to the Popsicle man for an entire summer for fear he was the Boston Strangler.

I finally saw in the distance, an outpost—a gas station, and, fearing it may be the last for another thousand miles, I pulled in only to be accosted by two frolicking mongrel pups who swirled and tumbled over my feet, over each other, nipping and panting puppy play in the dust. A month ago, maybe even just a few hours ago, I might have been tempted to scoop these two pups up and reminisce about Griffin's and Harley's childhoods, but instead I scrambled back into my truck and sped off into the threatening horizon besieged by an ancient fear of rabies.

Rabies was not prevalent in the Memphis of the 1950s and 60s, but the combination of a timely perusal of *Old Yeller* and my mother's lifelong paranoia about this horrible disease, cast a shadow of fear over an entire summer of my youth—a fear that culminated in my ducking when sparrows I mistook for bats flew over my head and running home to wash my bare foot after stepping on a slug I feared may be carrying the deadly virus.

This ridiculous rabies thing receded and I suddenly had a burning desire to escape from my truck—but as quickly as the feeling was upon me, my claustrophobia gave way to agoraphobia, the likes of which I hadn't felt since I was twenty-four and experiencing the nothingness of Kansas for the first time.

But this felt infinitely worse.

I glanced to my left and saw a scarlet face in my window, following me like a low-slung harvest moon at seventy miles per hour. It was a face I recognized. It was the serial killer I saw in Kansas nine years ago, trying to coax his way into my car with sad lies and I beat at him with my fist, saw my hand in the glass, saw the face was mine.

I roared through this deserted landscape, careening every day to another destination that meant nothing to me, and I realized my agoraphobia was not my claustrophobia's opposite at all, but was actually a grandiose version of it. As long electrical fingers of lightning bolted from black clouds and stabbed the empty space ahead of me, I realized the marriage of my two phobias left me feeling trapped in my own body, in this country, in this universe. I deftly extracted two Valiums from my black bag and dry-swallowed them, breaking my promise again not to use while driving. There were no more rules. I was crazy. This was anarchy.

Centuries later the clouds relieved themselves and in the distance were a few twinkling lights. I relaxed knowing soon I would terminate my third day on the road in Williams, Arizona.

ALPINE GLOW

I liked my Holiday Inn room. I had come to love hotel rooms. I loved traveling light, getting up each morning and throwing the few things I had used back in my bag and moving on, not worrying about the dirty towels or sheets or unmade bed, or the blobs of toothpaste in the basin or the wads of tissue that littered the floor, my having repeatedly failed to hit the basket.

I lay on my bed that first evening in Portland having kicked off my shoes after enjoying a huge, free meal that was brought to me by room service. I had a memory of my mother and father. How old could this memory be? I remembered it from a baby's perspective, flat on her back, legs in the air and my mother is fussing over my body below the waist, not looking at my father while she speaks.

Daddy says, "The kids should get to see the mountains at least once."

Mama says, "The subject is closed."

"Is it just hotels, Bear? Is that all you're afraid of?"

Mama screams, "You know what mean men do to kids in those places. Don't be a stupid ass!"

And Daddy gives up.

Since this argument appears to have taken place over the diapering table, it would predate the 1960 release of *Psycho*. Mama's fear of travel lodges must have existed before Hitchcock gave it validity, although she wasted little time using this film to reinforce her point, taking our family on a rare evening out to the movies to see it when I was four.

I would be told repeatedly the dangers of "mean men" who hung out looking for little girls in schools, churches, Sears stores—everywhere a child might wander from a trusted adult. My mother's ominous warnings that provided little detail but obvious implications would keep me from daring to stray far in public places. I always felt an especially profound thud of panic in my chest when we passed a hotel, or someone said the word, or I read it somewhere.

As I lay on this comfortable bed in this room that felt secure, I thought, *Hey, Norman Bates didn't do anything to a little kid. How did Mama get away with using him to instill that fear in us?* Then I glanced down the length of my grown-up body and thought, with a slight flutter of panic, *But he did do it to an adult, an adult female.* Then a moment of debate started in my head. *Yeah, but she had stolen all that money—yeah, but Norman didn't know that—yeah, but God and the other powers that be knew it—so you're saying she got killed because she was a bad girl?—I'm not on the road because I did anything wrong. So I'm perfectly safe, right?*

I sat up on the bed and took a deep breath. "Casey," I said, "Mama is dead, her fears were exaggerated, you are safe, this is not the Bates Motel. You are seven days from Memphis, a trail of rented rooms you have loved and left behind you—and there was not, is not, a mean man in one of them."

I sighed. I guessed these little glimmers of fear were normal. Mostly I felt free, lucky to be young with a little money and dependable wheels and guts. "You're a real pioneer, Case," my father had said, clapping me on the shoulder as I bid him goodbye, then waxing poetic about the wagon train days and how those great explorers, Rodgers and Hart, had battled disease and starvation blazing the Oregon Trail.

I laughed at my father, but sometimes I had to admit the man made some uncanny observations in his oddball way, albeit inadvertently, or maybe not. I turned my head and gazed out my eighth-floor window, mind blank for a few moments, then slowly began formulating a thought. *It's almost ten o'clock and night hasn't completely fallen yet.* I got up and perched myself on the air conditioning unit and took in an unobstructed view of Mt. Hood, all pink and drizzled white, like a baby girl's birthday cake.

"Alpine glow," my brother would later say, providing me with the official name for the mountain's twilight attire.

"It's ten o'clock," I whispered. "I'm on the West Coast. We're the last to see the sun." I laughed and shook my head. "Rodgers and Hart. Hey, I battled some disease and starvation of my own to get out here. Mama wasn't the only person ravaged by her cancer." I pulled up my shirt and grabbed a piece of the little belly I was starting to sport thanks to seven days of high caloric road food—still not enough to offset the spindly wrists and skinny neck and thighs, absent butt, and protruding ribs I had acquired during the two years of watching my mother die.

I let go of myself and stared at Mt. Hood until it disappeared in the darkness that finally came, even to the West Coast—totally unaware on that innocent evening that disease and starvation were not one-time demons I had conquered, but were poltergeists that would visit me again and again.

PREMONITIONS

Williams is one of those places that, if you drive through a traffic light or two, you've driven through the whole town. I learned quickly that Williams has three motels, all in a row, and yet I found myself driving the length of the town again and again in the rain, inexplicably reluctant to pull into any of the three for the night.

A flicker of fear bled through my Valium. I stopped on a deserted roadside where the town peters out to search my mind for clues that might explain my apprehension. Once the truck was stopped with the wipers off, I was completely awash in the relentless storm which relaxed me with its sensory-depriving, soft, dark, steady beat—and I stretched my right leg out over onto the passenger floorboard and slumped in my seat.

Williams, Arizona, I said to myself several times. I knew Halcion fries your short-term memory, but I was fairly certain I had only been there for about half an hour, and that I hadn't gotten out of my truck—nothing bad could've happened yet—and my long-term memory was completely unimpaired and I was positive I had never been anywhere near Arizona in my whole life. Off the top of my head, I couldn't remember any prominent serial killers who operated down there. Nothing stood out in my memory to taint Arizona for me.

Maybe the steady egg diet was catching up with me, skewing my biochemistry into perceiving danger where none existed. I saw a prime rib restaurant on one of my passes through town. I vowed I would make an attempt to eat there that night.

Jimi Hendrix is dead!

I pulled myself up in the seat, glanced behind me, then giggled. Whoa. That was Beale's voice, clear as a bell, and the memory, a long-term one, was just as clear.

"Jimi Hendrix is dead!" my next door neighbor, Beale, shouted that late summer day in 1970 as he ran toward our front lawn where the rest of us congregated. As usual, he tripped and fell several times before reaching us, every time getting back up and rolling on as though nothing had happened, as though we weren't laughing our asses off at him. Beale had a learning disability, although our descriptions of his intelligence were far less politically correct at the time, and he wore glasses with a strap behind his head because his motor skills were also below par and his middle-class family couldn't keep up with the repair bills otherwise.

When he finally reached us, he was all hands flailing wildly and spit flying from his foamy mouth and grass stains on his knees and he kept shouting, "Jimi Hendrix is dead!" We all hooted at him, one of the big boys gave him a rough shove, he went away, and nothing else was said.

Until two days later.

Two days later, we were all congregated on the lawn again, excepting Beale—and David, the oldest boy and our appointed leader, was standing in our center, as solemnly as the rest of us, with the morning's *Commercial Appeal* dangling in his hand, the front page headline clearly visible: *JIMI HENDRIX IS DEAD.*

Flash to older memory. 1960. Our new neighbors have just moved in next door and their two-year-old, still in diapers, keeps toddling over and spitting on our carport. By the end of the day, I am one weary four-year-old and I stand before my mother and say, in reference to this baby who will one day be my best friend, "I hope Sophie falls off her trike and busts her head open."

My mother delivered her famous reply, "Don't even *say* things like that or they just might come true!"

Then, it was 1990 again, and my short-term memory blinked back on. I remembered sitting with Allie on the porch, smoking a cigarette as the sun set on the last day of the garage sale. "Are you sure you don't want me to come along?" she said. "I can fly back. It's no big deal."

"No, really, I'm not afraid to go alone."

"It's a long trip." She squeezed my forearm and peered at me over her wire-rimmed glasses, raising her eyebrows. "You're not in great shape."

"I know, I know. I appreciate the offer, really. I just don't feel like it's going to be a problem. I mean, I did it before, you know, in '81—and believe me, I was pretty wasted then, too."

"I know. Okay."

I laughed. "I'll be fine, as long as I don't accidentally check into the Bates Motel or something."

Allie slapped my arm and shivered. "Don't even *say* that!"

Now, as I sat at night alone in a downpour in Arizona, my dead mother's voice finished the rest. My hands flew to my door locks and depressed them. I gripped the steering wheel, then held my palms out toward the windshield in a gesture of halt. *Wait a minute, wait a minute. The Bates Motel wasn't in Arizona.*

Yes it was, this little bitch who always thinks she's right said softly in my head, and the argument was on.

No it wasn't.

Yes it was.

No it wasn't. Marion stole the money in Phoenix, but she drove to . . . she bought a Los Angeles Times *at the used car lot—and the car she bought had California tags. The Bates Motel was in California.*

But it was raining hard, just like tonight. . . .

Oh, shut up.

And you know why she got it. . . .

My shoulders slumped. *I know, because she did something bad. Okay, you've made your point.* My heart beat a rasping thud in my ears. I had seen the movie a dozen times, and, to my dismay, one scene surfaced in my memory above the rest.

The boyish, quirky Tony Perkins is sitting across from Janet Leigh in his parlor, revealing a bit much about his life with mother as Janet delicately nibbles buttered bread. He says, "She just goes a little mad sometimes. We all go a little mad sometimes. Haven't you?"

Janet, reflecting on her recent financial indiscretion, says, "Yes . . . sometimes just one time can be enough." Then she indicates to Tony she will be going back to Phoenix tomorrow to right her wrongs—but, of course, he and his mom have other plans for her.

I was sitting in my truck surrounded by the Arizona rains, contemplating the world according to Alfred Hitchcock who seems to have meant to imply: *Sometimes when you misstep, repenting is not an option.*

The location of the Bates Motel, I decided, was completely irrelevant.

THE DEVIL'S CHURN

I parked on the street in front of the three motels, none of which I could see clearly because of the rain, but I remembered their names from my many drive-bys. The Range Motel. The Canyon View. Val-U Inn. All had vacancies. Although I suspected my destiny was already carved, my mind played its games—suggesting I go with my first choice, then, no, think about it a little, which has the best name, which *feels* like the right place—then, I knew no matter which one I picked it'd be the wrong one. Or the right one. Whichever way you want to look at it.

I thought about driving another hundred miles to Flagstaff, then immediately rejected the idea and stopped thinking altogether. I dashed into the closest lobby, The Range, and was greeted by an elderly man with a kind smile. I pulled out my wallet as he thumbed through his keys. "Well, we only got two rooms left—uh, less see, well the one's pretty big. It's jess you, huh?"

"Right."

"Well, it's more for a fambly, uh . . ."

"How much?"

"Sevendy-five."

"Oh, well, what about the other one?"

"Wellll. That one's real little. It didn't got no sharar."

"Excuse me?"

"It dudn't got no sharar, you know." He mimed washing his underarms.

I burst out laughing. "No shower! Are you serious?" I noticed he looked kind of ashamed and I felt badly, realizing he couldn't possibly know why that struck me funny. "No, no, I'm sorry, that's fine—no shower's no problem."

He guffawed and I followed him to the room. It was furnished with a cot and a chair and a toilet behind a tattered curtain and it smelled of piss and cigars. I looked at the old man, thinking, *God, the Donner party wouldn't have taken this place*, and I said, "Oh, gosh, it *is* small. I'll check next door. Thanks! Sorry!"

The dark-haired man behind the front desk at the Canyon View was young, lean, and slightly stooped but otherwise looked nothing like Anthony Perkins and his story was oddly similar to the first guy's—two vacant rooms, one large for $85 and one small for $22.

"Does the small one have a shower?" The man stared at me vacantly and nodded his head. Something felt strange. "I think I'll check with the Val-U Inn, thanks." I turned to go.

"No vacancies there," he said behind me.

I turned around. "Oh, their light was on earlier."

He gestured out the window. "That was earlier." He grinned, his parted lips revealing teeth that looked like Indian corn.

I glanced at the extinguished sign outside and turned back to him. "Wow, okay, well, I guess I'll take the smaller one." As he filled out the form and ran my Visa card, I nervously made light conversation both for genuine fact-finding purposes and to somehow reassure myself that this guy wasn't psycho, that he was perfectly nice and normal.

"So, hey, is there something going on in town? Seems like all three motels are pretty booked for this time of year." He shrugged and didn't look up. "Hmmm. I guess out here there just aren't many towns to stop in so people stop here a lot or whatever." He still said nothing. "So, what's to see in Williams, Arizona anyway?" I was amazed at how much I sounded like my father, the ultimate let's-take-the-scenic-route kind of guy.

The man still didn't look up, just gestured with his pen toward a rack on the wall. "Take some litrichure if ya like." I took some tourist pamphlets and scurried off to my little room.

The rain continued to fall in great sheets and I was wet up to my knees by the time I bounded into my room and slammed the door behind me. I drew the curtains closed, checked the door and window locks several times, then shed my soaked clothes and headed for the shower. A thought kept running through my mind like a tape loop—*I can't get to Memphis any faster than I can get there and I can't get back to Portland any faster than I can get to Memphis*—and my anxiety about being stuck in the middle of time and space was out of control.

I decided to take a shower without closing the curtain.

I turned the spigots and the head shuddered and thumped and three impotent rivulets of cold water that never warmed dribbled out. As I twisted my skinny body to get the soap off I realized that even tender-footed Norman couldn't sneak up on me under these circumstances. I climbed out and into the bed, snuggling deep under the covers until I was warm enough to decide what to do next. I decided to call Kris, but when I peeked out from under the covers, I noticed the room had no phone, so I took a Halcion and read the literature from the motel office.

Williams, Arizona, it said across a picture of a one-horse town surrounded by barren desert. *Magnificence on the Grand Canyon's Southern Rim.* One of the pictures inside was of the yawning Canyon itself, shot as though you were standing right there in Williams and gazing down into its depths. I was awash with a dizzying fear of heights, fear of not being able to control the urge to fling myself off an extremely high place such as the one pictured, a fear that threatened to loosen my bowels or bring up whatever might be in my stomach. My mind searched for silly games to ward off the impending purge my body contemplated.

I stuck my hands out in front of my face and counted aloud the number of letters in Williams, Arizona. Then I counted how many states I had ever been in—eighteen and Canada. By the time I tallied how many beds I'd slept in over the past year, including this one, and arrived at twelve, my vertigo had subsided.

I smiled and pulled my fists to my mouth. Closed my eyes and treated myself to a good memory.

———

Kris and I are on the Oregon Coast. The sky is heavy with gray clouds, the sea is stormy, the tide, high. There's a lookout point off Highway 101 and we pull in, step out of the truck and Kris, who has only one muscle in her whole body that's weaker than mine, stops to pee in the foliage over the first coastal ridge. It is winter and no one else is around as we lumber down a beaten path that is gentle and lined with log railings for safety, belying the untamed waters at its end.

The Devil's Churn. We approach it for the first time, amazed that once we are on its treacherous edges there are no railings, nothing but self-control and extreme caution separating us from its hypnotic rhythm and awesome violence. The Churn is a deep crevasse that the sea has cut over eons into the rocky cliffs that allows the high tide to swirl into its confines, foam and rage, only to swirl back out in an endless lashing of water against earth that never subsides, only calms slightly when the tide goes out.

At high-tide's peak, the cold, salty sea roars up the sides and sprays our feet as we stand just inches away from sure death—a death that, with one misstep, would come only after a human body was sucked below the current, spewed back up to the spiky surface, spun in maddening circles and dashed mercilessly against the hard rock sides until all the bones were shattered, the skin flayed—and no one, not even the best swimmer, could beat this watery devil and save the soul that had teetered into its maw.

Kris sees me creeping closer across the slimy rocks that are not immovable monoliths but infirm stepping stones, and, as I lean farther over the edge, she exhibits rare terror and slips her fingers into my belt loops.

"Oh honey, oh please," she wails over the beating din, incapable of articulating her fear. I laugh and point at a huge piece of driftwood, something that was once a tree's rooted trunk, battering the sides, going under, bobbing back up, swimming close to the opening out to sea only to be dragged back into the cauldron. Kris doesn't think any of this is funny, and her fear drags her to her knees as she throws her substantial weight back, holding onto me so I can't fall.

Back safe in our home, I tell Kris what Elvis said, marveling that this is something I've never told her before, incredulous that his prediction was so accurate. I know Kris is as astounded as I, but her need to dismiss the inexplicable evokes a typical wry Kris response. "That's great. The problem is, no one was holding onto *my* pants."

————

If there are no guard rails at the Grand Canyon, will anybody be holding onto my pants?
This thought came with a flicker of anxiety just as the Halcion's first hypnotic effects kicked in—then promptly went. I stayed in bed for a few more minutes, thinking about how to spend the rest of my night in Williams, Arizona.

MISS ETHEL AND THE VOLCANO

I had always been intimidated by maps, so, although I had a city map, I didn't bother to take it out of my glove compartment on my first full day in Portland. Instead, I drove aimlessly around, hoping I would intuitively know where I should look for an apartment, hoping I would be lucky enough to find my way back to the Holiday Inn that night.

I drove up and down 82nd Avenue and didn't like the endless string of used car dealers, fast food restaurants, and gas stations that lined it, or the squat, boring houses that flanked it to the east. I passed over the Sellwood Bridge with its funny signs: *Men Below: Please Don't Throw*—didn't like the look of the cheaper dwellings close by and knew the manors surrounding Reed College were out of my range. Based on my Memphis experience, I didn't even consider it possible to live downtown, so I didn't look there at all. I liked the inner Northeast but thought those houses looked a little pricey, too. I began to settle comfortably in the Southeast quadrant once I crossed Burnside many times in a panic, unable to figure out how I was on Southeast 20th one second and Northeast 20th the next. Finally, I stopped at a 7-Eleven and a cashier kindly explained that Burnside is the street that divides the city north and south.

The first place I stopped was on Belmont and 20th—a multistoried building with a *For Rent* sign hanging out front.

I rang the manager's bell and an elderly woman took me to the fourth floor in a hydraulic cage elevator reminiscent of the one that delivers Frankenfurter to Brad and Janet in *The Rocky Horror Picture Show*. She led me down a dark hallway and showed me a one bedroom that had disintegrating plaster and little light, but that was cheap—just $35 a week. We took another elevator ride to the fifth floor and she invited me into her apartment—a cluttered place that smelled like cigarettes, cinnamon, and Chanel No. 5 with a northern window that framed a consummate view of Mt. St. Helens.

"Wow," I said, staring at the mountain while the woman rummaged through a battered rolltop desk for the application. Her husband sat in an easy chair with an oxygen tank on the floor to his left, a tube leading from it into his nose, and a cigarette burning in his right hand. He smiled at me and weakly gestured with his left hand.

"Nice view, huh?"

"That's Mt. St. Helens, right?"

"Yup." He wheezed for a moment, then said, "Oh, Reenie, show the girl the pitchers Billy took."

The lady handed me the papers to fill out and dug through another drawer. "Oh, honey, yes—our youngest boy, Billy—well, he's thirty now, but he was right here when she went off that morning, May 18th last year—and he had his camera with his telescope lens and, look." She thrust a stack of impressive pictures into my hands and hovered at my elbow as I flipped through them. "See, it looked like an atom bomb, you know, like a big ol' mushroom in the sky. See, it was white, then gray, then black, just rollin' outta the top, see, and—"

"Tell 'er about Miss Ethel," her husband interrupted.

"And see," the woman continued, "this was when finally the smoke cloud died down you could see—the mountain's just gone." She pulled another picture from the bottom. "This is what she looked like before. Perfect, just a perfect round snowball. Beautiful. She just took her whole top right off."

"Tell 'er about Miss Ethel."

The woman became excited, fluttering her hands, her face flushing. "Oh my, Miss Ethel was right down the hall, in 509—"

"Go show 'er."

"You got a minute?"

"Sure," I said, following her down the hall.

As she fumbled with the keys with her knotty fingers she continued in a hushed tone. "Mr. Cedar—he's the landlord— he still ain't rented Miss Ethel's place—I like to think outta respect." We entered the dim, empty apartment. "But mostly I think cause word travels in this town and I'm not sure he can rent the place, 'specially since the stain won't come out."

I remained silent as she led me to a small room with a window that also looked out over the mountain. There was a broad window seat. The remains of curtains still hung on rods close to the ceiling—mere inches of tattered fabric fringed with erratic, singed edges. The tiny room smelled of woody smoke and something else, something cloying and dank. The window seat was painted white, but marred by a dripping, reddish-brown stain. The old woman put her fingers as close to it as possible without actually touching the wood, then looked out the window toward the volcano, then, intently, back at me.

I donned a look of grief I didn't feel. "She died here."

The old woman's eyes looked just like my own—cobalt blue shot through with chips and cracks like a smooth marble someone has carelessly dropped and broken. "Oh, she died here all right. On that morning, May 18th of last year, Miss Ethel . . . she was near ninety, near blind. She lived here for fifty years and, before her sight failed her, she used to love to watch that mountain out this window. That morning, she was watching it 'cause, of course, she knew it was there, though she couldn't hardly see it no more, you know. And you know what happened?"

"Uh, no." Reenie pursed her lips and said nothing, forcing me to ask, "What happened?"

"Well," she said, whispering, "when ol' Helen blew up, so did Miss Ethel."

"Oh, that's weird," was all I could manage to say, but as I left the building I thought, *This definitely is not a safe state for old women to live in.*

I talked to my aunt long distance from the hotel that night and her oddly negligent response to this whole story was, "Casey, don't ever take a place that rents by the week!"

She was right, of course, and a week later I found my first Portland home—a yellow duplex on a hill on the corner of 22nd and Yamhill that the locals called "The Castle." My one-bedroom perch on the top floor with its bright western windows and cool northern exposure that looked out over a cemetery was known as "The Eagle's Nest."

With a week's lead time for moving in, I settled back in at the Holiday Inn and planned my adventures in the great Pacific Northwest.

DOUBLE JEOPARDY

The Halcion, and my recalling the daring self who cheated death on the edge of the Devil's Churn, gave me the courage to get dressed and walk through what had become a chilly drizzle to Williams' prime rib restaurant. I took a seat and ordered a balanced meal that I couldn't eat. A giant painting of a Brave on horseback spearing a terrified buffalo whose nose spewed drops of blood hung over my table. I asked for a doggie bag and took my dinner back to my room, where I threw all of it away except the baked potato.

I took another Halcion and got into bed and wrote in my journal:

I wonder if I will ever be happy again. Things that have made me happy: getting colored Band-Aids in my stocking at Christmas and sticking them all over my baby dolls, getting stoned and making out with my first boyfriend and eating pancakes with blueberry syrup at the IHOP, dancing at the bars with my gay friends in the seventies, lying naked alone in Judith's house on her couch watching the sun set with Penn at seven pounds sleeping on her stomach on my chest, tubing on Mt. Hood with Kris and Harley and Griffin, everything about Harley. She's the only thing I've ever wanted and gotten that turned out to be as good as I dreamed it would be. See, I try to think about happy and no matter what it bleeds into sad. I miss Harley. Griffin, too, but not like I miss her. I'm not even sure if I miss Kris. I'm afraid I don't love her as much as I need her, and I always thought she wouldn't ever let me fall, but I think she might be about to let go. What is this paranoia? She begged me to come back to Memphis, but I have this horrible feeling that I'm going back there to die. I know she hates me for what I did to her, to us. Maybe she's luring me back to finish me off, to get some kind of revenge.

Oh well, I'm halfway there with nothing to go back to anyway.

One thing I never asked Alex was where she got the courage to try to kill herself. I wish I knew, wish I could really know I could do it if I had to. How bad do things have to get? I'm afraid I can't wait much longer for another food pellet.

I'm getting sleepy. Halcion makes me happy, but I know it's delusional, temporary—seems too good to be true, therefore it probably is, but why not enjoy it while it lasts? Is it possible that ultimately you have to pay big time for everything good in your life? And the bad stuff, you don't ever pay that shit off.

———

I never achieved deep sleep in Arizona. One eye stayed open monitoring the strange shadows in the dingy room, and bad dreams danced behind the other. In one dream I was in a small country house with Anthony Perkins and he said he was sorry but I would have to identify the body. He led me into a chapel with an open coffin at the altar, and I peered inside and Alex lay there, looking perfect except a trickle of blood was coming out of her nose. I told Tony it was Alex and he respectfully lowered his head and thanked me. I gently laid my hands on the side of the coffin and the whole thing tipped over and Alex came tumbling out onto the floor. "I'm sorry, I'm sorry," I babbled, fearful of being punished, and Tony took my arm and led me outside.

"It's okay," he said, "the maintenance men will clean it up."

In another dream, I was on *Jeopardy* and the host was Ted Bundy. We chatted and I said, "You're not still dangerous are you?"

He flashed his charming smile. "Oh no, not really, not with all these people around."

"But, how am I going to get to my car?"

"We'll think of something," Ted said, grinning, his teeth small and colorful like Indian corn.

CONTEMPLATING THE FALL

The next morning I checked out and headed toward the Grand Canyon only to discover that the literature had exaggerated Williams' proximity. It was fifty miles or so south of the Canyon, not exactly *on* the rim. The ascent was steep, through mountains I hadn't noticed in the distance as I left the motel; and, as my loaded truck chugged up the passes, I began to shiver in my thin T-shirt, finally flipping on the heat. Everybody had warned me about the blistering sun of Arizona and how miserable I would be in my unairconditioned vehicle. But, so far, this state had been nothing but threatening skies, driving rain, chilly temperatures day and night—and now things were getting downright frigid.

When I pulled up to the lot that abuts the Canyon, I dragged my Thinsulate jacket out from behind the seat. As I was wriggling into it, the sky erupted in a thundering torrent of walnut-sized hail that pelted my truck and blanketed the ground—stopping five minutes later as abruptly as it started.

As I got out of the truck and headed down the stony path to the Canyon's rim, huge flakes of snow began to flutter around me. By the time I reached the crest of the ridge from which the alarming expanse of the Grand Canyon is visible, the snow was falling furiously and sticking to the trees and to the rocks and to me. I ventured out to the edge and couldn't believe there were no guard rails and I remembered what Elvis said. That somebody would always be holding onto my pants. But did he say just in Oregon? Was I safe here?

I gazed down into the Grand Canyon and remembered stories of people falling—down here, off bridges, off buildings. They say some people die before they ever hit bottom. Some don't. I wondered which type of person I would be. I had a dizzy spell, so I forced myself to spend a little time dwelling on slightly safer subjects.

MEETING THE SEA

—

I swam in the Holiday Inn pool, soaked in the hot tub, bellied up to the buffet tables and shamelessly overfilled my plates, slept whenever I felt like it, and basked in the knowledge that no one in town would be calling me with any demands or unpleasant surprises. After three days of this, I decided it was time for me to venture out and explore my new world, so I called my brother. Martin had a whole bookshelf full of state and city maps and atlases—and huge maps of the United States and the world on his walls. He had even drawn his own maps of the ancient hills and valleys of the Ozarks he so passionately loved.

"Hey," I said. "How do you get to the ocean?"

He told me in precise detail.

"How about Mt. Hood?"

Ditto.

"How about Mt. St. Helens?"

"You can't drive up there," he said.

"Why not?"

"Because it's totally destroyed! All the animals and trees are gone, the Toutle River is sludge, and besides, the damn thing's probably going to erupt again."

"Wow, really?" I made a mental note to figure out a way to go up.

"Go to Mt. Rainier," he said.

"Where's that?"

"In Washington."

"How do you get there?"

For some reason he didn't have all the information I needed to get to Mt. Rainier, but he assured me, "You can't miss it. It's huge. Bigger than Hood. It's like 14,000 feet." I figured I'd find it once I got close enough to see it. "And, oh, go to Lost Lake."

"Where's that?"

"It's on the eastern slope of Mt. Hood," he said, mumbling vague directions as he pawed through his maps.

"By The Dalles?" I proudly showed off my new found geographical prowess.

"Yeah, probably close to there," he said, pretending like he knew what I was talking about.

On Wednesday morning I got up early and stood outside of my car for a few minutes enchanted by the phenomenon of foggy breath swirling out of my warm mouth in July—remembering with my hands cupped around the goosebumps on my arms the oppressive summertime air of Memphis, sticky wet and buzzing with insects. I hadn't even seen a housefly since I got to Portland, much less a mosquito—and I was yet to discover the pleasure of sleeping on summer nights with screenless windows open wide, cuddled under a blanket to protect myself from the crispness that came even after the warmest day. I stopped at a Plaid Pantry and purchased a

Styrofoam cooler, filled it with ice and Cokes, then followed my brother's directions to the Pacific Ocean.

I had no memories of the Atlantic Ocean that we visited when I was little—but even if I had, they wouldn't have compared, or prepared me for what I saw that day. My disappointment at the flat, boring landscape quickly dissipated as I passed Hillsboro and North Plains and began winding my way toward the coastal range. I had unpacked my car but not my trunk, and the Corolla sputtered at the challenge of the Sunset Highway's gentle ascent.

At the junction of 101 I made the spontaneous decision to take the left to Cannon Beach rather than the right to Seaside and Astoria, then drove ignorant of what lay past the dense forest that lined the road. Finally, just outside of the first coastal town, I crested a ridge and, with no trees blocking my vision, the gun-metal-gray whitecapped ocean appeared. I did one of my now famous dangerous careens off the highway and spilled out of the car. "Oh my God," I said, clapping my hands over my mouth, then jumping back in and speeding ahead.

That day I strolled up and down the northern Oregon coast—perched myself on some rocks on Arcadia Beach while the tide rose and lashed them, wetting my clothes, totally unaware of the danger, of how lucky I was that the day was clear and the sea relatively calm. Only as the years passed would I understand my good fortune as, every few months, the news would feature a story about the untimely death of some careless beachcomber, drowned trying to sit out the high tide.

In Cannon Beach I ate my first veggie sandwich—nutty avocado, tomatoes, bean sprouts (which I had never seen before and was highly suspicious of and which, that day, I threw to the sea gulls), Jarlsberg and cream cheeses, lettuce, and black olives with mayo on a fresh croissant. This would become my coastal staple for the next nine years. I had my first rich, gooey

Linzer torte, and took back to the city a pound of salt water taffy. I saw sea lions basking on rocks not far off shore on Indian beach, then heard their frantic barking and watched them suddenly disperse—noticing long after they did the tall fin of a circling shark some distance out in the water. *This is heaven,* I thought, *and I deserve to be here.*

It would be a year later before I'd see my first whale—a mammoth, mottled Gray cutting the water followed by two others. I would be standing that day on the rim of the Devil's Punchbowl at Otter Rock, holding three-month-old Penn, sheltering her blinking eyes from a salty breeze.

I watched the deep orange sun disappear below the undulating emerald horizon well after ten o'clock—stared out to sea until the gray water faded and the whitecaps looked like points of light dancing on the edges of a vast black hole. *I am twenty-four and standing on the westernmost edge of the United States.* I cocked my head and listened to the dull roar that didn't sound like the ebb and flow of the ocean's tide now that I couldn't see the water. It sounded like something big moving toward me, then moving away. I wouldn't be here if Mama hadn't died, I realized, then wondered, *does everything you get have to be at somebody else's expense?*

On Friday the sky was clear and the sunlight brilliant even in Portland, and I drove across Mt. Hood to the east where the cloudless blue and piercing yellow bouncing off the bright, white snow was blinding. As I wound toward Lost Lake I disappeared into a narrow, winding forested corridor that took me deeper into darkness until I was beneath a canopy of towering, gnarled, prehistoric trees that allowed no light at all onto the road I traveled.

The air was hushed and frigid. I parked long before I got to the lake and walked as far as I dared into the forest, running my hands along the damp, rough bark. I half expected these trees to begin to move and talk, to reach down with their full arms and scoop me up, cradle me and show me their magic if

I was worthy—dash me to the ground in a broken heap if I was not.

I had a vivid memory of Rod Serling talking about stepping into another dimension—some story about parallel universes where everybody thinks you're you, but you know you're not where you used to be—and I felt like this might be what that would be like. If anybody I knew could see me now, they would recognize me, but I didn't. The Casey standing alone in these woods, twilight at midday, was unafraid, untethered—had no city life, no one to care for, no one to lean on—no past, no future. I believed, that day, that whole other worlds existed I had never imagined before and that everything in them was conscious. I remembered Phillips' theory about inanimate objects being not mass but energy, and for the first time in my life I wondered how delusional my sense of control might be. I felt, that day, it just might be the world that moved me.

Lost Lake itself was twilight blue and quiet as ice.

When I got back to the Holiday Inn, I fell asleep wondering where Portland would take me, and whether I had any power to choose my destination.

PORTLAND, OREGON

I spent a week settling into my apartment and exploring Portland, my new city, my new home. I began what would be a long relationship with Pacific Northwest Bell and Portland

Gas and Electric—and I enjoyed a long honeymoon one-stop shopping at the Fred Meyer store, Freddy's, once we became intimate, where I could buy everything from frozen food to 501's to file folders. I discovered the best place to see Mt. Hood on a clear day—the east side of Mt. Tabor—and the best place in my neighborhood to get a deli sandwich—the German Bakery on Hawthorne.

There was a Safeway supermarket five blocks from me, and clean, well-lit self-service laundry facilities a block past that. I bought freshly baked bread that was dark and dense with nuts and seeds and possibly sticks and grasses at the Daily Grind—and various cafes served strong, fancy coffee and exotic foods that for a long time I dared not eat, such as falafel and hummus. It was also possible to find Coney Island hotdogs in Portland, Oregon.

In public, in southeast Portland at least, nearly as many fathers as mothers seemed to be their children's primary caretaker, and parents of both sexes carried their infants in soft cloth sacks tied to their chests or backs. Men wore cords and plaid shirts—women, peasant dresses, or cords and plaid shirts—and a lot of people still wore bell bottoms. There were moments in Portland, a city I found to be different beyond my imagining, when I definitely felt like I had stepped into a time warp. A surprising number of females had leg and underarm hair as lush as the men. Some appeared to be lesbians—could all of them be?

Portland's streets were cleaner than Memphis'—its downtown livelier, apparently even livable. Police car doors were stenciled with long-stem red roses. The streets were safer, too, I believed, and I fearlessly walked them alone in the wee hours of the morning until 1984 when the Bloods and Crips and Neo-Nazi skinheads started making headline news.

My job would open up other new ways of seeing the world. I didn't know there was any such thing as a lesbian community. I wouldn't have thought of even putting those words together, being more likely to describe those of us in Memphis as an errant band of homosexual outlaws, living on the hard edge of the Bible Belt's buckle. In Portland, I discovered women's bars, women's bookstores, women's music festivals. I saw women spelling women *wimmin*. I saw pink triangles on car bumpers and pictures of women kissing on T-shirts.

At a party with my work friend Eddy, I would take a wrong turn on my way to the bathroom and enter a room in which an ultra femme with heavy makeup and spiky dyed hair was draped across a bed clad only in seatless leather pants being spanked by a large butch wielding a thick wooden paddle. I had heard stories about men and S/M—I was astonished to discover that dykes did it, too.

I had never heard of lesbian separatists, much less eavesdropped on one of their heated debates about whether dyke mothers should be allowed to bring their infant sons into "wimmin only" spaces. Portland, I found, was a breeding ground for alternative thinking—and, an entire decade before this became a nationwide catchphrase, I would be dunked into the pool of political correctness, most often only to sink like a stone.

My first dousing came one evening when, having been promoted to night manager, I was supervising the Friday night rush at Judith's when a disheveled woman tore in the front door screaming amid this heavily lesbian crowd, "I need a man!"

She approached me and I glanced at Sue. Sue was a waitress who, by day, studied high colonics, an alternative healing procedure which, she claimed, not only would rid the body of its toxins, but which would often transport the recipient onto higher levels of consciousness inconceivable to the unclean masses. Sue found my comment that I'd just settle for a few scotch and sodas to be unspeakably plebeian. But if this encounter got my feet wet, I was about to drown in the face of this distraught woman and her singular cry, "I need a man!"

The bar being in the gentrified northwest section of Portland but still just blocks from the large transient community of West Burnside, another new sight for me, we were often visited by the homeless mentally ill, and I prepared to defuse this incident as I had before.

"Can I help you?" I asked.

"I need a man!"

"What for?"

She began gesturing wildly. "My car's outside. I've got a flat and my friend's trying to change it but he's physically challenged."

I laughed. "Hey, if I was trying to change a flat I'd be physically challenged, too!"

Sue yanked me aside to explain this new term for what I had always called handicapped, as a gallant dyke pushed aside her café latte, followed the woman outside, and removed the lugnuts after helping her quadriplegic friend back into his wheelchair.

While PC Portlanders found me oafish, others thought me to be a downright hick. One asked me if we had running water in Memphis; another assumed for some odd reason that I had never eaten pizza. Few were inclined to believe me when I noted that Memphis was almost twice Portland's size.

One day a fellow transplant and her Oregonian girlfriend sat at one of my tables, and the former adeptly identified my accent as Tennessee. "How did you know?" I asked.

"Well," she said, "I'm from Maryland—that's the south, isn't it?"

I honestly didn't know, and the only way I could think of to ask was to say, "Was Maryland below the Mason-Dixon Line?"

The girlfriend's jaw hit the table and she exclaimed, "Oh my Goddess, do you people still talk about *that*?" I knew at that moment this modern metropolitan dyke saw us riding our Thoroughbred steeds across vast antebellum fields of white cotton, wielding with power and privilege our well-worn whips.

But, it seemed, for every Northwest native who found me weird beyond words, another was attracted to the cute new Southern girl in town with her exotic accent thick and rich as *sear-up*.

"*Sur-up*, you mean?" I'd drawl, and they would clutch their crotches.

SANGRE DE CRISTO

The sudden snow caked on my head and shoulders and shoes, and lowered a thick, white curtain over the Grand Canyon, obscuring its depths. I decided Elvis did not intend for me to assume anybody would be holding onto my pants in Arizona, so I drove the quarter mile back to a tourist's cafeteria and ate my standard breakfast, treating myself to a carton of chocolate milk that tasted funny and gave me stomach cramps that lasted the rest of my way through the state.

I stopped only twice—once to fill my gas tank, once to throw up in the sand at the base of a colossal, multi-armed Saguaro cactus—before leaving Arizona for good.

New Mexico was cold, too, and, for the first half, gray. I wound through mountains in a snowstorm that was heavy enough to slow my progress significantly and sensory-depriving enough to give me entirely too much time to think. Grabbing my Trip-Tik, I spotted New Mexico and my eyes lit on three pretty words—*Sangre de Cristo*. I didn't look long enough to see that these mountains were far to my north—not the ones I was driving through at all—but it mattered little where I really was at this point. I experienced a brief moment of pride as I translated the Spanish words in my head. *Blood of Christ*. Pretty good, considering I had one year of Spanish in the tenth grade which I failed after being barred from attending the final quarter for instigating the infamous third-story textbook toss. But somebody was being hard on me in my head, denying me even the vapid joy of thinking I knew a couple words in a foreign language.

You knew Sangre because you know Sangria is that fruity red wine that means blood, and any idiot could figure out Cristo. My cynic was genderless and ageless.

I sighed and continued navigating the crunchy road conditions, conceding that the voice was right, pretending that I didn't care. I managed in my mind a brief moment of silence before the chattering began again.

When did I get to be such a wimp that I can't even stand up to myself? I asked myself.

Maybe it's not yourself.

Then who is it?

Everybody else.

Well, they should just leave me alone. Maybe I've lost my mind but I still have a heart and it hurts.

Nobody with a heart could break somebody else's like you did mine. That was Kris' voice.

I did to you what you should have done to me four years ago when I stopped having sex with you.

You said things would get better.

How long were you willing to wait for God's sake?

Forever . . .

"That's stupid," I mumbled aloud, figuring I could say that because apparently I couldn't hurt her worse than I already had and, also, she wasn't really there to hear me.

You broke my heart, too. Now Alex was joining in.

Oh, shut up.

I made believe my mother was sitting next to me, because I needed to feel safe traveling through these strange mountains in snow that was showing no signs of letting up, and she was my last hope.

"Mama," I said, immediately remembering what I told the Mojave and feeling badly about it. "I'm sorry what I said to the desert. Now that you're dead, can you understand? You loved me too much—you couldn't let me go. And now I can't let you go. I kept looking for you in Portland. I feel like you saw everything so I don't have to name names.

"God, Mama, I fucked up. And now I don't know what to do. I'm heading home, but I don't know what's waiting for me there. There's not really an answer to anything is there? What did you want that night when you came into my bedroom? I'm sorry I was afraid of you. I never thought I would be. If it was to tell me to go somewhere other than Portland, isn't it true that if it hadn't been there, it would have still happened wherever else I went?

I laughed. "Remember in Idaho, when Elvis talked to me through the ashtray? A lot of what he said has turned out to be right. Hey were you there when he was saying that stuff? I remember, you went to Humes High School with him, didn't you? I guess you were a couple years ahead of him, but I remember you telling us about how the whole school was talking when the new boy from Tupelo with the ducktail and weird clothes showed up.

"That night in Alex's apartment, I couldn't remember what he said about the denial stuff, but now I do, and I think I get it. Three times I would be denied. Judith denied me life. She really tried to orchestrate things so I wouldn't have a life outside of her, Penn, the business—and when I asserted myself and tried to go to Memphis, she kept stopping me. And when I finally succeeded, well ... She couldn't have known Kris was there waiting to happen to me, but she must have known there was some threat, because that night before I actually went, I guess she panicked and, well, you know what happened that night, what she did when everything else she had used to control me failed. . . .

"Kris was number two, huh? The one who denied me breath. She loved me so much, but there ended up being so many strings attached that it was like living in a cocoon. Suffocating. I'm sorry, but she was the most like you. I know neither of you wanted to hurt me—you were just protecting yourselves. But it's like that old cliché about the bird in the hand—or about letting something you love go free and if it comes back . . . oh, whatever. You know, Daddy was always the one in the family who was good with clichés.

"And I guess Alex did, in a way, deny me death. She always said, 'Don't die, don't die'—at the same time she drove me so crazy it was like she wanted me to die. Still . . . you know, the closest I came to killing myself was that night just a couple weeks before Alex left. Do you know how I ended up with Grandpa's straight razor? Anyway, I got it out, opened it—it was so big and so sharp, unbelievable—Alex was out on the town with one of her ex's and I got the razor and my Percodan. I really wasn't interested in the pain. The perfect plan seemed to be, take about four pills, which I did. That was sure to kill any pain. Run a hot bath, which I did. Open up my arms with the razor and climb in the tub—I wouldn't feel anything, and the hot water would draw out the blood quickly. I was sitting on the side of the tub when I made the first nick and I didn't feel it at all—but the blood instantly ran right off my wrist into the water and what I saw was how it stayed together in this red, snotty string for a minute, then started to spread out pink, then more dripped in and you know what I saw? I saw Janet Leigh in *Psycho* with her face smushed against the cold bathroom tile, her dead eyes staring, brown clots swirling down the drain. Then I saw what I would look like when Alex found me later that night, or the next day—white, like a fish's underbelly, slackjawed, staring, floating in a tub of cold, red water. As much as I had come to loathe her in those last weeks, I just couldn't do that to her. So yeah, maybe she did deny me death, whether she meant to or not.

"Elvis also said I wasn't alone, that someone I thought I left behind in Memphis was tagging along? I remember I thought he meant you, then when you showed up I was sure he did. He wasn't talking about *you* was he. He was talking about me. How did he know so much? I wish you could tell me if you were in on this.

"So much has happened since you died, to me, to everybody, the whole country. Remember disco? Remember Tim? Both of them are dead now. Obviously you know I'm gay—all of us were. I always kind of thought you knew, even when I dragged my 'boyfriends' home and you hinted what good sons-in-law they would make. I remember when I got the call that Tim was dead, being stunned because he was so young—and just thinking, *what the hell is toxoplasmosis?*

"So many times I wished you were there when Penn was a baby. You would have been so proud of me. I changed her diapers a million times and never gagged once. I could drive myself crazy thinking about this, but that night you came to Portland—I had my first migraine the next day. If I could have let you near me—were you going to take me with you so I'd never have to go through that pain like you did? That's what I was afraid of that night, that if you touched me I was going to die. Of course, if I had known, I might have wanted to come. Because it was the migraines that finally bound me so tightly to Judith, with me not able to work much and all. I bet that night you already knew what it was going to take for me to get away from her. So maybe that was the first time in my life you tried to give me a hand and I didn't take it.

"And now look where I ended up. Kris got me away from Judith and Alex got me away from Kris and now to get away from Alex I'm going back to Kris or something like that. Who's ever going to get me away from me?"

Mama didn't speak, so I imagined she ruffled my hair which, right then, was good enough. My rear wheels slipped on the icy road, and when I regained control my mother was gone.

I more than made up for the lost time when the snow stopped just east of Albuquerque, flooring it through this flat, straight country—and I finally checked into a clean, comfortable motel room in the tiny desert town of Cuervo—a Spanish word I didn't know how to translate.

SPECIAL DELIVERY

The motel in Cuervo was the best yet, maybe the best ever. I was on the bed looking out my second floor window at the desert bathed in every hue of red imaginable in the dying sunset. Red. That is New Mexico. I remembered driving out to Oregon, eons ago, assigning colors to all the states. I think I picked red then, too, but whichever state that was, it couldn't have been redder than this one.

I felt calmer than I had anywhere else so far. I almost felt like I could eat some real dinner, and I wished it could appear magically so I wouldn't have to go out and get it. I closed my eyes and was tempted to go to sleep. Then I realized in this tiny town, at this hour, I'd better go get something or forget it. I sat up and reached for my keys by the telephone—noticed a menu on the table and picked it up. My mouth watered and my stomach growled as I read down the list. Then I saw at the bottom, below the desserts and beverages, the cursive offer—*We Deliver to . . .* followed by the names of three motels and mine was one of them.

Pastor Barker from my childhood Sunday school days reminded me, *Ask and ye shall receive.* I made the phone call.

Twenty minutes later, a beautiful boy who looked fourteen with precision-cut raven hair, obsidian eyes, and lashes so long they brushed against the glass in his wire-rimmed frames delivered hot chicken and dumplings with a Coke and a piece of strawberry-rhubarb pie. I gave him a ten for the four dollar meal.

"Thank *you*," he said in a voice that wasn't yet cracking with change.

I ate as much as my shrunken stomach would hold. Then I took a hot shower. I was digging through my black bag for the Halcion bottle when there was a soft knock on my door. I jumped to answer it, then stopped halfway across the room. *I'm in a motel in Cuervo, New Mexico. It's ten o'clock at night.* I sat on the bed staring at the door and there was another knock.

"Hey, it's me," a small voice said. It sounded like Alex, and my heart pounded. *No fucking way.* I shook my head and ran my fingers through my hair. *Am I dreaming? I haven't taken any drugs all day. Maybe it's the housekeeper. It sounded like a woman. What is there to be afraid of? And what do I have to lose?*

I opened the door and the delivery boy was standing there with his hands in the waistband of his faded 501s and my first thought was: *Money. Shit, I didn't give him enough. Or I gave him so much he's back for more. What would I do in New Mexico with an extortionist?* He pulled his right hand out of his pants and thrust it toward me. I touched it lightly, and his crimson lips parted in a huge grin.

"My name's Quay," he said, and I realized he was a girl.

"I'm Casey." I let her into my room.

"I know."

I towered over this person and I felt physically awkward and uncontrollably suspicious. She sat on the bed and patted the spread next to her, and I sat down as close to the edge as possible.

"I have a proposition for you," she said. I looked at her incredulously. "I'm not weird or anything."

"*This* is pretty weird, wouldn't you say?"

"When I was here before, you looked sad."

"Well, I wasn't." She pursed her lips and nodded. "I hope you don't think this is rude," I said, finally really looking at her, "but how old are you?"

She laughed. "Twenty-two. I know you don't believe me. How old are you?"

"Thirty-three."

She shrugged. "Good, I don't believe you either."

"What do you want?"

She looked hurt. "I don't want anything. Well, yeah I do. I want to show you something that I think will make you feel better."

"I feel fine."

"You're lying."

"You're right." I smiled at her boldness. "You say what you think, don't you—and I bet you do whatever you can get away with."

"I do, whenever possible. So, will you go with me?"

"Where?"

"Out there." She pointed into the now invisible desert outside my window.

"What for?"

She took my wrists and stood up, pulling me gently. "Have you ever been to New Mexico before?"

"No."

"Have you ever walked in the desert at night before?"

"No."

"Well, here you are. Let's go." I refused to stand. "What are you afraid of?"

"You're a stranger."

"So's everybody else until you get to know them," she said, starting to show signs of exasperation. "Why are you afraid of me?"

"You might be a serial killer."

She frowned. "There aren't any female serial killers."

"That's debatable."

"Well, I'm not one." I got my jacket and followed her into the night.

Just past the parking lot, when I could still see part of her face in the reflected light from the motel office, I turned and said, "Look, I'm sorry. I know I'm being wimpy, but please tell me what we're doing, okay?"

Quay sighed and reached up, speaking as she softly ran her fingertips across the nearly-shaved hair behind my ear, a gesture so tender it almost made me cry. "White people are so ruined." She didn't take her hand from my head, but turned her eyes toward the blackness to her left, pointing with her fingers spread. "There's something wonderful out there."

"It's so dark, though."

"I've been there thousands of times. I could get there in my sleep. I *have* gotten there in my sleep. Nothing's going to hurt you. *I'm* not going to hurt you. Please trust me."

I did, and I had no idea why.

After a few minutes, when the motel lights no longer illuminated the scenery, my eyes adjusted to the moon's glow and, when I could see the desert around us in some detail, I relaxed.

"Are we going somewhere specific?"

"Yeah."

"How long a walk is it?"

"Long enough for you to tell me why you're so sad."

We walked silently for a few moments. Finally, I said, "What are you?"

"What am I?"

"Yeah, I mean . . ."

"You mean like a boy or a girl?"

"No." I laughed. "Well, I *did* think you were a boy."

"I know, everybody does—which is fine with me. I feel much safer that way."

"You probably are," I said. "Usually."

"So, are you afraid I'm a ghost or . . ."

I couldn't believe I had the nerve to ask her what she was, and now I was too embarrassed to ask directly. "No, I meant, what, uh, what's your, uh—earlier you said something about white people."

"Oh, you mean what am I, like, as opposed to a white person?"

"Yeah."

"Why didn't you just ask? I'm an Indian. More? Navajo. Enough?"

I trembled as I imagined the PC police pouring out from behind the cacti and tumbleweeds to berate me for asking such a blatantly racist question—and, just as was my way at the crisis line, I stayed silent in an attempt to ward off committing another, possibly worse, semantic crime.

"What's the matter?" Quay finally said. "You're about five shades whiter than you were five seconds ago." What I was thinking spilled out of me. When I was done Quay said, "They really reamed you didn't they? You can call me a woman of color if that'll make you feel better."

"What does Quay mean?"

"I like that even better," she grinned. "A quay's—you know what a quay is. A pier or wharf, you know, where ships dock to load or unload or whatever."

"Oh. Well, why did your parents name you that? I mean, does it mean something else?"

She laughed. "That's what I mean about white people—or should I call you people of *no* color?" She tapped my temple. "You think too much."

"Lately I've been feeling too much."

"Not enough. That's why it feels so bad."

"What's that?" I pointed to a pile of bleached bones we had nearly stumbled right into.

"A cow."

"What happened to it?"

"I don't know. It died." I wanted more of an explanation— I wanted to know the story of this cow's life and its demise in the desert—but no more was forthcoming. She hooked her arm through mine and we trudged forward. "So what happened that made you so sad?"

Realizing this was a woman whose train of thought could not be derailed, I gave in. "I'm in big trouble."

As we walked deeper into the desolate terrain, the shadowed rock shelving on the horizon never seemed to get closer, and I told her why tonight I was alone in a motel in New Mexico. By the end of my monologue we had stopped walking and we were sitting against huge rocks some spectacular geological event from long ago haphazardly tossed into a jagged pile. Quay straddled my lap and wrapped her arms around my waist, resting her head on my chest. She rocked us gently, silently, for a few moments, then looked up at me.

"Why did you stay with Judith for so long?"

"Well, Penn, number one. I mean, I really couldn't have cared less about having a baby until she was born, then . . . it was like instantaneously I couldn't imagine living without her."

"But you could have kept seeing her. You did after you finally moved, right?"

"Yeah, but while I was there Judith . . . well, a few times when she got really crazy she said stuff like 'Go if you want but don't plan on ever seeing Penn again.' Mostly though, it was the migraines. It's hard to explain now because once they were diagnosed and treated, well, now they're totally manageable. But that wasn't until after I was already with Kris. With Judith I was sick as shit and . . . she took care of me. She paid for everything." I shrugged. "She also had all these connections, and I was desperate. I thought I had a fucking brain tumor or something. I mean, the pain was so horrible, so consuming. I would've done anything to make that constant pain go away. After the regular doctors did all their brain scans and tried all these sinus medications that didn't even make a dent, Judith gave me a long list of people she knew, and I began subjecting myself to every alternative healer in Portland. I swallowed a hundred dollars worth of vitamin, herb, mineral, and enzyme pills a month on the advice of a naturopath. I lay still as a stone in a dark room full of tiny needles an acupuncturist had tapped into my skin in search of my *chi*. A chiropractor yanked and jerked my head, neck, and back—finally convincing me I was a prime candidate for a 'nasal specific.' So I let her stick deflated balloons attached to an air pump up my nose which she then inflated, causing this blinding pain that was supposed to rearrange my allegedly misaligned facial bones that were fucking up the proper blood flow to my brain.

"I gagged down glasses of muddy sludge that tasted like pureed sticks mixed with damp tree moss and pond scum. This dishwasher at work named Blue, who had an orange Mohawk hairdo, fixed me macrobiotic food that I couldn't eat because, when I opened the Rubbermaid containers, the air that puffed out smelled like a huge fart. I hung my head upside down off my bed for fifteen minutes twice a day, stopped smoking, stopped eating cheese and chocolate. Needless to say, none of this made a damn bit of difference as my migraines marched on. I stopped short of high colonics. Use your imagination."

Quay shivered and laughed. "No thanks."

"Then one night, as if I wasn't already terrified enough about the state of my health and this mysterious ailment of mine nobody could figure out, my sister called. 'God,' she said. 'I hope you don't have that thing that's happening to gay men!'

"'What are you talking about?'

"'Are your glands swollen?'

"'Yeah, they're always swollen.'

"'This is serious,' she said. 'These guys, I think it's mostly guys—it's gay people anyway. They've all got this disease like cancer but they get really sick over a long period of time—sort of like the flu, but it won't go away.'

"'Then what happens?'

"'They die!' Clara was never one to spare anybody the truth.

"'Jesus Christ,' I said. 'How do you get it?'

"'Nobody knows, that's what's so scary.'

"I remembered an allergist telling me that the Native Americans in the Northwest called Portland 'Sickness Valley' because, he said, viruses and bacteria thrive in the moisture of the Willamette River. After we hung up, I knew there was no getting away from Judith until I got better, or until I died—and I fell asleep thinking: *How in the world can a disease figure out we are gay?*"

"So you were afraid if you left nobody would support you, and you couldn't take care of yourself right then?"

"That, and it was just so confusing. No one had ever treated me like she did and I couldn't even see it all clearly, much less figure out how to fight back. It was weird, like, I couldn't eat after ten at night because the sound of dishes, the smell of food cooking would wake her up. I couldn't turn on the heat after ten either, because she said the noise of the system cycling on and off disturbed her, too. One night while Judith was paying bills I was reading and she told me that the sound of my breathing was bothering her and she wished I'd be quiet. I know it sounds absurd in retrospect."

"What finally made you leave?"

I grinned. "She hit me."

"Shit."

"It was one night in February '84. I had been trying to go to Memphis for six months. Every time my plans were set Judith came up with some reason I couldn't go. One time she fired four of our best employees for reasons that were inexplicable to anyone else—then told me I couldn't go until we stabilized the staff. Finally, I had my ticket, I was packing, and I guess she had run out of ploys. She hadn't spoken to me all night. All of a sudden, she came into my room, grabbed me by my shirt and slammed me up against the wall. Then she delivered this roundhouse punch and knocked the crap out of me. I stayed there that night, but I didn't sleep. The next morning I went to Memphis and the rest, as they say, is history."

Quay stared off into the desert. "God, you just don't think about women doing shit like that to each other."

"Yeah, I know."

Quay looked back at me, her fingers toying with the lapel of my jacket. "You know what?"

"What?"

"I'm glad you were hungry tonight."

"I did five hundred miles today. I almost stopped in Gallup and again in San Felipe. Maybe it's true that you end up where you're supposed to be."

Quay beamed. "Ready to go?"

We walked and, after a moment, I stopped abruptly and turned to her. "Are you real?"

She laughed. "What do *you* think?"

"I really don't know."

"What kind of proof do you need?"

"I don't know. I know that if I tell anybody about you nobody's gonna believe you were real."

"What would it take to convince them?"

"I guess if they could see you."

"Has your father ever seen your house in Portland?"

"No."

"Does he believe you really have a house in Portland?"

"Yeah."

"So he trusts you, right?"

"Yeah, but houses are everywhere. Lots of people own houses, but very few people meet strangers and wander into the middle of the desert with them."

"So, consider yourself one of the lucky few."

"Man, you are impossible," I said and giggled. "I'm not supposed to say 'man' like that."

"Why not?"

"It's sexist according to you-know-who."

"You're kidding! Man, those people have their heads up their butts." She was silent, picked up a handful of small rocks and hurled them into the void. "It's not exactly like you're honoring males when you say 'man' instead of 'fuck' or 'shit' or something."

"Hey," I said. "Two points."

"What?! Two points? That sounds like something a person with a penis would say!"

I playfully punched her arm and we danced around each other like boxers, then she hooked her elbow around my neck. "Do you know 'Higher Love'?"

"Is this a philosophical question or music trivia?"

She let go of my neck and grabbed a microphone from the air with her fist and began singing Steve Winwood's song. She had an adorable voice and, at first, I was too shy to sing along with her when she stuck her fist to my mouth; but as she danced in the moonlight and dragged me with her, I lost my inhibitions and joined together with her in this sexy, joyous song. By the end of the tune Quay had jumped into my arms, her legs encircling my waist. We were both sweaty and laughing and we collapsed panting in the sand. I ran my hand through the gritty dust, picked it up and let it sift through my palms. "I don't remember the last time I laughed like that . . . the last time I had fun, without feeling guilty." I thought of another happy night long ago—a full moon on Mt. Hood, a first kiss, an unforgettable fuck.

"Casey," Quay whispered. "We're getting close. Ready to go the last mile?"

"Mile?"

"Figure of speech." She laughed and pulled me up. We walked holding hands and singing 'You're All I Need to Get By.'

"It's right here," Quay said, finally, gesturing toward what looked like another heap of strewn stones. She had to duck to get through the opening. I had to crawl on my belly. By the time I wriggled through, she had lit a candle and I saw we were standing in a room half the size of mine at the motel with a sand floor and stone walls. She lit another candle and glued the two with their own melted wax to the small rocks in the corner.

"Wow," I said as my eyes took in the etched, carved, and painted walls. "It's like the Pyramids."

She sauntered over to me and laid her hands on my hips. "Only my favorite people—" I blanched and pulled away from her, turning toward the opening that from this angle did not look like an exit. I heard her sigh behind me. "*Now* what did I say?"

I felt a flash of rage and spun to face her. "I don't ever want to be anybody's only, first, best, cutest, smartest, anything ever again, ever!" I was shivering, feeling guilty, feeling like an idiot as Quay silently turned and pulled wool blankets and handsewn quilts from a duffel bag against the wall, then arranged them into a makeshift pallet on the ground. She retrieved a dark, unmarked bottle and two battered tin cups from the bag and set them next to the blankets.

"Casey," she beckoned me toward her, "come here." When I was standing over her she uncorked the bottle and poured inky fluid into the cups. She patted the pallet and I knelt down as she handed me a cup. "You need a fucking break, baby."

"I'm sorry," I whispered as she dipped her fingers in her cup and touched them to my lips. The wine was sweet and thick.

"My dad made this," she said, running more of it into my mouth with her purple fingers. "Tastes like it belongs on hot-cakes, doesn't it? But it'll knock you on your ass if you're not careful."

"You're cute," I said before I could stop myself. I couldn't stop staring at Quay in the candlelight in her faded, torn Levi's and white buttondown man's shirt and weathered leather jacket.

"Thank you. You're cute, too." She held up her hand to ward off an imaginary blow. "But definitely not the *cutest* woman I've ever met, oh no, not the cutest, no way!"

"Oh shut up," I said, slapping her knee. She took my hand before I could remove it from her leg and gazed at me, slowly pulling her glasses off.

"I want to make you happy," she said.

"I don't know who you are or why we're here or why I feel like I can tell you what I'm really thinking but . . ."

"But . . ."

"But . . ." Her eyes were so lovely I couldn't bear to look at them when I said this. "But I don't want to make love with you."

Without hesitation she said, "Is making love the only way to make you happy?"

"No!"

"Well, then, good, 'cause that's not what I want to do."

"Really?"

"Really. Not that the thought hadn't crossed my mind. But tonight's for you. Still trust me?"

"Yeah."

"Take your clothes off."

"What?"

"You heard me."

"What for?"

"So I can make you feel good."

"How?"

"Trust me."

"Are you gonna touch me?"

"Yeah, I am."

"Don't if you don't want to."

That little look of exasperation flitted across her face again. "What is the matter with you? I'm not going to attack you. And the wolves at the door can't get in here." I looked at her with my mouth open. "Uh-oh, what?"

"I used to have a dream about wolves." I giggled. "I thought Kris would protect me from them—only in the dream Kris was Kraft Macaroni and Cheese."

"*You're* the weirdo. Now, take your clothes off and lie down on your stomach." I took off my jacket and shirt, then I wrapped my arms around my chest. "Keep going."

I shook my head. "I can't, I . . . I just can't."

"Are you shy?"

"No."

"Please tell me the truth."

"The truth . . ." I laughed. "I'm thinking."

"Too much again, obviously."

"You know what I'm thinking? I'm figuring I'm gonna get my clothes off and, based on what you've hinted at, you're gonna do something, uh, nice—or something that feels good, something for me or to me that feels good—I know not sex—I'm not afraid you're lying about that. I'm figuring you're gonna do something exotic, or mystical and . . ."

"And you're right! How did you guess?"

"That's the problem. I think that's racist."

"What!?" She raised her voice higher than I'd heard it all night.

"I'm afraid that's racist for me to assume because you're a, an, uh, Native American, you know."

"A Navajo?"

"Yeah, that you're gonna, I don't know, introduce me to the spirit in the sky or some racist shit—you know?"

She was shaking her head with her mouth open. "What'd they do to you?"

"And if what you do is something just for me, I don't know, like rubbing my shoulders or something, then it's like slavery."

"Slavery?!"

"Like I'm this privileged white person and you're, you know, a minority person and it's your place to service me, like slavery, oh God, I don't know."

"What did they do to you?" she whispered.

"They explained things, and I got it. I really did get it." I looked into her eyes. "And I know it's important, but it's so much. I don't know what to do with it."

"Casey," she said, touching her fingers to my bare neck. "You know what I think is racist? I think it's racist for you to think you can't let me make you feel good just because our parents were different colors. And you know what else I think? I think it's *inhuman* for you to think my making you feel good somehow demeans me."

"I'm so fucked up."

She gently knocked on the side of my head with her fist. "Isn't there somebody in there who knows how good it feels to do something that makes somebody else, even a stranger, feel good?"

"Penn." Quay nodded. "But she was just a baby."

"Growing up doesn't mean we don't get to feel good anymore. Stand up." I did, and she slipped off my pants. "You have a handsome body. A little too skinny, though."

"Will you take your clothes off, too?" She did. "You're very, very pretty. The sex thing, you know, it's nothing personal."

"Roll over." She pulled a bottle of cloudy liquid out of the duffel bag, poured it into her hands and held them for a moment over the flickering flame. It smelled like coconut milk. She touched the thin leather strap around my neck. "Can we take this off?"

"I'd rather not."

"Is this from . . ."

"It's a crystal, for good luck on the road." I felt a little foolish. "My friend Allie gave it to me the night before I left Portland."

"Good friend," she said, starting to work the oil into my neck. "Don't let her go."

"She's in Portland."

Quay patted my back. "She's in here. Don't let her go."

"That lotion you're using . . . before things got bad, when Penn was still a little baby . . . Judith let me suck her breast one night. It tasted like that stuff smells."

"Somebody loves you. Somebody will always love you. Say goodbye to Judith." Quay applied steady pressure to my shoulder blades.

"Does Kris?" I asked as she refilled her palms and touched the soft spots above my road-sore kidneys.

"I don't know. Maybe, but she's not the only one. Do you want to say goodbye to Kris?"

"No. I don't know. No. I love her—sometimes I think since before I even met her, you know?"

"Um-hm," Quay murmured, pushing her thumbs into my lower back.

"I didn't want to leave her. I just wanted to *move*—it wasn't her, it was inertia. We weren't *doing* anything except running in place. She's a wonderful person, but—"

"Even caviar gets boring if that's all you've got to eat."

"Yeah. It was just such a shock, though, going from caviar to beans and hotdogs. Ohhh," I responded in spite of myself as her slick hands caressed my ass.

"Ummm," she sighed. "And Alex?"

"I hate . . . despite everything that happened . . . I hate to admit—sometimes when I think about her, I still get wet."

"It's okay."

"I hate admitting that all I wanted from her was *that.*"

"Sometimes that's all there is."

"Why did I have to pretend like there was more?"

She was working my thighs. "Because you felt like there should be. Do you want to say goodbye to Alex?"

"Oh God, yes!"

"Goodbye Alex," Quay said, pressing her thumbs deeply into my calves. Our silence was prolonged, finally pierced by a lonesome howl far in the distance, then another, then a chorus. "It's a coyote party," Quay whispered, placing her warm oily palms on my feet.

I gasped and jerked away. "I'm sorry, did that hurt?"

"No."

"May I have them back?"

She stroked my feet. "I used to rub my mother's feet," I laughed, choking back a lump in my throat. "And it didn't do a damn bit of good."

"You're not your mother. And I'm not you." Quay finished her massage.

I lay still, unable to move. I heard one candle sputter and die and Quay lit another to replace it, then came back and lay quietly next to me, her hand resting on the small of my back. The coyote howls died, and I turned on my side and raised my head. "I'm thirsty," I said, and Quay started to move toward the wine. I slipped my hand behind her head and kissed her lips, used my tongue to part them. "I'm hungry," I whispered, trailing my fingers down her smooth belly, lightly touching her black down.

"Oh, Case," she said, raising her leg and draping it across my hip. Moving down between her thighs, I made love to her. After she came, with her fingers still gripped in my hair, she looked down at me and said, "Somebody loves you, Case."

We didn't get much sleep, and the next morning the bottle of viscous wine was empty. We got back to the motel room and took a shower together. With a soapy hand, I fondled the lump in my groin I had neglected to let a doctor examine and I asked Quay to feel it. She did, facing me, then her brow furrowed and she moved behind me and felt it some more. Finally, with her other hand, she felt the other side of my groin and laughed. "Silly, that's a bone. You find all kinds of interesting new things on your body when you lose too much weight. Here, feel." She took my fingers and put them on the other side so I could feel my lump's sister. I hoped I would remember to tell Kris this good news.

With a little time left before check out, we lay naked on the bed in each other's arms and talked.

"So what did last night mean?" I asked.

"That nothing has to mean anything . . . white person."

"You're something."

"Is that a politically correct term?" I slapped her ass. "Ouch," she said, and we kissed for several minutes.

"Are we ever going to see each other again?"

"If we're supposed to we will."

"Are you going to stay here in Cuervo?" I said, fishing.

"Oh God, no."

"Where are you going?"

"To NYU in the fall."

"Really?"

"Yep. Film school."

"Really?"

"Yep."

"I'd really like to see you again."

"Well, I'll tell you what. You go to Memphis and write a book and put me in it, and I'll go to New York and make a film and I'll put you in it—and I'll keep an eye on the bookstores and you keep an eye on the movie theaters and when we both get rich and famous, *at each other's expense,* we'll come looking."

"Deal."

"Probably with lawyers."

"No way. Well, I know whatever *I* say will be favorable." I glanced at my watch on the bedside table. Quay started to rise and I stopped her. "Five more minutes," I said, and she nestled next to me. "What does *Cuervo* mean?"

"You mean in English?"

"Yeah."

"*Cuervo* means crow, or raven."

"Really?" I said, tickling the soft, short ends of her black hair that stuck up like a little boy's.

"I probably shouldn't tell you this, your being a white person and all," she said, poking a finger in my ribs. "In some tribal legends the raven is the mischief maker."

I stiffened. "What do you mean?"

"He plays tricks on people, he . . . oh no . . ."

"So last night . . ."

"I'm not the raven, and last night was not a trick."

We dressed and I threw my few things together and tossed the room key on the bed. She walked me out to my truck. We both kicked sand and pebbles around with our shoes. Finally,

Quay fingered a lump in her pocket. "Oh," she said, tugging inside. "This is for you." She handed me something that looked like a small beehive.

I rolled it around in my hand. "What is this?"

"Goofy city girl. It's a rattle. Off a snake."

"Oh wow." I shook it against my ear.

She slipped her arm in mine and glanced around the empty parking lot, then gestured for me to lower my ear to her mouth. "It's a Navajo thing." She winked and we both burst out laughing. When we quieted, Quay curled her hands around mine that held the rattle and looked at me suddenly with an expression so serious I felt a brief flutter of the initial anxiety I had when we were strangers. "This is from my father," she said, "from his father. I don't even know how old it is."

I felt the ridged roughness squeezed into my palm. "I can't take this, Quay."

"You have to take it, Casey. It's for the best of luck—umm, not luck—it's bigger than that. I don't even know exactly how to describe it to you. It's for luck . . . forever—and ever. Do you know what I mean?"

I didn't know what to say, so I pulled my hands from hers and pushed the rattle deep into the inside pocket of my jacket. I wrapped my arms around her shoulders as hers wound around my waist. We kissed. Then she looked at me and said, "You gotta go."

"There's one thing, one thing I'd like to say." I squinted into the sun. "One thing I'd like to say because . . ." I looked in her black eyes and removed her glasses. "Because I want to because . . . because it doesn't mean anything more than what it means right now."

She cocked her head.

"I love you."

Her smile was so wide it uncovered crows' feet that wouldn't easily be revealed on her delicate face for another ten years. "See ya in court," Quay said, and we kissed each other goodbye.

THE LAST LEG

My New Mexico high carried me into the Texas panhandle, through a night spent at a comfortable motel in Shamrock where I devoured a Pizza Hut pan pizza and watched MTV and remembered how luxurious is the anonymity of the road.

The next day I drove into Oklahoma which was oppressively hot, scenically boring and, by Oklahoma City, horribly humid—and my troubles returned as I perceived I was close to being back in the South. I stopped in this state just once—to pee at a McDonald's—a suggestion of Kris' that I had taken many times on my trip. "You know they're going to be relatively clean," she said that day in Portland when she came back to take the dogs. "And the place is always so crowded nobody's going to notice you just came in to go to the bathroom. And, of course, you can always get a burger if you're hungry."

I was astonished to discover that, at this late date, there was something about me Kris didn't know. I had never had a McDonald's hamburger. It never occurred to me that I might be the only thirty-three-year-old American who could make this claim until one night when my friend Elaine found out and suggested I call *The Guiness Book of World Records*. I spared her the explanation—that my mother believed ground beef purchased anywhere other than Baker's Big Star in Memphis, Tennessee—beef prepared and eaten anywhere outside of her kitchen—was a primary evil—and that I was probably the only child ever severely traumatized in a restaurant by the appearance of three fat meatballs sitting on top of my spaghetti.

Or, on top of my *pasta*, as the culinary elite in Portland would have me say.

Oklahoma's outstanding feature, in my mind, is signs along I-40 that say: *Hitchhikers May Be Escaping Convicts.* I experienced a brief moment of panic when, misinterpreting the poor sentence construction, I took this to mean motorists should pick up hitchhikers to save them from the convicts they may be escaping. I realized my error before I picked up anybody in striped pajamas.

I stopped for the night in Russellville, Arkansas, the scene, I recalled, of a mass murder a couple Christmases ago.

At bedtime I took a Halcion and a Percodan because the memories of Quay were unraveling and the pain was coming back. Before I got too stoned to focus, I retrieved the toilet paper wrapper from the bathroom trash can and wrote on its blank underside.

———

It's hot here and humid. I had forgotten how wretched the air is in the South. I hear large insects screaming in the weeds and flinging their hard bodies against the windows.

Tomorrow I'll be in Memphis. With Kris. I wonder who we are to each other now? And Griffin. And Harley. I can't wait to see Harley again.

Please don't let me forget Quay. Please let me remember her until I get a chance to write it down. This is my prayer.

Walking back through the New Mexico desert that morning—that morning—it was just yesterday. Seems like forever ago. She said, "Who do you talk to when you need to?" Nobody. Used to be Kris, but now I'm figuring out that she only put up with me because her fear of abandonment was bigger than her dissatisfaction. Now when we talk she keeps her lips tight, her words seep out from her clenched teeth. I think we both got something out of sticking around, but, for the time being, I have to take all the guilt because I'm the one who got laid while we were still married.

I can't believe I admitted to Quay that I talk to Mama. But she didn't make me feel like an idiot. In fact, she said, "Great—that's a great start!"

"What?"

"She's dead, right?"

"Yeah."

"Then that's a good start. If you can talk to one dead person, it's only a small step until you can talk to other dead people—any of them, anytime you want—and there are millions out there, and they really will help us if we ask."

Some people would find that disconcerting, but it made me feel better. Everything about Quay made me feel better. But, in a way, I'm glad she wouldn't tell me how to keep in touch with her. I have to be very, very careful around people who make me feel better.

"Somebody loves you," Quay said. I liked that, but I pretended I didn't.

"Yeah, probably a bunch of dead people," I said.

"Well, hey, you're gonna spend a lot more time over the years with them than you are with the living."

I am over 2000 miles from Oregon now.

Tomorrow I'll be in Memphis. With my family I destroyed. Oh, God help me. Or if you can't, send some dead person who can.

———

The drugs had worked, but suddenly I was overwhelmed with guilt so powerful it shot through their gauzy curtain. It was Kris' thirty-first birthday and I had forgotten. I dialed her number, got her answering machine, and hung up. I just couldn't say happy birthday after the beep.

The air in my room was stuffy and dank but I can't stand sleeping without a blanket so I cranked up the air conditioning before turning off the light. In the dim glow of the motel lights that seeped through the thick drapes, I reached for my jacket, slipped Quay's gift out of the pocket, and held it against my lips long enough to whisper a brief prayer that went something like: *Oh God, whoever you are, please help me.* I set the rattle on the bedside table and climbed beneath the covers. Deep sleep was moments away when I heard a woman's high, pleading voice, "Why are you doing this to me?" —and I had a vision of a burly Arkansan lumbering through a sprawling farmhouse as his mother, wife, and children try in vain to dodge the blows of his hatchet.

"Why are you doing this to me?"

I saw myself, my neck and back and wrist and jaws inflamed from making love with Alex until three a.m. at the crisis line, my throat raw from too many cigarettes, my knuckles scraped bloody with carpet burn from kneeling between the legs of my former client—and all my physical soreness can't distract me from the despair I feel in the face of Kris, her eyes swollen from a solid week of sobbing, her disappointment and anger undisguised as I miss my third school graduation.

"Why are you doing this to me?" she demands to know, and I have no answer for her.

But, in a half-sleep in an infamous Arkansas town, the bloody faces appeared and their voices said, *"You buried us alive in your mother's grave. We have dug out and found our way home. We are a steaming cauldron of putrid grief, rank despair, fetid anger, and rancid love—all of us spoiled by neglect and denial, oozing out to destroy everybody who dared try to replace the only woman who truly loved you, to murder you for letting them try."*

"Wake up, wake up," I was mumbling as I became aware of the motel room around me. My fingers were curled beneath my nostrils and they smelled like Mama's—formaldehyde and dead flesh. I sat up quickly and gagged and coughed and gagged and bolted for the bathroom. I was conscious of the stickiness between my legs before I noticed the dull ache in my ovaries. On the toilet, I wiped blood from my thighs and inserted a tampon, filled a plastic cup with water, swallowed two more Percodans, and went back to bed.

Thirty minutes later, I was high enough to watch the images that floated above me without feeling any anxiety.

———

Kris is leading me with my eyes closed to my graduation present. We sit together on the bench and she teaches me to play "Heart and Soul." "I still love you," she says. "I will always love you."

The lilting piano tune segues into the faint strains of a lullaby—my mother's sweet voice singing "I love you a bushel and a peck." as she holds a screaming baby, her tiny hands pressed hard against her infected ears—still too young to trust that the opiate Mama gave her will work and the pain will go away.

Then, I'm standing with Kris in a downtown Portland square on a bitterly cold, late October night. Alex is waiting in the shadows a respectful distance away. Kris grips my shoulder and says, "If you're not home in thirty minutes, it's finished." I watch her taillights merge into the traffic on Broadway, then disappear. I don't move a muscle until I feel Alex's arms encircle my waist from behind. I turn, hang my head, say nothing. Alex presses my face into her chest and rocks me gently while I cry, then she leads me to a bench where she opens her jacket so I can warm my freezing fingers. Words of love melt into tender kisses and we make love in the backseat of my car. Hours later, before Alex and I part for the night, I say, "I want you, but I need her. How am I supposed to choose between those?"

"I think you just did," Alex says.

Shortly before dawn, Kris meets me at the door. "Hi, honey," she says, smiling, allowing me to enter the house before her. I turn to face her as I back in, afraid of having her behind me. Inside she retrieves a fat envelope from her desk and hands it to me; but before I can get my fingers around it, she lets go and it falls to my feet. I don't pick it up. "It's a suicide note," she says. "I wrote it last night. Do you know you have fifty-seven Halcions in the medicine chest?" I don't answer her. "Well, anyway, I've got to get some sleep. Read it if you want, then put it back on my desk, okay? Oh, and by the way, rather than kill myself, I decided to go back to Memphis. I'm leaving Friday night."

She goes to bed. I read the note. The last lines say, *"You've done a terrific job of destroying everything. Still, I know you, and I figured you would have trouble finishing things off. So I'll do this piece for you. Consider it my final favor."*

On Friday evening, Kris is in my arms in our king-sized bed, neither of us knowing that this will be the last time I will sing my spouse to sleep. "I love you a bushel and a peck, a bushel and a peck and a hug around the neck, a hug around the neck and a barrel and a heap, a barrel and a heap and I'm talking in my sleep about you."

It's midnight as we kiss each other on the lips goodbye and she boards her flight. I stand at the frosted windows with my hands pressed against the glass watching the flickering lights fade gently into the foggy October night.

———

The last image I saw before real sleep came to me in Russellville, Arkansas, was our house in Portland, completely empty of furniture, full of police officers and Multnomah County officials. I was standing in the middle of the living room, soaked with blood, a dripping hatchet in my hand, staring incredulously at the coroner who was squatting next to the dismembered body, which was stacked like cordwood on the hearth. He was filling out forms in triplicate deeming Kris' death a suicide.

THE SUDDEN STOP

—

Kris had secured a rambling ranch-style home in Fox Meadows through friends of her mother's, an upper middle-class couple who was divorcing unamicably and desperate to rent the property that neither of them could afford alone. My face puckered like I'd eaten a grapefruit without sugar when I realized it made me feel better to know other people's lives were as wrecked as mine. How could I have forgotten Winston's words so quickly?

I left the Ozarks behind and would have driven the rest of the way through ugly eastern Arkansas with my eyes closed if I could. Fox Meadows. One of the first subdivisions built for those of my parents' generation who had a few bucks and wanted everybody to know it. My family could never have afforded a house there in its wildest dreams. The person I was before moving to Portland wouldn't have lived there if somebody had paid me to. And it still didn't make me happy to think about it now. But Kris had done her best to get us a place where we could be back together to . . . what?

Resolve. Dissolve.

I had seen more dead animals on the road in the past hour than I had in the previous seven days put together. "Road pizza," Alex would say. A spray of bitter stomach acid shot up into my throat.

As I drove across the Memphis-Arkansas bridge in traffic that shattered my fragmented nerves, I pulled out a piece of paper Kris sent me with directions to the Fox Meadows property. I looked at my watch. Thirty minutes. I'd be there in about thirty minutes. I realized I was thinking: *If I don't die in the next thirty minutes, I'm gonna be one of those people who lives until impact.*

I remembered a funny line from somewhere that didn't sound so funny anymore. "It's not so much the fall as it is the sudden stop."

I realized I was thinking: *Being back with Kris is hitting bottom. What am I doing this for? Who am I doing this for? I've got to stop thinking like this.*

I bypassed the city. The interstate took me well past the neighborhood of my childhood. I got off at the proper exit, drove down Mt. Moriah, Mendenhall, turned on Fox Run, then again on Fox Burrow. Saw the numbers getting close to the ones on my paper. Saw the curbside mailbox numbers that matched.

As I pulled into the driveway I had one of those mental images—like they say right before you die your whole life flashes before you. Well, it wasn't my whole life, but one very specific incident—and it did come in an instant, in full detail.

———

I am a senior at Memphis State, working on a final project for my video class. I have checked out the equipment from the audio/visual office, loaded it into my '64 Volkswagen, and driven out to shoot scenes in an old graveyard—its cracked and leaning tombstones covered with virgin snow. Speeding back to the school with reckless disregard for the treacherous road conditions, I lose control on a curve approaching Walnut Grove, not far from my grandmother's house, and my Bug's rear end goes into a long skid that whips me and my little car around and around before we finally slam head-on into a ten foot brick wall surrounding someone's corner property.

On that silent, snowy afternoon, I sit stunned in my crushed car. I feel warmth and taste salt and see red drops landing on my shirt. I see my feet plastered against the pedals, the toes of my hiking boots concealed by a chunk of metal that has been shoved over them. The gear shift is bent around my right knee which is pressed against my left knee which is wedged between its sister and the door. My hands are pinned to my lap by the crumpled steering wheel—the right one bent at the wrist in a manner one only normally sees on a cartoon character.

I am hurt, I know, as I lap blood off my lips and wait for some kind soul to happen by and help me out. I am hurt, I know, but I don't feel anything.

————

The front door flew open, it seemed, by itself, and the first thing I saw was a manic flurry of brown fur—Griffin shooting into the yard and throwing his paws up on my truck. I unfolded my stiff legs from the seat and stepped out, petting him, and I looked up and Harley came out, lumbering toward me, tail down, looking at Griff. I said her name and she looked up and stared for a moment. Then her tail started wagging frantically and I knelt and pulled her into my arms. Griff was jumping on my back.

"Oh I love you I love you I love you," I said. Then Harley was chasing a bee and Griffin was peeing on a tree and Kris was standing on the porch. She blushed and barked at the dogs to get back in the house and both of them totally ignored her.

I stood up slowly, looked at Kris shyly, and a small smile started to rise from the corners of her lips. Griff zipped past her, his head turned away in deceit, and she grabbed his scruff. "What the hell is *this?*" Kris said, prying something from his mouth. She stood and held her palm out to me. "What the hell *is* this?"

It was Quay's rattle, broken beyond repair.